MW00613044

TANNER

The Stewarts of Skagway #1

KATY REGNERY

New York Times Bestselling Author

Please visit my website at www.katyregnery.com
Cover Designer: Marianne Nowicki
Editing: Tessa Shapcott and Ellie McLove
Formatting: Cassie Mae

First Edition: January 2024
Tanner: a novel / by Katy Regnery—1st ed.
ISBN: 978-1-944810-93-1

This book is dedicated to Diane Tapley Gilliam.
Some as good (unlikely), but none better.
I love you so much, Mom.

xoxoxoxo

chapter one

Tanner

HELP!

SM, 29, seeks SF, 24-34.

Let me be straight with you:

I'm not looking for love.

My psycho ex-girlfriend is coming back to town, and I need someone to pose as my fiancée so she leaves me alone. I'll pay your R/T transportation from the Lower 48, can offer free accommodation, and I can guarantee you a seasonal job in retail, hospitality, or tourism—your choice. Help a guy out! Doesn't someone want to spend an all-expenses-paid summer in beautiful Skagway?

I cringe at the bluntness of the personal ad, but I don't know what else to do.

Time's running out.

Ramona will be here any day, and in a town of a thousand people with a total area of nine square miles, there's nowhere to hide.

I press *Enter*, and a new screen pops up, asking for my credit card information. As I type in the digits, I wonder—yet again—if what I'm doing is rash.

When I first met Ramona De Alicante last summer, to my shame and woe, I was a typical guy, blown away by her gorgeous eyes and voluptuous body. I jumped into bed with her, clasping my hands in prayerful thanks that she found a bearded mountain man from Dyea so appealing.

Twice a week, I found heaven between her thighs when I stayed over at her apartment in town. And on her days off, I'd spirit her down the dirt road from Skagway to Dyea in my bright red RAV4, where we'd skinny dip in the river behind my cabin and fuck for hours in the sunshine.

She sure did look pretty butt-naked in the sunshine.

Yes, indeed, for about three weeks, it was perfect.

Until it wasn't…

It was little things at first: her insisting that I stay over every night of the week instead of just a couple. And when I said no, that I couldn't, that I needed to get back to my family's business, she wouldn't let it go with a shrug and smile. She'd yell. She'd scream. She'd throw things.

One time, she threw a mug at my face that read, "I left my heart in Skagway."

A few hours later, as I had my nasal septum repositioned back to the middle of my face at the local clinic, I wondered half-heartedly if there was another mug reading, "I lost my mind in Skagway." If so, it was surely meant for Ramona.

Heading home from the doc's office, I wished that I could chalk up the mug incident to a fiery disposition but found I couldn't. It was just too crazy. I prepared myself to bid farewell to red-hot Ramona and went back to her place the next day—my nose covered in bandages—to break things off clean.

But she dropped to her knees in the doorway of her apartment...and let me tell you: a good blow job can surely mess with a man's head and thwart his better intentions. We made up instead of breaking up and fucked all afternoon instead.

She never said she was sorry.

I never said I forgave her.

We let our bodies do the talking, and a blissful unity was found.

Back to our twice-a-week-at-her-place-and-once-a-week-at-mine schedule, without a reprisal of crockery violence, I hoped that we'd found a groove to take us to the end of the summer season.

...until the Tuesday evening I had to cancel on her for work.

My family's been running a campground on the old Dyea Road almost continuously since the Gold Rush days: a dozen cabins are available to rent with two meals included a day and evening campfire s'mores accompanied by stories of days gone by. During the day, we entertain our guests with bear tours, salmon tours, fly-fishing tours, Yukon tours, dog mushing tours, historic gold rush tours, or you-name-it tours available upon request. And while my younger brother, Sawyer, generally takes on the two-night tours up north, he had a dentist appointment in town on a Wednesday afternoon and needed me to step in for him.

Knowing Ramona was in the middle of her shift at the

King Kone, I sent her a text, explaining that I had to work and wouldn't be by that night. Then I loaded up the passenger van with a family of six and headed north to Whitehorse. It was only when I arrived in Whitehorse, five hours later, that I received Ramona's texts.

The first was a photo of her, face streaked with tears, holding up a carving knife in one hand.

The second was of the carving knife against her wrist.

The third was of her hands, covered in bright red blood, waving goodbye.

Frantic that she had killed herself over my cancelation, I called my sister, Harper, and begged her to drive into Skagway and check on Ramona. A call from Harper half an hour later indicated that Ramona was fine, and an excess of grenadine syrup had been wasted on theatrics.

But, man, I was shaken.

First a split nose, and now a staged suicide?

Far away from Ramona's tight pussy, I could think clearly. *We are finished. Over. Through. No more*, I promised myself. No matter how good a blow job she gave, we were over…which is exactly what I told her when I arrived back in Skagway on Wednesday afternoon.

"So, you're going to abandon your child?" she asked me, eyes narrowing, spittle gathering in the corner of her lips.

"What child?"

She pointed to her flat stomach. "The one in here."

I may have blacked out for a second. For sure, I almost fainted.

"W-We used p-protection," I finally blurted out.

"It's not foolproof," she said, nostrils flaring. "And you're a fool."

"No, I'm not," I had the presence of mind to tell her. "I always check the condom after. We were safe."

She shrugged. "So get a DNA test in six months. You can come down to Sacramento and meet my family when you do."

This is a trick, I thought. *No way she's pregnant.*

"I'll see you in hell first," I said, heading back downstairs and through the door onto Broadway, the main Skagway thoroughfare.

"Damn it!" I bellowed.

"Rein it in, Tanner," said my older brother, Hunter, exiting the Ace Hardware at the exact moment of my outburst. He clapped me on the shoulder, steering me toward the Purple Parsnip Saloon. "Let's get a beer."

"Don't want one."

"Sure you do," he insisted.

Ten minutes later, we sat side by side at the bar, the last of the day's cruisers paying up their tabs before returning to the Norwegian Sun or the Princess Emerald or the Carnival Clownhouse.

"Parker said you're having trouble with a seasonal."

"Parker always *could* keep a secret," I mumbled, frowning at the foam crown of my beer.

"Better'n Harper," he pointed out.

We are a family of six kids altogether, born in boy-girl, boy-girl, boy-girl order: Hunter, Harper, Tanner, Parker, Sawyer, and Reeve. When I asked my momma why Reeve was

5

called Reeve and not Archer, Miller, or Wheeler like the rest of us, she said that my daddy needed a "The End," or he'd keep after her to finish the story.

My little sister, Reeve, who's almost eighteen, was my parents' finale in more ways than one: my mother died a year after she was born.

"Anyone keeps a secret better'n Harper," I agreed.

"So tell me what's up."

I told Hunter about meeting Ramona—about the sounds she'd make in the dark and the way she made my body feel. And then I told him about how she broke my nose and pretended to kill herself. And today, how she claimed she was carrying my kid.

"She's lying," said Hunter, his lips thin.

"Yeah. I know." Except I didn't. Inside I was scared shitless that one of my swimmers had broken free, and I was about to be bound to this lunatic woman for life.

"You make her any promises?"

"Not one."

"You tell her you loved her?"

"Never."

"Used protection?"

He knows my history. "Always."

"So it was casual."

"I thought so."

"Looks like you thought wrong," said Hunter, gesturing to the bartender for another round.

"Damn it, Hunt! You don't think I know that?"

"You tried to break it off?"

"Yessir."

Hunter took a deep breath and sighed. "You gotta leave town."

"What? No. No. Come on. She'll…she'll stop."

"Nope," he said softly. "She's crazy. Crazy don't stop." He scratched his beard in thought. "Heard from Parker today. Uncle Frank and Aunt Petunia could use an extra hand until October."

My middle sister, Parker, was working as a summer musher at a dog kennel in Juneau. Tourists will pay a pretty penny to be dragged around by huskies on a golf cart in the middle of June, and the dogs don't mind summer training as long as it isn't too hot.

"Ain't going to Juneau all summer." I picked up my beer and downed it, relishing the bubbly burn against my throat. "I'll handle Ramona."

"If you say so."

But two days later, Ramona showed up at my family's campground unannounced. It took one glance at the car that drove her there to realize she'd hitched a ride with the local sheriff. It took me an extra second to realize her arm was in a sling.

"Morning, Tanner," called Sheriff Joe, exiting the cruiser, his face graver than usual.

"Hey, Joe," I said, changing direction from the campfire ring where I was headed to his car. Joe and I were in high school together—*my* graduating class had consisted of Joe's cousin, Sandra, and me. His, two years before, had consisted of him and Harper. "What can I do for you?"

"Miss De Alicante claims you roughed her up on Wednesday night."

I whipped my eyes to Ramona's, my heart thundering with denial. "No, sir, I did not. I'd never, ever lay hands on a woman in anger."

"She's all bruised up. Showed me her arm."

"Then she did it to herself," I cried.

"Liar," she snarled. "You shoved me against the wall, saying you hated me, saying you hated our baby, you—"

"Our *fake* baby—"

Sheriff Joe stepped between us, taking off his hat and scratching his head. "Okay, folks. Okay now. Sounds like you two have some things to discuss."

"No, sir. There's nothing to discuss. She's not pregnant. It's a lie."

"It's the truth," she declared, placing her free hand over her washboard abdomen.

"Then it's not mine."

"Like hell, it isn't," she shrieked.

"How do I even know you're pregnant? Prove it," I said. "Let's go into town, and you can pee on a stick!"

"You can't order me around, you goddamned—"

"Folks!" thundered Joe again. "Let's stop the yelling and talk calmly."

"She pretended to kill herself!" I blurted out. "Did she tell you that?"

Two red spots colored her cheeks. "He can't take a fucking joke."

In my peripheral vision, I could see my grandmother and

8

Reeve step out onto the porch, watching the spectacle. Lord almighty, I was going to have a lot to explain.

"Not a very funny joke," Joe observed, glancing at Ramona appraisingly.

"You can say that again," I agreed.

"No one likes being dumped," she whined.

"Dumped? We were barely going out!"

"We sure did a lot of fucking if we weren't going out!"

I know she said that extra loud so Gran and Reeve could hear, and it made me hate her all the more. I could feel the heat creeping up my neck, flushing my face red.

"I don't know what's going on here," said Joe, "but for now, I think it'd be best if you took some time apart and gave each other some space. Miss De Alicante, I don't want you bothering Mr. Stewart. Not by text, not by phone, and not in person. That clear?" Ramona had a pout on her face, but she nodded. "Same goes for you, Tanner. Understand?"

"A hundred percent. In fact," I said, "I'm heading out of town for a job in Juneau. Won't be back until the fall."

Ramona's lips parted in surprise. Her eyes filled with tears.

And me? Dumb me? I actually felt sorry for her for a second.

"What?" she asked, her voice all soft and breathy. "When did this—"

"Yesterday."

"Oh." Her shoulders slumped as she searched my face. "I didn't want..." She cleared her throat. "I mean, I only wanted..."

I lifted my chin and looked at Joe, who stared at Ramona with confusion.

"You only wanted…what?" he prompted.

"Nothing," she said, turning back to the squad car. "Nothing."

She sat down in the back seat and pulled the door closed with a slam, leaning her head against the headrest with her eyes closed.

Joe leaned forward. "The bruises on her arm look bad."

"I didn't touch her. You can't believe a word she says. She's nuts, Joe."

He took a deep breath. "I don't know about that, per se, but something doesn't feel quite right here."

"Something's not quite right," I agreed. "And it's her."

Joe gave me a look.

"I never touched her aggressively. I swear to God. I swear on my momma's life. You *know* me, Joe! You've known me forever!"

He scanned my face for a second before nodding. "I believe you. But I also think it's a good idea for you to leave town for a while. Get some distance. Let the air clear."

"Will do."

He popped his hat back on his head, then looked over my shoulder. "Howdy, Miz Stewart. Hey, Reeve!"

"Hey, Joe. Hi, Joe," they answered, still watching the goings-on from the safety of the main lodge's wide porch where my grandparents, father, and Reeve lived; my brothers, older sisters, and I had claimed cabins as our own personal digs. Joe's eyes slid back to mine. "Ain't seen Harper in a spell."

"She and Sawyer are doing the Yukon tours this summer. Left for Whitehorse this morning."

"Whitehorse, huh?"

"Uh-huh. Then up to Stewart Crossing."

While my great-great-grandfather had stayed in the Dyea/Skagway area and set down roots here, his two brothers had headed north into the Canadian Yukon, founding settlements at Stewart Crossing and even further north and more remote in Eagle Plains.

"Long ways up."

"She loves it."

Joe lingered for a second, grinding his teeth before grimacing. "Yeah. She does."

I gestured to the stone fire ring, which had the charred remains of last night's campfire and needed to be reset. "Gotta get back to work."

"Sure thing, Tanner," he said, rounding the hood of his car to open the driver's side door. "Sorry for the bother. Good luck in Juneau."

All in all, Juneau had worked out pretty well. Though I hated leaving my family in Dyea, it felt good to help out my momma's brother; she would've liked that. With Parker around to bother me and two dozen dogs who needed to be fed, exercised, and picked up after, the summer flew by quicker than I expected. And best of all, I didn't hear from Ramona. Not once. I assumed she had found someone else to torture for the rest of the summer.

My sister and I returned home in the fall, reunited with

our family once again, to wait out the long winter with intermittent hunting bookings and occasional winter wilderness tours, the days short and dark until the cruise ships started arriving again in the spring.

Like clockwork, right around the first of May, the summer recruits started arriving in Skagway to open shops, sweep out storerooms, and brush up on Gold Rush history. The little village of 800 souls would swell to over 2,000 by June first, ready to meet the over one million tourists who'd arrive by seaplane, ferry, tour bus, car, and cruise ship between May and September. And my family, with our cabins, campfires, and tours of all kinds, would be there to greet them.

It was Hunter who heard about Ramona's return first. He'd been at the Ace Hardware—the only year-round store in town—buying pitch to seal a new outhouse, when he'd overheard Andi Jones, owner of the King Kone, talking to Phylicia Olson, manager of Wild Alaska Gifts and Sundries.

"Any repeat offenders this summer?" Phylicia had asked Andi with a chuckle.

"Yes, indeed. I have the Sutter girls from Homer staying in two of the bedrooms above the store, a new girl name of Caswell coming down from Fairbanks—her uncle was a teacher over at the high school a few years back, remember?— and that odd duck from last year…Ramona from California. She'll be back, too. Handful of drama with that one, but she already knows the ropes. How about you?"

Hunter had raced from the store and jumped in his truck, breaking the Alaskan land speed record to get back to the campground and find me.

"She's coming back!" he yelled over the motor of the leaf blower I was using to clear pine needles out of the barn.

"What's that?" I asked, taking out my earbuds and turning off the motor.

"She's coming back!" he panted, sweat breaking out on his forehead. "Ramona!"

"What? When?"

"For the season."

"You sure?"

"I was at the Ace," he explained. "I overheard Andi and Phylicia talking about summer help."

"Shit," I snarled. "Shit. Shit. Shit."

"Yeah. Shit. What are you going to do?"

"We have an idea."

I had looked over my shoulder to see Harper, Parker, and Reeve standing in the doorway of the barn's double doors.

"Oh, yeah?"

Harper held up a copy of *The Odds Are Good* magazine, a picture of a shirtless lumberjack on the cover.

"What the heck is that?" I demanded.

My oldest sister smirked. "A solution."

"I don't know what it is, but it won't work."

"Yes, it will," Harper assured me. "Even psychos like Ramona respect 'girl code.' If you're taken, you're off-limits."

"But you have to be *good and taken*," added Parker.

That was two hours ago, and here I am now, sitting at my keyboard, a desperate ad written with the help of my sisters and my credit card information entered into the magazine's website.

Fake fiancée needed. Lord. How has my life come to this?

I scan the page one more time…

and press Enter.

chapter two

McKenna

"Please reconsider," I murmur, staring at my toes.

"No."

"I need this job," I say, biting my cheek to keep myself from cussing her out.

"Not badly enough to follow protocol."

Protocol? Give me a break.

"Ma'am," I say, "my grandmother is—"

"Your family is your personal business, Miss Cabot."

"But she's dependent on me for—"

"I'm sorry to hear that, but rules are rules, and personal smartphones are not allowed in the warehouse. You knew the rule. You broke it. You're out."

Jo Berwick, Nile.com warehouse manager, stares at me, bug-eyed and thin-lipped in her bland, puke-green uniform. She looks like a frog: a fat, ugly frog covered in pond scum. That thought almost makes me grin.

"Hand over your ID, please."

"Ms. Berwick—"

"Enough, Miss Cabot."

"I'll…I'll beg."

"It won't do any good. We have a zero-tolerance policy."

At this point, Jo's lips tilt up. Only slightly and only for a moment, but enough for me to understand she's enjoying this. Like every other person in the world with an inferiority complex and a tiny bit of power, she's a bully when she gets the chance. It makes her feel big. And important. And I hate her for it.

I never wanted this job. I was happy working for a museum in Montana. I never wanted to move back to Seattle, let alone work for the biggest online department store in the country. I certainly didn't aspire to being a warehouse supervisor at said store, but beggars can't be choosers, and my anthropology degree from UDub hasn't gotten me very far in the three years since I graduated.

The *only* thing that ever could have persuaded me to return to Seattle was Mimi. She was there for me when my father was arrested and my mother fled the state for three long years. She was there when my parents came and went from my life, never sticking around for long. She was there to buy me my first bra and my first box of tiny tampons to celebrate my acceptance to UDub, and she was the one invited to my college graduation a few years later.

She got confused on her way to my commencement and ended up missing it, but instead of looking closer at why a born-and-bred Seattle native would have trouble making her way to an iconic location like Husky Stadium, I screamed at her for missing my big day and left town for a job in Montana.

After a lifetime of feeling abandoned, I reasoned, the one person who'd always "been there" for me had abandoned me, too. It had wounded me to my very core, blinding me to reason and perspective.

It was only when Mimi's neighbor, the aptly named Mrs. Peepers, tracked me down on Facebook to tell me that Mimi was hanging laundry in the nude, taking midnight strolls wrapped in her comforter, and having loud, nonsensical conversations with herself on the back porch, that I finally returned.

Sure enough, losing her way to my graduation two years before had been a warning sign: Mimi had Alzheimer's and was already approaching the dreaded middle stage, requiring at-home treatment or a residential treatment center. She was no longer able to live on her own.

It was a terrible blow for me, made all the more painful by the shabby way I'd treated her over the past two years. I promised her (and myself!) that I'd do better. I'd do whatever I could to be sure she knew she was loved and to guarantee that she was comfortable and safe.

In-house care was a possibility after her diagnosis, but Mimi wasn't an easy patient, and over the next few months, she went downhill quickly. She always knew who *I* was, but she pushed back against the anonymous *(to her)* nursing staff who I paid to come and help her while I was at work. She couldn't remember her address or phone number. She had trouble getting to the bathroom in time. She was restless at night and prone to wandering.

Her doctor advised me that it was time to find her a

memory care facility.

Her savings, in addition to the proceeds from selling her house and my deceased grandfather's VA benefits, would get her into a decent facility, but the one I found in Seattle wasn't what I wanted for her. Yes, it was clean. It was professionally staffed. It was safe. But it didn't have some of the bells and whistles I wanted her to have while they still mattered.

It didn't have a swimming pool, hot tub, or gym; just a small, windowless room with a few exercise bikes and a treadmill that had seen better days.

The dining room meals were simple and nutritious, but nothing special; nothing that would give her foodie brain some sensory pleasure in their taste.

There was a TV room but no organized movie nights, and because the place was in the city, there was no garden where Mimi could sink her arms into the earth up to her elbows.

I wanted her to have better, and better existed outside of Seattle, in a newer facility located in a nice suburb with yoga classes and a hot tub, with bingo nights and gardening.

I'd already quit my job in Montana and sold my little apartment there. After selling Mimi's house to optimize her care, I found a small, cheap apartment near the university, but if I wanted Mimi to move to a better place, I needed to make money. Enough for me to live on and a little more to make her life as comfortable as possible.

I found a teaching job at one of the local community colleges, and while my benefits were good, my salary was not. I'd need more to give Mimi the care I wanted her to have.

That's when I heard that Nile.com was hiring…and not only that, but they were also paying thirty dollars an hour to warehouse supervisors, sometimes thirty-five dollars on the night shift. It was too good to pass up.

For a while, that was my life: teaching at Seattle Community College from eight a.m. to one p.m. Monday through Friday, then working as the night supervisor at a Nile.com warehouse from four p.m. to midnight, Wednesday through Sunday. Not much of a life maybe, but when I moved Mimi into a beautiful memory care unit at a center in Yakima, WA and left her potting flowers in their perennial gardens, I knew I'd made the right choice.

So, I can't lose this job.

I can't.

"*Please*, Jo," I murmur, reaching for her arm, then stopping when she flinches away. I put my hands in my pockets, lest I get it in my head to smack her stupid, smug face. "What if it was *your* grandmother? *Your* mother? *Your* child?"

"My grandmothers are both dead. My mother is self-sufficient, and I have no children." She holds out her hand. "Your employee badge, please."

I yank it off my lapel and slap it into her palm.

"Good riddance," I say, turning away from her.

"My thoughts exactly."

I swing around on my heel and face her, giving her the finger. "Fuck you, you pious, pretentious, past-your-prime, malicious, malignant, middle-aged old hag!"

She looks affronted just long enough to give me a mite

of satisfaction, then marches back to her office.

***

"I couldn't help it."

"You could've," says my best friend, Isabella. "You chose not to."

"She deserved it."

"Did she, Ken?"

"Yes! The phone number was from Yakima. I had to answer it. What if Mimi had fallen? Or gotten her meds confused? Or...or...I don't know! I had to answer."

"I get it." Isabella takes a sip of her merlot. "You're an awesome granddaughter, and your Mimi is really lucky to have you. But before you burned the house down at Nile.com, you could have gone to bitchy Berwick's manager and asked for a second chance. He wouldn't be very likely to give it now, would he?"

Isabella's right. Ethan, the general manager of the Nile.com Seattle warehouse, could've reversed Jo's decision, but it was definitely too late now. I'd thrown a proper tantrum on my way out the door.

"She was a sadist," I mutter.

"You broke the rules."

"Oh, god, what am I going to do, Iz?" I ask her, swirling my wine around in my glass. "I paid Mimi's care up through March, but another bill's going to come in June, then September, then December...God, it's never going to end, and my teaching salary is never going to cover it."

"Calm down. Drink your wine. We'll figure this out."

"How? Teaching barely covers *my* expenses. Where am I

going to find another overpaid second job to cover Mimi's?"

I flatten my arms on the bar and lay my forehead on my wrists. I know I'm being dramatic, but my situation is as heavy as my head feels. Mimi's care depends on me, and I just lost an annual salary of $60,000 extra dollars. Fuck. Fuck. Fuck.

"I have an idea."

I don't bother looking up. "I'm not answering phones for your creepy brother-in-law."

"He couldn't afford you anyway. No. I have a different idea. Hear me out?"

"Sure."

"Look at me, Ken."

I raise my head and sigh. "Fine. What?"

"Remember my cousin's kid, Beto, who worked on a crab boat in Alaska last winter?"

"I'm not working on a—"

"Gah! You are so annoying! Can you just listen?"

I pretend to zip my lips and throw away the key.

"So, Beto worked on a crab boat and made, like, thirty thou in three months. He's eighteen, Ken. High school grad. So, that's a ton. Anyway, he was at my abuela's last weekend, and he's telling us that he's going back up to Alaska to one of the big cruise ports this summer because he can make a lot of money driving a van for tourists. Apparently, it's a big money maker. Three months of work, beautiful scenery, cool summer, and you make, like, a few thousand dollars."

I blink at her. "Um…let me get this straight. Your bright idea is for me to move to Alaska and—"

"No! Not move. Never move. Just…go. For a little

while. From Memorial Day to Labor Day."

"I'll lose my teaching—"

"That's the best part! No, you won't. Your teaching job ends in mid-May, right? And starts up the Tuesday after Labor Day?"

I open my mouth to argue, then promptly close it.

Huh. She's right. She's totally one hundred percent right.

As a teacher, I have the option to teach summer school, or I can have my summer off. And if I have my summer off, that means I'm free to work another job.

"And you can even make an extra couple of bucks if you sublet your apartment for the summer!"

"What about Mimi?" I moan. "I can't abandon her."

"She's in Yakima. That's two hours from here on a good day. You go visit her ...what? Once a week? Once every two weeks?"

"Yeah. About that."

"So I'll go."

"To Yakima?"

"Sure. I'll visit her every other week and give you an update. And I'll be, like, her local emergency contact. If anything happens to Mimi, I'll be there!"

Tears spring into my eyes, welling until they spill over. What would I do without Iz? I hope I never find out.

"You'd do that for me?"

"For my ride-or-die best friend who punched Becky Beavers in the face in fourth grade for making me cry? Uh. Yeah. I'd be happy to."

"You're the best, Iz."

"I am, aren't I? Next round is on you." She chuckles. "Oh! Look at this." She reaches into her handbag and pulls out a rolled-up magazine. "Beto brought this to the BBQ and left before I could give it back to him. It's…interesting."

I unroll the magazine to find a shirtless beefcake on the cover. My eyes slide to the title. "*The Odds Are Good.*"

"Yeah," says Isabella. "I guess that's an old saying about Alaskan men: the odds are good, but the goods are odd." She grins at me. "Who knows? Maybe someone will catch your eye?"

I haven't had the time to *think* about dating since moving back to Seattle, let alone *go* on a date, and Isabella knows it.

"The odds *aren't* good," I tell her.

"You never know," she says in that singsong way that makes me roll my eyes.

I shove the magazine in my handbag and gesture to the bartender for another round.

***

The next evening, when I'd usually be at work, I'm sitting at my laptop researching summer jobs in popular Alaskan cruise ports.

Sitka.

Ketchikan.

Juneau.

Skagway.

Seward.

Homer.

These six towns recur over and over again online, and so far, I've seen jobs ranging from $15-$35 an hour, which is pretty good for seasonal work.

Seasonal housekeeper for $23/hour! Seasonal tour van driver for $25/hour! Seasonal bartending for $28/hour plus tips!

Hm. I don't have a bartending license, but the bus I take to school every day advertises a way to get one. It's a two-day course, and you finish "Certified to Serve!" If my math is right and I work my ass off, I can make at least $100 in tips per shift. That means I could make about $6000 a month bartending in Alaska. That's $18,000 from the beginning of June until the end of August and would take care of Mimi's extra expenses for *nine months!*

I surf "Skagway seasonal jobs," intrigued by a blog post entitled, *10 Great Reasons to Get a Summer Job in Skagway.* Among the perks mentioned? Skagway is "summer camp for adults" flush with "tourist money and tips," with "no boring people in sight," and a "wealth of Gold Rush history."

I can't lie. There isn't a word in that description that sounds bad to me. It's been too long since I had fun making money, and the fact that Skagway is historically rich only adds to its allure. As an anthropology major, the human experience—especially in terms of harrowing historical narrative like the Gold Rush—appeals deeply to the scholar in me. Perhaps I could even do some research while in Skagway and add a new section to my fall courses.

Of course, I'd need to pay for housing, but these little port towns—Skagway, especially—seem to offer discounted housing to those working seasonally. Three months' rent would barely bite into my earnings.

A picture of me and Mimi on my sixth birthday sits on

24

the corner of my desk, and I pick it up, looking at the way I'm leaning into her. There's a giant cake in front of me and a bunch of kids making a semi-circle around the cake, but it's Mimi's lips on my cheek that I'm clearly relishing. She was my everything. I loved her.

I *still* love her. Today. Right now. Right this second.

I sit back in my desk chair and rub my burning eyes.

It was hard to call her care center today and add Isabella to my meager list of approved visitors and emergency contacts. Even though Mimi's two hours away, it's been comforting to me to know that I could jump in my car and get to her quickly in an emergency. I'm so grateful to Isabella for helping out, but it hurts me to think of being so far away from Mimi if she should need me. There's no way to get back to Washington except by boat or plane.

Out of the corner of my eye, I see the beefcake magazine Iz gave me sticking out from my purse and pull it free. Lying down on my bed, I take a guilty peek.

Oh. Wow.

Page after page of hot, bearded guys stare back at me boldly, muscles bulging and testosterone zinging off the paper. Flannel shirts abound, more than one man "looking for love" rests an axe on his shoulder, and several made the smart choice to have themselves photographed with sled dogs, their bright blue eyes alert and ears pricked. My mood lifts a little, and I'm at the end page all too quickly.

About to close the magazine and start applying for the jobs I've found online, a small ad on the back page catches my eye:

HELP!

Grinning with amusement, I read one man's brief, but hilariously blunt, plea for a fake fiancée. I can't help but wonder if his ex is more of an Isla Fischer from *Wedding Crashers* or a Glenn Close from *Fatal Attraction*, and for whatever reason, both ideas make me giggle aloud. I mean, how psycho are we talking about here?

My amusement fades as I read on:

I'll pay your R/T transportation from the Lower 48, can offer free accommodation, and I can guarantee you a seasonal job in retail, hospitality, or tourism—your choice.

Free transportation, free housing, *and* a guaranteed job?

The shrewd caregiver in me can't deny the appeal, and what was broadly funny a second ago now feels personally relevant.

Without having to pay over a thousand dollars for a round-trip air ticket and another four hundred dollars a month for a room, I could afford an extra month of care for Mimi. And for what in return? Wearing an engagement ring around Skagway and pretending to be someone's girlfriend? He clearly states he's not looking for love, so presumably he won't get creepy with me, and if he does? The deal's off. Plus, I'll knock his block off. I didn't get my black belt for nothing.

I go back to my desk, open my laptop, and paste the email address provided into a new message.

Dear HELP! I type. *When's the wedding?*

chapter three

Tanner

Her name's McKenna, she's twenty-four, from Seattle, and willing to pose as my girlfriend. She'll be here today, and Ramona isn't due until this weekend.

My sisters' crazy plan actually appears to be working.

Though my ad didn't get a ton of responses—I guess not every woman wants to walk into a situation that includes a psycho ex-girlfriend. *Go figure!*—McKenna was the best of the bunch. Her answer was well-written with a sense of humor, and she agreed to my terms with the added caveat that if I stuck my tongue down her throat, she'd karate chop my face with her hand. Unenthusiastic about adding a broken cheekbone to my recent list of facial injuries, I assured her that our physical contact would be limited to handholding and the occasional peck on the cheek. Anything else would be subject to negotiation and agreed upon in person.

She requested that I find her a job bartending, so I reached out to the owners of the Skagway Brew Pub and the Purple Parsnip Saloon—both locals, both of whom I've known my whole life. She settled on the Purple Parsnip because, she said, she liked the historical element of a business that had been in operation for over a hundred years.

I liked that. I did.

I felt that asking her for a photo would send the wrong message, so I have no idea what she looks like, and to be frank, I don't care. Chasing after a hot woman last summer got me in a heap of trouble. I'd just as soon McKenna was sensible and plain, the kind of girl I could be friends with over the next few months, without any complications or entanglements. I just need her to hold up her end of the bargain convincingly and pretend to be my fiancée. My sisters assure me that even crazy Ramona will respect "girl code"—once she understands that I'm engaged, she won't bother me anymore.

God willing.

Because I promised McKenna housing, I moved a cot into my brothers' cabin, where I'll bunk this summer. McKenna will have my cabin—at the end of the row and a little nicer and more private than the rest. Hopefully she won't mind my driving her into town for work and picking her up at the end of her shifts, because it's too far to walk from Dyea to Skagway, and I need my car during the day. But Harper said it was a good thing. It'll make our story more convincing if McKenna's seen getting into and out of my truck a couple times a day.

"What time's her flight arriving?"

Reeve sits beside me in the front seat chewing gum and blowing bubbles.

"Fifteen minutes," I mutter.

"You nervous?"

"Hell, yeah."

"It's not every day you meet your bride for the first time," says Reeve, grinning at me.

My youngest sister is all sass.

"Why'd you wanna come with me again?"

"Because she'll be less creeped out with someone else in the car. Especially if that someone is young and female. And if you get weird, I'll smack your leg as a warning."

"Well, hell, Reeve. What am I gonna do for the other twenty-three hours of the day when you're not here to police my behavior?"

"Get yourself into messes like the one with Ramona."

Damn that sass!

I pick a parking spot close to the terminal building and cut the engine, turning to my sister. "Wait in the car."

"Like hell." She opens her door and hops to the ground, charging into the tiny waiting room.

"Reeve!"

I'm distracted by the roar of the seaplane engine above the clouds before I see it descending, but once it's in range, landing is quick and easy. I hustle inside the squat building to find Reeve standing by a giant, stuffed grizzly bear, shifting her weight from foot to foot as she looks through the glass windows at the tiny plane taxiing to a stop on the single runway.

"Guess I'm not the only nervous one," I say from behind her.

"Shut up, please," she says without turning around.

29

As a baggage handler unloads the three or four suitcases in the hold, a side door opens for the passengers to deplane.

"You ready?" murmurs Reeve.

"Not even a little," I whisper back.

A family of four climbs down the little stairs—mother, father, and two sons—and then…no one. I stare at the plane in confusion, but as the family walks toward the terminal building, the pilot pushes the stairs back up, then drives his puddle jumper over to the hangar.

Reeve elbows me. "What's going on?"

"I don't know…"

My eyes slide back to the family approaching the arrivals door. The mother, father, and younger son are making their way together toward the terminal, but the older boy is lagging behind. Like most teenagers, he's wearing an oversized sweatshirt, loose jeans, and sneakers. He's short and slight, like a good breeze would blow him away, the kind of kid who probably gets a lot of crap for being so small. *Really* small. Huh. My eyes narrow, registering something seminal before my mind can process it completely, but I think it's this: his gait is, well, *dainty*, for a teenage boy. A baseball hat shields his face, but just before he follows his family through the terminal door, he—*fuck! She!*—looks up. And while there's nothing about her body in loose clothes that would identify her as female, her *face*—with a fringe of dark bangs covering her forehead, huge brown doe-eyes framed with long, curled lashes, and pink, bowed lips—is unmistakably feminine.

She walks through the door, takes off her cap, and pauses to glance around. Spying me to her left, she raises her chin, locking her eyes on mine.

"Tanner?"

I thought I didn't have any expectations, but I guess I did, because she definitely isn't what I expected. She's short and tiny, with dark, close-cropped hair and a sharp, direct gaze. She reminds me of someone. *Who? Damn it! It's on the tip of my tongue!* Who the hell does she remind me of?

"Yep. He's Tanner. I'm Reeve," says my sister, stepping up from behind me and shaking McKenna's hand. "His sister."

"Hey, Reeve."

"Did anyone ever tell you that you look exactly like Alice Cullen from the *Twilight* movies?"

Alice Cullen from the stupid Twilight movies! That's it! Small, but mighty. Little, but fierce.

McKenna nods with a little chuckle. "Yeah. I get that every so often. Especially when my hair's short and dark like this."

"It's uncanny," says Reeve.

I offer McKenna my hand. "I'm Tanner."

"McKenna Cabot."

Her hand is small and cool in mine, the tiny bones like a bird's. I feel oafish shaking it, scared that if I use too much pressure, I could break it.

She stares up at me thoughtfully for a second. "This is weird, right?"

"A little, yeah."

"You got a ring for me?" she asks, sliding one hand from mine and holding up the other.

"Uh. Yeah. I got it, um—"

Damn it. I'm so nervous, I forgot which pocket I put it in.

"Did you already lose it?"

"Shut up, Reeve," I mutter, relieved to feel the little box tucked safely inside my jacket.

McKenna chuckles. "Might as well make it official right from the start, huh?"

With twenty different souvenir shops in town, half a dozen of them that specialize in jewelry, I had my pick of rings. The one I chose was the cheapest I could find that would actually pass as an engagement ring: a simple ten-karat yellow gold band with a bright white opal in the middle and two diamond chips on either side. Three hundred bucks well-spent if Ramona leaves me the hell alone this summer.

As I slip the ring on McKenna's finger, I realize I've made a big error in sizing it. While it would have fit a more average-sized woman like my sisters or Ramona, it practically dangles from McKenna's slim finger.

"We can exchange it for a smaller size," I tell her.

She fists her hand to keep it in place. "Good idea."

Out of nowhere, I hear myself ask her: "Do you like it?"

"Mm-hm. I do. My grandmother had one—*has* one— just like it, but in silver. She hasn't worn it in a long time, but I remember it well. I loved the way the opal caught the light. Sometimes it looked like there was a whole universe inside that tiny stone."

"You talk like a poem," says Reeve, and I sense something akin to heroine-worship quickly developing in my youngest sister.

"That's a great compliment," says McKenna, hefting her backpack up on her tiny shoulder and shoving her hands in her jean pockets. "Though I doubt my students would agree."

"You're a teacher?" Reeve asks.

"I am. At a community college in Seattle."

"Wait. You're a *professor*?" I ask her.

"Technically, no," she says. "I don't have a PhD. But I do teach at the college level. Sort of a gray area."

Again, not that I had any well-developed expectations, but her being a college professor somehow wasn't what I expected either. What is she doing here? Why come all the way to Skagway when she has a decent job teaching in Seattle?

Reeve clears her throat loudly.

"Well, I guess we should get going," I say, taking the hint. "Got any luggage?"

McKenna puts her baseball cap back on her head, gesturing toward the baggage claim area where two maroon suitcases sit side by side. "Those two are mine."

"Reeve," I say, "be useful, huh? Show McKenna where the car is while I get her things."

My sister grabs McKenna's hand, as she would Harper's or Parker's, and tugs her toward the terminal exit. I watch them go—Reeve taller and bigger next to McKenna, who could still pass for a teenage boy from behind.

Not that I have a right, but I feel disappointed.

She's not my type. Not by a long shot. Not even a little bit.

I like a little more meat on the bone, a fully feminine

33

figure with long, wavy hair that can drag over a man's naked torso as she kisses her way south. Not to mention, even in modern times, Alaska can be a brutal place, and it takes a strong, sturdy person to make it here. McKenna's *wispier* than wispy; she's just a slip of a girl.

And yet, she's here.

She came all the way to Skagway, Alaska, to pose as my fiancée, and I'm determined to find out why. No, I have no interest in fucking her, but I can't deny that she intrigues me as a person. I want to know what she's running from...or to. And on the plus side, she's obviously smart; when she takes off that baseball hat and looks you straight in the eye, there's no mistaking her intelligence. I sort of doubt it, but maybe she's made of stronger stuff than I think.

She reminds me of the poster on Reeve's bedroom wall:

Though she be but little, she is fierce.

I grab her bags and say a prayer.

Please, God, just let this work.

***

McKenna

Reeve insists that I sit in the front seat, and a moment later, Tanner emerges from the terminal building, carrying my bags like they're filled with feathers.

In point of fact, they're definitely *not* filled with feathers. At the Seattle airport, I could barely roll them from the outside curb to the check-in line inside, and I had to pay extra because they were both overpacked and overweight.

Tanner opens the trunk, plops them inside, then sits

down next to me in the driver's seat.

"All buckled up?" he asks. "Road to Dyea can be bumpy."

Not quite as cute as Charlie Hunnam from his "Sons of Anarchy" days, Tanner Stewart is still a very attractive man by most standards. Huge and blonde, like some sort of Viking lumberjack, he's the kind of uber-masculine stereotype that makes most women weak in the knees.

Most women…but not me. He's not my type because, attractive or not, he's messy, and I don't *do* messy. The first half of my life was messy enough without making the second half a wreck, too. And this guy? Tanner Charlie-Hunnam Stewart? He has 'MESSY'—in bold type, all caps, highlighted with yellow neon marker—stamped all over his life.

"So," I say, riffing aloud on the same theme, "tell me about your ex."

"Oh, man," mutters Reeve from the back seat. "Here we go."

"Her name's Ramona," says Tanner.

"*Crazy* Ramona," adds Reeve. "She's *totally* unhinged. She pretended to kill herself when Tan broke up with her. I'm not even kidding. Isn't that *nuts*?"

"That's pretty nuts," I have to agree. "What happened?"

"We dated last summer, and she—" Tanner takes a deep breath and lets it go slowly. "I think you need a little background, okay?"

"Sure. Go for it."

"Okay. So, my great-great-grandfather came up here from California in 1897 to mine for gold, but once he understood that he'd be *walking* to the Canadian Yukon—five hundred miles with his mining supplies on his back, a tiny fact that the newspapers of the day had forgotten to mention—he cut his losses and used his connections in Sacramento to open a mercantile here instead."

"In Skagway."

"No. In Dyea."

"Dyea," I repeat. "Where's that?"

"So, there were two places of entry for prospectors during the Klondike Gold Rush: Skagway and Dyea. Skagway had a deep port that could accommodate larger boats, and Dyea had a shallow beach that only allowed for ships during high tide. But Dyea had the advantage of being the trailhead for the Chilkoot Trail, an existing Tlingit trade route that was used by prospectors whether they arrived in Skagway or Dyea." He sighs, like what he's about to say weighs heavy on his heart. "But when the trains settled on Skagway for a depot, Dyea died."

"What do you mean 'died'?" I ask. "Don't *you* live in Dyea?"

"Oh, it died," says Reeve. "We're the *only* ones who live in Dyea."

"Reeve, do you mind?" asks Tanner, shooting her an annoyed glance in the rearview mirror. "We're not the *only* ones. There are a few other homesteaders. But we own the only business in the Dyea valley. That's for sure."

"You own...a campground, right? For tourists?"

He nods. "Yes. On the original site of my great-great-grandfather's store. Even when prospectors and tourists started going to Skagway instead, he didn't abandon or sell the land. He passed it down. There was always some sort of dwelling or business on the original spot."

"I checked out your campground online," I tell him. "Looks nice."

"It is. We work hard to keep it up. There's the main lodge: restaurant and meeting rooms downstairs, while my father, Reeve, and grandparents live upstairs. Plus fifteen cabins," he says. "Twelve available to tourists, one for my sisters, one for my brothers, and one's mine."

"How come you get your own?"

"Because I bought it. I own it outright."

He's proud of this fact. I can hear it in his voice, and I approve. Heck, I'm about a million miles away from buying myself a house, and we're only a few years apart in age.

"So…how many siblings do you have?"

"There are six of us," pipes up Reeve. "Hunter, Harper, Tanner, Parker, Sawyer, and me."

Workers, I think, remembering a course I took on the etymology of names. Hunters hunted. Harpers played harps. Tanners tanned hides. Parkers maintained parks for noble families. Sawyers sawed wood. And Reeves—it takes me a second to remember the details from my class—*ah, yes!* Reeves were stewards.

Keepers.

Just like Reeve is Tanner's, I think with a grin.

"Who named you guys?"

"Our mom," says Tanner, his voice soft and final.

I sense a story, but not one he wants to tell. I don't push

it.

"So you're in the tourism business," I say.

"Yep. We maintain the lodge, restaurant, and cabins. We also have a barn with a couple of mountain goats."

"One's three-legged," says Reeve. "She got hit by a tour bus. Now she's ours."

"Poor thing," I say.

"Don't pity her. She's happy as a clam," says Reeve "Name's Trinity. Her boyfriend is—"

"Let me guess! Neo?"

"Yes!" cries Reeve. "How'd you know?"

"Old *Matrix* fan," I tell her.

"So is Tanner. He's our sci-fi nerd."

"Thanks for that, Reeve," says Tanner. "Anything else you want to share?"

"That you're ornery AF," mutters Reeve.

Tanner clears his throat, then continues telling me about their business. "We run tours anywhere our clients want to go: up north to the Yukon, in the footsteps of miners on the Chilkoot Trail, outback to see wildlife. Fishing and hunting packages—you get it. Whatever the guests want to experience. Plus, we host the occasional wedding, family reunion, et cetera."

"We're rated real high on Trip Advisor," says Reeve, pride in her voice. "Had a corporate retreat come in last spring. Big muckety-mucks from Anchorage."

I smile at that expression. *Muckety-mucks*. It's one Mimi uses often. Or used to.

"Sounds great," I say, turning slightly in my seat to smile

at her. "Keeper."

"Huh?"

"Your name. Reeve. It means steward, or keeper."

"It does?"

"Sure," I say. "All of your names are jobs people used to have in old England."

"What was a Harper?"

"Someone who played the harp."

"And a hunter? Let me guess: someone who hunted?"

"Bingo!"

"And tanners tanned, of course. My brother's got a good one."

It's on the tip of my tongue to say, *Not that kind of tan*, when Tanner beats me to it.

"Don't be a dingbat, Reeve. Tanners tanned hides for clothing and furnishings. Like PawPaw does when he gets a deer."

"Your father skins and tans what he hunts?" I ask, the anthropologist in me sitting up and taking notice.

"Not our father. Our grandfather. He's Tlingit. Whatever he hunts, he eats or uses everything."

"You're native," I say, wondering why he's left this interesting detail out of his story.

"Nope. Not technically. PawPaw's my Gran's second husband. But we don't remember our biological grandfather. PawPaw's all we ever had."

"Gotcha," I say, noticing that we've left the paved roads of Skagway behind and are driving on a dusty dirt road now, the car bumping over ruts and rocks. "I think I get the family dynamic. Now, tell me about Ramona."

His face tightens and on the steering wheel, his bronze knuckles go white. Wow. I already knew she was trouble, but she sure did a number on this guy.

"Ramona was seasonal help. She worked at the King Kone last summer—the ice cream place in town."

"In Skagway."

He nods. "If we say 'town,' we always mean Skagway."

"Okay. Go on."

"She was hot."

I file that information away. Whatever Ramona looks like, she's Tanner's type.

"Uh-huh."

"She was hot, and I was an idiot." He huffs softly, glancing in the rearview mirror. "Reeve, cover your ears."

"No chance!"

"Fine. She was hot, I was an idiot, and without really getting to know each other, we started…sleeping together." He shakes his head like he's trying to chase away memories. "At first, it was great. Fun. Then…she started getting clingy."

I bristle at this. Something in me rebels against this description of a fellow woman. It's too easy to get sick of someone and call her "clingy" to make her look like a psycho and get rid of her. I mean, is there any chance *he* gave *her* the wrong signals? Lead her to believe there was more on the table?

"Clingy?" I know my tone is sharp, but I can't help it.

"She wanted me to stay over at her place every night. She wanted to spend every second together."

"Well…what was your arrangement? Did she have a *right* to expect more from you?"

"I never promised her anything. We were attracted to each other. Into each other. I got to her place, and we ripped each other's clothes off. We didn't have deep conversations about our thoughts and feelings. We barely talked at all. We didn't chill out together, watching movies or anything. I mean, pardon me for being crass, but we were screwing. That's it. That's *really* it. We got together and screwed."

A declaration like this one deserves a moment. I process it quietly before asking: "And she was on the same page?"

He throws up his hands. "Apparently not."

It isn't the right time to quibble over Ramona's right to expect more from Tanner. I want to hear as much of the story as possible before we get to the campground.

"Okay, so…she got weird about things?"

"She got…*psycho* about things."

"How?"

"She broke his nose!" says Reeve.

"She faked her own suicide and sent me photos over text."

Oof. That *is* pretty crazy.

"Wow. Okay. Anything else?"

"She came over with the sheriff and claimed I smacked her around. Had bruises all over her arms."

"No chance you…" …*might've been rough with her?*

He looks at me, his eyes grave. "I'd *never* touch a woman in anger. Never."

I believe him.

"And she said she was knocked up," added Reeve. "Big fat liar."

I glance at Tanner, who's clenching his jaw so hard, it's liable to pop.

"Any chance…?"

"None," said Tanner. "I had a scare once. I *always* check to be sure there aren't any leaks."

Hard to be a hundred percent positive, I think, but don't say it aloud.

"So, she broke your nose, pretended to kill herself, tried to have you falsely arrested, lied about you beating her and faked a pregnancy?"

"That's right," he says. "All in the space of a few weeks."

"What a nightmare," I mutter.

"Tanner left town and worked the rest of last summer in Juneau with Parker," says Reeve. "We never thought Ramona would come back."

A large wooden sign up ahead reads: Stewart Pass Campground and Conference Center.

"But she did," I confirm.

"She'll be here in three days," says Tanner, his voice low and tight.

We bounce down another dirt road until a grand, old, rustic resort comes into view. A generous-sized, Swiss-style lodge stands tall and proud before us with split log rockers on the porch, window boxes overflowing with red geraniums, and red gingham curtains in every shiny window.

"Oh, wow." I sigh as he parks in front of the lodge. "The pictures don't do it justice."

Reeve jumps out of the car and runs up the porch stairs, yelling, "Gran! PawPaw! Come meet McKenna!" I turn to Tanner, who's staring out the windshield, a troubled expression on his face.

"I may be little," I tell him. "But I take shit from no one. Including this Ramona person. Don't worry, okay? We've got this."

He turns to me, his handsome face softening.

"Little, but fierce," he murmurs, his blue eyes locking with mine.

Shakespeare. Huh. I wouldn't have guessed it. I decide then and there: he may look like a beefcake mountain man, but there might be more to Tanner Stewart than meets the eye.

"That's right," I manage to murmur, my cheeks growing warm from the look he's giving me.

"Welcome to Alaska, McKenna Cabot," he says. "I can't thank you enough for coming."

chapter four

Tanner

After a quick hello to Gran, I grab McKenna's suitcases from the back of my car and walk her to my cabin.

All fifteen of our cabins are situated in a wide circle around a central campfire, carefully landscaped and freshly-sealed every April. But mine is nicer than the other fourteen cabins because I own it, and I've made my own modifications to it. Unlike the others, which are powered solely by the solar panels mounted on each of the roofs, and therefore subject to the whimsy of the Alaskan sun, mine also has a dedicated generator so I'm never out of power. I also have a full kitchen, a small living/dining area, a shower *and* a bathtub, my own dedicated hot water heater, a wraparound porch I built myself last fall, and a wood-fired hot tub out back.

My cabin is a home, not a vacation spot, and I don't ever intend to leave.

"It's the one at the end," I tell her as we walk down the gravel pathway.

"They're in a circle," she points out.

"The furthest one from the lodge," I clarify.

"With the porch?"

"Uh-huh."

As she trudges behind me, I try to see our campground through her eyes—the handcrafted log cabin construction, complete with Tlingit carvings on the ridgepoles, and the stone-circled campfire with its tree stump seating. The style is overwhelmingly "rustic Alaska," but that's what our clients want. It's served us well for generations.

"I bet you do a good business here," she says, as though reading my mind.

"Always have."

"What are the cabins like inside?"

"Two twins or one full-sized bed in each, with end tables, lamps, a bureau, a coffee maker, and a shower-stall bathroom. Snug, but comfortable."

"Are those solar panels on the roofs?"

"Yep."

"Dyea doesn't seem like the sunniest place."

"It isn't. We get about eighty-five sunny days a year. Luckily, most of those are in the summer when the tourists come."

"What do you do for the other two hundred and eighty days?"

"We have a few portable generators for off-season guests."

She sighs. "How often will I be without power?"

"Never," I tell her, swinging her suitcases onto my porch. "My place has its *own* generator. The lodge does, too. You'll always have power."

She stands at the foot of the stairs looking up at my cabin, those big brown eyes taking in everything. Her lips quirk up into a grin as she catches my gaze. "That's a relief."

I reach into my pocket for a key and unlock the front door, holding it open so she can precede me inside. We enter the living/dining area, where I roll her bags against the back of the couch. It faces an old cast iron stove I found in Fairbanks two years ago and painstakingly restored.

"When I get that stove going, it warms up this whole cabin in fifteen minutes."

"So I won't be cold either."

"Kitchen's over there," I tell her. "I stocked the cabinets, fridge, and freezer with some essentials. Anything else you want, feel free to raid the lodge."

"Cool. Thanks."

Crossing the small room, I open the bedroom door. She peeks in from behind me.

"I thought you said the beds were full-size."

I glance at her from over my shoulder. "Mine's a king."

"Clearly," she says, sliding past me to get into the room. She stands at the foot of the bed with her hands on her hips, and my caveman brain flashes to a picture of Ramona in a similar position, with her rounded butt pressed against the footboard and her full tits spilling out of her T-shirt. Ramona had looked sturdy and voluptuous in the same spot—she stood tall in proportion to the dimensions of the room. She wasn't dwarfed by it as McKenna is.

A sudden stab of uncertainty makes me nervous. Are

people going to believe that the same guy who dated Ramona De Alicante last summer somehow ended up engaged to McKenna Cabot this one? She's just not my type. Not at all.

"Something wrong?" asks McKenna.

I must be frowning.

"Nope," I say, clearing my expression as I gesture to the door in the corner of the room. "Bathroom's through there."

She opens the door and looks inside. "A bathtub? I didn't expect that."

"I love a bath," I tell her, my cheeks coloring because it sounds stupid.

"Nothing wrong with a hot bath," she says with a little shrug.

"There's a hot tub out back, too."

"Really? Nice."

"Yeah. And the Taiya River beyond that."

"A bathtub, a hot tub and a river. Are you a water sign, by any chance?"

"I don't know what that is."

We stare at each other for a second, strangers facing each other in a strange place with a strange mission before us. It feels weird to be standing in my own home, acting as the tour guide. It feels even weirder to be showing my place to a woman who's supposed to be my fiancée.

We don't know each other, and we're not comfortable with each other. How in the world are we going to pull this off?

"Do you drink?" I blurt out.

Her eyes widen. "Drink…what?"

"Anything. Whiskey?"

"No," she says.

"Beer? Wine?"

"Wine. Beer. Sure."

"Red wine? White?"

"Red."

"Good. Settle in, then meet me at the lodge, okay? I think we need to get to know each other a little better before we head into town tomorrow."

She looks down at the ring on her hand, then clenches her fist and nods. "Sounds like a plan."

I take one last look at her, then sigh, turning on my heel and heading back to the lodge.

"Reeve says she's here!"

I look up to see my sister, Parker, coming out of her cabin. Although we're side by side in birth order, she's actually eight years younger than me, which makes her the oldest of the second three Stewart kids.

"She is...and this is *never* going to work," I mutter, keeping my voice low.

"Why not?" Parker walks in step beside me, her long legs easily matching my strides.

"She's tiny and strange and a college professor."

"What's wrong with being a college professor?"

Nothing.

"She's little," I add. "Like a teenage boy."

"But she's *not* a boy. So what's the problem?"

"She's not my type, Park. Not at all."

She ignores this. "Why do you think she's strange?"

I stop walking and put my hands on my hips, staring at my sister. "Why is she here? Why did she agree to this? She has a good job in Seattle teaching college. What's going on with her?"

My sister squares her shoulders, crossing her arms over her chest and looking at me with something bordering on disgust. "What's wrong with you, Tanner? How about a little faith and gratitude? She's here to help you out of a jam."

"I know it."

I take shit from no one.

As the words flash in my head, so bold and firm, I think that they're a shocking contrast to her stature, and yet, I believed her when she said them.

"You're smiling." My sister tilts her head to the side, staring at me with narrowed, appraising eyes. "Why are you smiling?"

"She said she doesn't take shit from anyone."

Parker nods approvingly. "Then, little or not, you better watch it, big brother."

As my sister saunters away, I shake my head with annoyance and continue on to the lodge, where I check the bar at the back of the restaurant for a decent bottle of red wine. I'm no connoisseur, but I discover a Willamette Valley Pinot Noir from Oregon with a medal around its neck and uncork it so it can breathe for a minute.

While I prefer whiskey, it doesn't feel hospitable to let her drink wine alone, so I take two stemmed glasses from the kitchen and place them on one of the empty tables in the large, quiet dining room. Then I sit back in a chair and wait.

I take shit from no one.

I smile every time I think of her saying that because it was awesome. Here she is, this little, owl-eyed, college professor spewing swear words with aplomb. It's weird. It's strangely wonderful.

Fuck it. I pour myself a glass of wine and down the whole thing like a shot before pouring myself another glass, and one for her, too. Cheersing her *in absentia*, I take a sip of mine before placing the glass back down on the table.

"Started without me, huh?"

I look up to see her walking toward me. I didn't even hear the lodge door open and close. She's stealthy. Cat-like.

"Just a sip," I lie.

She sits down across from me, picks up her glass, and with a *glug, glug, glug,* she downs her wine as quickly as I did mine. She wipes her mouth with the back of her hand.

"You were saying?" she asks.

"You're going to get drunk if you drink like that."

"Don't worry about me. I can hold my wine."

I roll my eyes because she can't weigh more than a buck ten, and the math doesn't add up. "Is that right?"

"Yes. It is." She pours herself another glass, then leans back in her chair, swirling the garnet liquid around the glass. "I spent a year in Greece and Italy. I learned how to drink. I had to."

"Had to?"

"If you get drunk and lose control, bad things can…" She averts her gaze. "I mean, it's just safer if you keep your wits about you."

"Were you there during college?" I ask her, thinking it's as good a place as any to get to know her.

"Yes."

"Where'd you go to college?"

"UDub."

"And studied?"

"Anthropology and archaeology."

"Why?"

"What?" She looks up at me, her eyebrows furrowed. "What do you mean…*why*?"

"Did you want to be an archaeologist?"

She shrugs. "I'm interested in the past."

"What did you do after graduation?"

"I worked at a museum in Montana."

"Whereabouts?"

"Bozeman."

"You liked it there?"

"Yes," she says. "Very much."

I feel like I'm about to catch her in a lie, and my adrenaline rushes. "Then why'd you leave?"

She takes a deep breath and lets it go slowly. "My grandmother got sick. I went back to Seattle to look after her."

Huh. Okay.

Pieces start falling into place now. I couldn't figure out why someone with a steady job in Seattle would come here for a season, but caring for a sick family member can be an expensive business, especially if you love them and want the best for them.

"Your grandmother."

"Mm-hm. My Mimi." She takes a sip of her wine and nods slowly. "She raised me."

I want to search her face for clues, but she stares intently at her wineglass, her eyes downcast.

"What happened to your parents?"

She snaps her head up, her lips taut, her eyes sharp and wide. "Your turn. Where did *you* go to college?"

"What?"

"College. You. Where?"

"I didn't," I say, sitting back in my chair and crossing my arms over my chest. "College isn't for everyone."

She stares at me hard for a moment, and I get the feeling she doesn't agree with me but doesn't want to push her point. Finally she asks, "You went to high school here?"

I nod. "Yep."

"And then started working for your family's tourism business."

"Yep, again," I say, finishing the rest of my wine and pouring myself another glass.

McKenna looks around the empty dining room. "I thought it would be busier here."

"We *are* busy for so early in the season. Cabins are two-thirds full right now," I tell her. "Only feels empty because the days are full of tours. Got three cabins hiking the Chilkoot, three up in the Yukon until tomorrow, and three more whale watching in Skagway harbor."

Her expression softens. "Whales? Really? Wow."

"Yep. Juneau's better, but we've got 'em, too." I gesture to the kitchen. "My Gran and sister will start making dinner in an hour or so. The guests will all be back for dinner around six. And there's a campfire tonight."

"A campfire?" She grins at me like a little kid. "Like in the movies? With songs and s'mores?"

"S'mores for sure," I say, capping off her glass with what's left in the bottle and chuckling at her excitement. "Like the ones in the movies."

"No singing?"

"Sometimes, if the guests have some favorites and get a sing-along going. If not, we always have tales to tell."

"We?"

"My family and I."

"Sounds fun," she says.

"Guests like it," I tell her. "And whatever the guests like pays the bills."

"Don't *you* like the stories?"

I shrug. "I guess."

Honestly, I don't think much about it. The stories are part of the job, and I've been listening to them and telling them all my life.

Do I like them? Hmm.

I guess I do.

But even more—*way more* than the stories themselves—I like the guests' expressions and reactions when I tell them. I like the way they get excited about Alaskan culture and history. I like knowing that I did something to make history come alive for them as my parents and grandparents did for me.

We sit in silence for a second, and I mull over what I've learned about her in the short time I've known her.

She's educated, smart and motivated.

She has a good job in Seattle.

She's caring for someone who needs her.

Not as strange as I originally thought, I grudgingly admit. But there are big gaps in my knowledge of her, and I feel strongly we need to fill those gaps as best we can to be a convincing couple. She doesn't seem to want to talk about her parents, but if there's a story there, I'd like the broad strokes at least.

"Hey," I say, keeping my voice gentle like I used to when Reeve skinned her knees, "I get it that family stuff can be tough, but…I really think we need to get to know each other so we can field questions. I've lived here my whole life. People are going to be interested in us, know what I mean?"

She takes a deep breath and lets it go slowly.

"You first," she finally says. "And fair warning…I'm gonna need more wine."

***

McKenna

I understand what he's saying about getting to know each other. I do. And I signed up for this—no one put a gun to my head and forced me into this awkward situation. But I hate talking about my parents. I can't think of any topic on earth I like less.

As he rummages around in the nearby bar area for another bottle of wine, I let the wine I've drunk—about a glass and three-quarters—settle. It smooths my edges and mellows my anxiety. When he returns to the table, I fold my hands in front of me and meet his eyes.

"What do you want to know?"

He pours himself a fresh glass and refills mine.

"Why did your grandmother raise you?"

I take a big sip, then say: "Have you ever been to Seattle?"

"Sure. A few times."

"So you know about the drug problem? And the homeless problem?"

He nods, but his eyes don't leave mine, and in a strange way, his fixed, intense gaze gives me the strength to power through the sad details of my fractured childhood.

"My parents were—um, *are*—addicts," I say, all the words coming out in one breath of air, the sound of my voice thin and shallow by the time I finish. I take a deep breath before continuing. "My father was arrested when I was four. My mother fled the state and didn't return for three years. My grandmother got custody of me when I was five, and I lived with her after that."

He stares at me, his expression troubled, but steady.

I am reminded of a strange reality for the children of addicts: we read your faces like a book when we share our trauma. We know when you're disapproving and when you're repulsed. We know when you assume that the poison in our parents' minds and veins has been passed on to us. We know when you lack sympathy of any kind or when you have a little to spare. We've seen the gamut of facial expressions for our whole lives, and we continue our stories based on how you respond to us.

Tanner is neither disapproving nor repulsed.

He doesn't see me as "infected."

He is sorry, which means he is kind.

My muscles relax in one slow wave of gratitude.

"That sucks," he says softly.

"Yes, it does," I agree.

His eyes flick to my wineglass. "I'm sorry about—I mean, I shouldn't have suggested—"

"I love wine. I know how much I can drink. Don't apologize."

"Fair enough," he says. "Do you see them? Your mom and dad?"

It's weird because I don't call them "mom" or "dad." When I see them, which is next to never, I call them Sheila and Theo.

"Sheila lives in Phoenix, I think," I tell him. "Theo…" I rub my forehead. "It's been years. I have no idea where he is."

"Got it. And your Mimi?"

He doesn't hesitate before calling her "Mimi." I love that.

"She has Alzheimer's."

"Fuck."

"Mm-hm."

I don't tell him what a world-class bitch I was three years ago when I screamed at Mimi for missing my college graduation and left town just like my mother. I leave that part out. It's my greatest shame, my greatest regret; putting words to it and hearing them aloud makes me disgusted with myself.

"We sold Mimi's house, and since my grandfather was a veteran, there were a few care centers available to her in the city. But they…they weren't good enough for her. I was working at Nile.com for a while to supplement my income, and the money allowed me to move her to a better place about two hours outside of the city near Yakima. But that job didn't work out, so…"

"So you needed a way to make a lot of money fast."

"Exactly. Your ad was a godsend. I mean, this is the *perfect* job. You're in a jam, sure, but I'm only too happy to help you out. You flew me up here, I have a free place to live, free transportation to and from work, a good job, and—depending on how charming I can be—the opportunity to make big tips. All for pretending to be your fiancée for a few months. I want you to know how grateful I am, Tanner. The money I make here will keep Mimi safe in Yakima for months."

"And then?"

"I don't know yet, but it's enough time for me to figure something out."

He tilts his head to the side. "You're a really good granddaughter."

"No, I'm not," I mutter, swirling my wine and watching the long legs slide down the sides. "How about you? I met your grandmother. You said your step-grandfather is in the picture. Mom? Dad?"

"Dad's up in the Yukon with my brother, Sawyer, leading a tour today and tomorrow."

"Okay. And Mom?"

He clenches his jaw. I can tell because his facial muscles tighten, his cheekbones stark and highlighted, before he relaxes. "She died."

"I'm sorry."

"It was a long time ago."

"How long?"

"Sixteen years. She was leading a heliskiing expedition up north and got caught in an avalanche."

"Oh, my god…"

"Reeve was only one," he adds. "We don't do heliskiing excursions anymore."

"I'm really sorry."

He looks up at me, blue eyes sad but clear. "So neither of us have a mother, really."

"I have Mimi," I protest.

"I have my grandmother, too," he says. "But it's not the same, is it?"

I don't want to agree with him. I want to declare that Mimi was as good a mother—even better—than Sheila ever could have been. But in my heart, I know that I'd be speaking out of loyalty, not honesty. If I'm honest—both with him and myself—I know he's right. I'll never really know what I didn't have, but I'm fully aware I never had it.

"What next?" I ask him.

"Any brothers or sisters?"

"Just me."

"That's easy to remember," he says. "How'd we meet?"

"You're asking me?"

"Do you have any ideas?"

"We met through a personal ad, right? That's the truth. Maybe stick to it. The less we lie, the less we have to remember."

"It's so cheesy," he groans.

"Do you have a better idea?"

"How about we met while I was working in Juneau last summer?"

"I've never been to Juneau," I tell him. "The first person who asks me about my favorite restaurant or shop in Juneau is going to get doe eyes from me."

"You always have doe eyes," he says.

I'm not prepared for him to say something so personal, and it takes me aback. I stare at him, waiting for him to say more.

"Your eyes are big and brown, like a doe's," he says, two smudges of color brightening his cheeks. "And those long lashes…" He stares at me thoughtfully for a second, then chugs the rest of his wine and pushes the glass away. "I get your point. We'll go with the personal ad story."

Aside from my quick evaluation that Tanner is conventionally good-looking, I haven't really evaluated whether or not I find him attractive. He's massive, of course, which isn't something I generally look for in a partner. We'd look ridiculous together with me just clearing five feet and him at well over six. I haven't been with a lot of guys, but most of them were of a smaller or average build.

I wonder what it's like to be intimate with someone as big as Tanner.

This thought, which zings me in the groin unexpectedly, makes my face hot. I lick my lips, then chug down the rest of my wine.

"I guess I should go settle in a little more," I say, feeling transparent and embarrassed, even though he has no idea what I was thinking.

"Sure," he says, running his hands through his blonde hair. "Yeah. Um. Good idea."

I stand up and head for the door, looking over my shoulder before I leave.

"Thanks for the wine."

He looks up and nods. "Sure. Come back at six for dinner."

"Will do," I tell him, letting the door slam shut behind me.

 chapter five

Tanner

I listen to her feet on the porch, then skipping down the stairs. When I can't hear them crunch on the gravel path to the cabins anymore, I shake myself out of my trance.

For a second—for just a split second when I was staring into her eyes—I started to get hard.

Fuck.

Where the fuck did that reaction come from?

She's not my type. Not to mention, I'm not interested in fucking things up with the woman who's only here to save my ass. No how. No way.

However, it does occur to me—for the first time since I embarked on this ruse—that if I'm not hooking up with McKenna this summer, I won't be hooking up with anyone. At least not in Skagway where I could be seen or found out.

Fuck.

How did I not realize this while I was plotting a fake fiancée with my sisters? I have needs. Big needs. Needs that have been met every summer by seasonal help like Ramona or cruise ship day trippers stopping over in Skagway. What am I supposed to do? Go without sex for the whole summer?

I push my chair away from the table with a loud screech, grabbing the wine glasses so roughly that they crash against each other and break.

"Fuck!" I yell.

"You watch your dirty mouth, young man," says Gran, swinging through the kitchen door and into the dining room. She's holding a large tray laden with plates, cups, silverware, and napkins. "I raised you better'n that."

"I'm sorry, Gran."

"You should be." She places her tray on the bar and takes the broken stems from my hands. "Go get the broom and dustpan."

When I return with them a second later, Gran has already put the largest pieces of broken glass in the garbage and recorked what's left of the wine. I sweep up the little pieces and add them to the trash.

"What's got you cursing like that?" she asks me, handing me a stack of napkins as she starts setting the tables. I follow behind her, placing a napkin, fork, and knife to the left of each plate.

"Female companionship," I mutter.

"I just met your female companion for the summer. I liked her."

"She's not...I mean, she's just...Gran, you get it that she's just *posing* as my fiancée, right? I barely know her. She's not my...companion. Not in any *real* way."

"You never know," says Gran in a singsong voice.

"Oh, *I know*," I tell her. "She's just here to do a job. She made that very clear."

"Lots going on behind those eyes. Still waters run deep."

"Doesn't change the fact that she's not my type."

"And who is?" asks Gran, putting her hands on her ample hips. "That floozy from last summer with the big tatas?"

"Gran!"

"She was trouble and a half," says Gran, finishing the last table and bustling back into the kitchen.

But she was hot! my body screams. *So fucking hot and wet and loud and soft and—Damn it. Fuck.*

Maybe I can take a few Yukon excursions off Dad, Sawyer, or Harper this summer. There's a waitress up in Whitehorse—Miranda something-or-other—who works at the 98. A half day's drive from Dyea and Skagway, barely anyone would know if I indulged in some covert, consensual adult entertainment with Miranda, and heck, she'd welcome the attention. Every other time I've been up there, she's come onto me. She's not the cutest girl I've ever seen, but she always seems up for some no-strings-attached fun.

Then again, so did Ramona.

I shudder, taking the empty pitchers lined up on the bar and filling them with ice and water one by one.

Tomorrow around ten, I'm planning to drive McKenna into town to meet Bruce Franks, owner of the Purple Parsnip. He'll do a quick orientation with her, and she should be ready on Monday for the first big wave of cruisers to hit town. But best of all, the Purple Parsnip is just two doors down from the

King Kone where Ramona will be working—plenty of opportunity for my psycho ex to see me dropping off and picking up my lovely little fiancée.

I grin to myself as I cross the dining room with two full pitchers of water and place them on tables. I wonder what Ramona will make of McKenna. I wonder if my sisters are right about her backing off when she realizes I'm engaged. I wonder if McKenna could really be the answer to my prayers, just like my offer was the answer to hers.

I remember what she told me about losing her job at Nile.com and needing something quick and lucrative to make ends meet. She *is* a good granddaughter, no matter what she says. There aren't too many folks who'd take a job so far from home just to keep their grandmother in a nice memory care facility. I admire her for it.

I like her.

Earlier today, when I was waiting for her at the airport, I hoped that she'd be "sensible and plain"— the kind of girl I could be "friends with," "without any complications or entanglements." By some rare stroke of luck or grace, I think I somehow managed to get exactly what I wanted.

Except for the plain part.

McKenna Cabot may not be my type, I think, but with eyes like hers, no one could ever call her plain.

***

McKenna

I don't remember falling asleep when I got back to the cabin, but for all my big talk about holding my wine, I sure did pass out completely after unpacking my bags. When I woke up a few hours later, a dinner bell—gong, actually—was clanging loudly to call guests in for dinner. Recalling Tanner's invitation, I decided to join them, ditching my baseball cap for a bobby pin with an enamel hummingbird, and throwing on a simple cotton dress with a white zip-up sweatshirt over it.

On my way to the lodge, I pass the cabins of Tanner's siblings—one for the two adult girls and the other that he's sharing with his older and younger brothers—in addition to the cabins of the guests staying at the campground.

Trailing behind a large, multi-generational family, I listen to them chatter excitedly about the whale-watching cruise they'd taken this afternoon.

"Bubble feeding! Can you imagine? It's the crown jewel of whale-watching!"

"I thought we'd hit the jackpot when that mama and baby Orca pair came swimming by. Never thought we'd see a whole pod of humpbacks bubble feeding."

"Best cruise of my life," says an older lady. "I told y'all that you'd love it here."

"You were right, Mom…"

The family climbs the steps to the lodge, entering through the screened doors into the dining room and heading for a large round table set for ten.

It's not unusual for me to feel lonely or left out; when your family consists of you and only one other person, you enter a ton of rooms in your life alone. You'd think that would make it easier, but it doesn't. I feel conspicuously alone every time, resentful of sympathetic glances, and yet longing for the day I have a table to join where everyone knows my name and is happy to see me.

"McKenna!"

Maybe today is that day.

I look up to see Reeve racing toward me, arms outstretched. She bowls into me, grabbing me into a warm hug. Then, before I can fully regroup, she grabs my hand and pulls me toward a large round table in the center of the room.

"McKenna's here!" she announces.

Standing behind an empty chair, I look at the faces seated around the table, quickly identifying Gran and—I assume—PawPaw beside her, his skin tone and hair color darker than everyone else at the table. The Stewarts have an unmistakable family resemblance. Their eyes are various shades of green and blue, and their hair color ranges from medium blonde to light brown.

Reeve elbows me in the side. "You ready to meet everyone?"

"Sure."

"Everyone, this is McKenna," she says, beaming at me. "McKenna, you already met Gran. That's PawPaw next to her. Then, there's Dad, Harper, Parker, and Sawyer. The two empty seats just there are for Hunter and Tanner. They'll be back in a sec. Gran sent them into the kitchen to bring out the platters."

I give a general wave to the table, then pull out my chair and sit down.

"Good to have you here, McKenna. Always wanted a daughter-in-law," says Mr. Stewart, with a twinkle in his eye.

I grin back at him. "I'll do my best to make you proud, Dad."

"Ramona back in town yet?" asks Sawyer.

"I think she's coming in this weekend," says one of the two older girls. *Parker or Harper?* I'm not sure yet.

One of them turns to me. "How was your trip up?"

"Fine," I say. "Easy flight from Seattle to Anchorage and then a puddle jumper to Skagway."

"Yeah. It's not that bad."

"Did you spend time in the Lower 48?" I ask her.

"I got my degree from the University of Oregon," she says.

"I went to UDub."

"Oh, no!" She narrows her eyes playfully. "Go Ducks! Huskies suck!"

"Thank God you don't have any Milk-Bones!"

The rivalry between the Universities of Washington and Oregon is well-known among students and alumni. One of Oregon's favorite pranks is throwing dog biscuits on the field as the Huskies enter the stadium.

"Don't worry," says Sawyer. "You're not alone, McKenna. Mom went to U of O. Dad and Hunter went to UDub. Our family's split down the middle every fall."

"Who's on which side?"

"Gran, Dad, Hunter, Harper, and Reeve like Dub. Tanner, Parker, and I like the Ducks."

"What about you, PawPaw?" I ask.

"Ain't got a dog in that race," he says.

"Literally," says Reeve. "PawPaw roots for one of the

Iditarod teams every year, and that's it. If it ain't got a dog, it ain't a race."

"Well, between you and me," I say to Reeve, "I'd say he's more of a *Husky* fan, then!"

The rest of the table laughs as Parker gives her grandfather a look. "PawPaw, don't break my heart and side with the dogs."

PawPaw chuckles at his granddaughter's frown and tells her she's the prettiest duck he ever saw.

"So, Tanner's a Ducks fan, huh?" I ask.

"I smell marital trouble a'brewin'!" says Harper, winking at me.

The door to the kitchen swings open, and Tanner and his brother step into the dining room, massive metal trays balanced in each of their oven mitt-covered hands. They lay the trays on the bar, then go about distributing smaller platters to the guest tables. Tanner sits beside me as Hunter goes back to the kitchen for the Stewart family platter.

"Hey, there," he says. "All settled in?"

"Hey, traitor," I say, raising my eyebrow at him.

"Traitor?" Tanner demands, genuinely confused. "What'd I do?"

"We told her," says Reeve.

He tenses up beside me. "Told her what?"

"That you're a Ducks fan," says Parker.

Tanner rolls his eyes at his sisters. "Phew. I thought it was something serious."

"Oh, no," whispers Reeve.

"You don't think loyalty to the Huskies is a serious

68

matter?" I ask Tanner with mock outrage.

He looks a little nervous. "I don't really care about college football that much."

"Traitor!" yells Parker. "You always told me you were a Ducks fan!"

"Who's a dirty Ducks fan?" asks Hunter, placing a large trencher on the table and taking a seat between Harper and Tanner. He reaches a hand across his brother. "Hi. I'm Hunter."

Another Viking god. Good Lord.

"Hi. I'm McKenna."

"Tan didn't tell me you were so pretty."

A *charming* Viking god.

"Cut it out, Hunter," mutters Tanner, spooning meat and potatoes onto his plate.

"She's not *really* your fiancée, dumbass," Hunter points out. "You don't have to get defensive."

"I'm not being defensive," says Tanner. "Just shut up and eat your chow."

Coming from such a small family, I find that sitting at a huge table with a close-knit family of nine is…wonderful. Jarring, sure. But wonderful. I can barely keep up with the various comments and personalities, but I can't stop smiling at their antics, and I already sense I'm going to love living here this summer.

"So, McKenna," says Hunter, ignoring Tanner's request that he shut up. "What brings you to Dyea?"

"Marriage."

"I see," says Hunter, eyes sparkling much like his

father's. "Settling down with this old lug, huh?"

"It's what one does when one falls madly in love," I tell him, batting my eyes at Tanner in faux adoration.

"She talks like poetry," whispers Reeve to her grandmother. "I told you, right?"

"And you're in love with...*him*?" Hunter hooks his thumb at Tanner and scoffs. "Only 'cause you didn't meet me first."

"Stop being an idiot," says Tanner.

"*You* stop being grumpy," snaps Harper. "He's just joking around."

"Maybe she's not interested in Hunter's dumb comments."

"I don't mind," I say, wondering if I should be offended that Hunter calling me "pretty" is considered a "dumb comment" by Tanner.

Mr. Stewart asks Sawyer about taking a group to Whitehorse tomorrow, and I move my meat and potatoes around on my plate, trying to keep up with the various simultaneous conversations going on.

After dinner, the Stewarts clear their own table first, followed by those of the guests, who depart with promises to appear at the campfire in an hour or so. Though it won't start getting dark until ten or eleven, the campfire begins at a bright and sunny eight p.m. so everyone can get a good night's sleep after.

I try to help clear the plates, but Gran insists that I sit with PawPaw on the porch and relax.

"First night here. You're still a guest," she says. "Can't

put you to work just yet, McKenna."

Leaving the dining room, I find PawPaw on a porch rocker, packing a pipe with tobacco.

"Can I join you?"

"Sure," he says, his voice raspy with age. "I'm about to smoke my pipe."

"It's beautiful," I tell him, sitting down in the empty rocker to his left as I admire his pipe. The tobacco bowl is an intricately carved animal head.

"I carved it myself," he tells me. "Outta walnut."

"A Tlingit tradition?"

"That's right."

"I'd love to know more about your culture."

"I'll tell you anything you want to know, *digitgiyáa*."

"Well, first I need to know what *that* means."

"*Digitgiyáa?* Hummingbird."

I touch my hair pin as I grin at him. "A nickname. I like it."

"Nicknames are good," he tells me, scratching a match on the side of his rocker and lighting his pipe. The smoke is sweet and thick, rising above us in gray puffs. "They mean that you are accepted."

Accepted.

A nice word. A nicer feeling.

I always felt accepted by Mimi, and by Isabella and her family. I felt accepted by my friends and professors at college, and by my boss and coworkers in Montana. But I've never felt accepted by a family, and I blink my flooding eyes as I consider PawPaw's words. *You are accepted.* They are, perhaps, the sweetest words I've ever heard.

"The burn in your eyes is like the burn of my throat," he tells me softly. "After a few deep breaths, it goes away."

So I take a few deep breaths, listening to the ambient noises of families coming and going from cabins, of the Stewart clan clearing tables and washing dishes in a kitchen not so far away, of the creaking chair rocking gently beside me.

And he's right.

Little by little, I accept it all, and my eyes stop burning.

 chapter six

Tanner

Driving McKenna into Skagway every afternoon and picking her up every night is going to take about forty minutes away from my morning and evening chores, but on the plus side, it will give us a little bit of extra time alone to get our story straight every day.

As we bump over the dirt road from Dyea to Skagway, I glance over at my "fiancée," who insisted on helping with breakfast this morning.

I was surprised to enter the kitchen and see her standing at the stovetop, cooking a massive skillet of scrambled eggs beside Gran, who was flipping bacon slices and sausage links. Reeve was on baking duty, pulling fresh blueberry muffins out of the oven, while Harper and Sawyer were out back getting the 4x4 open-sided Jeep ready for a family who wanted to go on a search for moose and bears after breakfast.

"You put her to work already, Gran?" I asked.

"She insisted," Gran said with a smile of approval.

"Where are Hunter and Dad at?"

"Left early with hikers."

"And Parker?"

"Ran a lady to the clinic in town."

"Anything serious?"

"Bites of some kind. All swollen and mean-looking."

"Mosquito allergy?" I guessed.

"Likely," said Gran.

Mosquitoes in Alaska are no joke. Often dubbed "the *other* state bird," they're huge and greedy, and though they don't generally carry diseases, if one of them gets into your room at night, you can end up pretty uncomfortable by morning…especially if you're allergic to them.

I stopped behind McKenna.

"You don't have to do this," I told her. "It's not part of our arrangement."

She looked at me over her shoulder. "I don't mind."

"Which is why she's the best!" declared Reeve from across the kitchen. "She's already part of the family, Tan!"

Rolling my eyes at Reeve's exuberance, I'd picked up the platter of clean plates, cups, silverware, napkins and pitchers and headed into the dining room to start setting the tables.

But as I worked, my mind was full of McKenna.

When I first met her at the airport yesterday, she hadn't impressed me very much. She didn't wow me with her looks. She didn't blow me away with her humor or charm. But talking to her over wine allowed me to learn how much she'd had to overcome in her life, and watching her interact with my family at dinner, and later at the campfire, had given me a glimpse into a character I'm admiring more and more.

So maybe she isn't the sexiest woman in creation, I think, glancing at her in the passenger seat of my car. *But I think I lucked out when she agreed to help me.*

"Any questions for me before we get into town?" I ask her.

"Any chance Ramona got into town early?"

"I guess it's possible," I tell her, "though my understanding is that she's not coming in until this weekend."

"Okay. And this guy, Bruce, at the Purple Parsnip. He's a good friend?"

"I've known him forever, and he's quirky as hell," I tell her, "but he's a good guy. He and my dad went to high school together."

"Got it. And he believes we're engaged."

"He does. And he's a huge gossip, so half the town already knows, too."

She takes a deep breath, then bites her lower lip.

"You okay?" I ask her. "Nervous?"

"A little, but it's not that. I just...I don't love lying."

Panic makes my mouth go dry. "But that's what we agreed—"

"I'll do it." She's quick to reassure me. "I promised I would, and I won't go back on my word. But you asked if I was nervous, and the truth is that I am...because I don't love lying to people. It felt theoretical when I agreed to do it. Now it feels real."

"Now it *is* real," I say. "It *needs* to be real, or Ramona won't stop."

"I know," she says, reaching out to place her hand on my

arm. "I know, and I won't let you down, Tanner. Don't worry."

After a little squeeze, she drops her hand, and to my surprise, I find myself wishing she hadn't. I liked the feeling of her hand on my arm. It was oddly reassuring, plus I've always been a tactile person. Speaking of which...

"We haven't discussed, um..."

"What?"

The dirt road segues into a paved road, which means we're getting closer to Skagway.

"We haven't talked about, um...affection. Public displays of...you know, touching."

She shifts in her seat, and though I keep my gaze straight, I can feel her eyes on the side of my face. "So let's talk about it. What do you have in mind?"

"Um...hand holding?"

"Sure," she says.

"My arm around your shoulder?"

"Good luck," she says. "I'm five foot nothing. You're..."

"Six-two," I supply.

"A full foot taller than me!"

"I can still get my arm around your shoulders."

"Waist would work better," she says.

"Is that okay with you?" I ask, thinking that shoulders are less invasive than waist somehow.

"Sure."

"How about..." I don't want to press my luck, but wouldn't fiancés kiss? For the sake of seeming believable?

"Kissing?"

"What kind?" she asks.

"Cheek? Forehead?"

"I'm not Reeve," she says.

"I know that."

"So, how does a brotherly kiss on the cheek fit into the plan of selling me as your fiancée?"

"You said you'd karate chop me in the face if I 'tried anything.'"

"Because I don't like surprises...which is why we're having this conversation."

"I doubt you could hurt me with a karate chop anyway," I scoff.

"Want to try your luck?" she asks, her voice like a whip.

"No, ma'am."

"I'm okay with a peck on the mouth when you say goodbye and another when you say hello," she says. "That should work."

"A peck."

"Mm-hm. You slip me tongue, I just might bite."

Not that I have any intention of French kissing her, but her words surprise me, catch me off-guard, and make my stomach flip over in a way that feels...nice. *Fuck.*

"No tongue," I mutter. "Got it."

***

McKenna

While still in Seattle, I looked at pictures of the Purple Parsnip Saloon online, so I knew that it was an old building with a

Western-style storefront, typical of most buildings in well-preserved Skagway. Once upon a time the Purple Parsnip had been a bordello and dance hall for the thriving mining town, enticing prospectors with its loud music, gambling tables, cheap booze, and scantily-dressed women.

At its peak in the late 1890s, Skagway had no less than seventy bars and brothels lining Broadway, the main drag and a road that's about a mile long. Sure, there were also general stores, outfitters, hardware and drug stores, but vice was the biggest seller of all, and prostitutes—women of fortune who followed the miners north or wives who'd lost their husbands during the arduous trek to and from the Yukon—could make a lot of money in a short amount of time

I'm fascinated by the history of prostitution in Skagway; in a time when women had extremely limited options for work, they could make up to $3000 a year selling their bodies. To be clear, that's over $110,000 today. After two years in Skagway, a hardworking woman could return to the Lower 48, buy land or a business, and set herself up comfortably for life. Not that the profession was without its downsides. The climate was inhospitable, venereal disease ran rampant, and customers—lonely, burly men frustrated by the conditions for gold mining—could turn violent on a whim.

The Purple Parsnip had, at one time, been the premiere bordello of Skagway. With a dance hall and bar on the ground floor, and ten small rooms upstairs for sex trade, the working girls were more protected at the Parsnip than they'd be in standalone "cribs" on side roads. The madam, a former Montana cattlewoman named Diamond Lil, was rumored to have interacted with clients while wearing a diamond-studded bracelet that went up the entire length of her arm.

Today, the Purple Parsnip is a popular bar and restaurant downstairs and has a museum dedicated to the history of Skagway prostitution upstairs. It's also rumored to be haunted. I can't wait to start working there.

Tanner parks his car in front of the building and hops out. I meet him on the old-fashioned wooden plank boardwalk and stare up at the building's façade.

"Wow. This is cool."

The historical district of Skagway, a nine-block area in the heart of Skagway and walkable from the cruise terminal, has over a hundred historically-significant buildings from the Gold Rush era, twenty of them managed by the National Park Service. What sets Skagway apart, however, is that the buildings are not museums. Most of them, like the Purple Parsnip, are modern and lucrative businesses, operating in historic buildings.

It's a wonder.

"I heard one lady say Skagway's 'theming' is better than Disney World," says Tanner.

I look up at him and grin. "She was right. Disney World copies details like these. This is the real thing."

"Sometimes we get TV or movie shoots," Tanner tells me. "I grew up here, so I don't always see the 'magic' of it, you know? Skagway's just part of home."

"I assure you, it's really unique," I say, marveling at the details. A carved wooden Indian here. A barber pole there. A decorative store front three stories high in front of a one-story shop. Each building is painted a vivid color: yellow, pink, aqua or purple. "One of a kind."

"Come on," says Tanner. "I'll introduce you to Bruce."

We enter the vestibule of the lavender-painted building, pushing through saloon doors into the main dining room. To my right, there's a dark-wood bar that spans the length of the room with a cloudy mirror on the wall behind it and bottles of every alcohol you can imagine lined up like soldiers.

In the main room, there are two and four-person tables set and ready with mismatched maroon and white-patterned china, and maroon napkins. The floorboards are scuffed and old, the wall lamps look like they were originally intended for gas hookups, and four wooden ceiling fans make lazy rotations, framed by an open balcony on the upper level. In the back of the room is an old player piano that surely adds ambiance to the Gold Rush-era conceit.

In short, it's perfect.

"Bruce!" yells Tanner. "You here?"

"Have the cruise ships started arriving yet?" I ask Tanner. "Town seems quiet."

"First ships started coming last week. Only one or two a day at first. Wait until next week. You won't believe it."

The first wave of a summer million. It boggles my mind.

"But you're already half booked at the campground."

"Those folks came in by ferry. Ferry operates year-round. Bruce!"

"Coming!"

"Am I right that ferries leave from Seattle and come all the way up here?"

"From Bellingham," he clarifies with a nod. "You can get from Bellingham, Washington, to Skagway in about sixty hours."

"Sixty hours! That's two and a half days!"

"Actually, it works out to about three and a half to four days depending on how many stops you have, but think of it this way: for $500, you can fly from Seattle to Skagway in five hours with a stop in Anchorage or Juneau, or you can take a scenic and leisurely trip via ferry for the same cost and make a vacation out of it."

"A vacation? On a ferry?"

"They're not bad, actually. Some have private rooms with bunk beds and washrooms. All have lounges and dining rooms. Plus, all the wildlife you can see from the decks, and plenty of time to read."

"I guess it doesn't sound terrible."

"It's not," he says. "You should try it sometime."

"Hello, weary travelers and welcome to the Purple Parsnip!" booms a voice from the end of the bar.

A man appears—Bruce Franks, I assume—channeling the great Nathan Lane, and dressed in "ye olde bartender" attire: black pants, a white, long-sleeved shirt with maroon garters, a maroon, tan and black plaid waistcoat vest and matching bowtie. He also sports a handlebar mustache and monocle.

"Howdy-doo, Tanner Stew?"

"Hi, Bruce."

"And this must be the Magnificent Miss McKenna!" cries Bruce, grabbing my arm with flare and kissing the back of my hand with a loud smooch.

I stare at him in gape-mouthed surprise. I wasn't expecting an acting gig and period costumes when I agreed to a bartending job. What in the world have I gotten myself into?

Bruce pops the monocle into his breast pocket and leans against the bar.

"We do it up for the tourists," he whispers conspiratorially.

"Will I have to…?"

"Wear a costume? Come up with a character? Sling drinks like a Gold Rush-era bar wench?" He twirls one end of his mustache and leers at me. "All of the above, sweetheart."

"Tone it down, huh, Bruce?"

"I'm just being honest, Tan."

"Tone it down anyway."

Bruce gives me a once over, twisting one end of his mustache in thought. "You're small and slim. I'll have to see what we have in the back. Maybe knickers and a bustier?"

"How about pants and a shirt?" suggests Tanner, putting his arm around my waist.

"Pants and a shirt. I like it. Add a cap to the mix, and we have a sort of waifish newspaper boy thing going on."

"She's *not* a boy," Tanner says, steel in his tone, ice in his eyes.

Bruce appears to get the message that enormous Tanner is getting annoyed and quickly works to pacify him.

"Of course not! Of course not! Not with eyes like that," says Bruce. "But if you want me to keep her covered up…"

"Gentlemen!" I say, finally finding my voice in this

incredibly odd situation. I turn to Tanner, reaching up to caress his cheek. "Baby, you don't need to be so protective. I'm a grown woman." Then I turn to Bruce. "Find the smallest-waisted skirt you have, Bruce. I'll alter it to fit."

"And for the top...?" he asks, glancing meaningfully at my modest chest.

"How about a peasant blouse? Something billowy and comfortable? I'll belt it over the skirt."

"Ooo! A sort of washerwoman-frontierswoman-bartender combination! Yes! Oh, my dear!" he exclaims, cupping my cheeks in his hands. "You may have a knack for this!"

As he rushes away to find my costume pieces, I look up at Tanner to laugh at Bruce's antics, but the look in his eyes stops me.

"What?"

"Baby," he says, his voice gravelly and low.

"Huh?"

"You called me 'Baby.'"

"Oh," I say, feeling butterflies swarm my tummy and color pinken my cheeks. "Yeah."

His eyes search mine, darker blue than usual, so intense it makes my breathing shallow. "I...liked it."

Me too. "Good. That'll make it all the more believable."

Bruce saunters back into the room with a dull-brown skirt, cream-colored blouse, and wide leather belt draped over his arm and presents them to me. Boots dangle from his other hand. "Here you go! Can you work with these?"

"Sure," I say, stepping away from Tanner to take the

clothing and boots. "Do you have a needle and thread by any chance?"

"We'll stop at the hardware store," says Tanner from behind me.

"Anything else I need to know about the job?" I ask Bruce.

"You have a bartending certificate?"

"I do."

"Okay. Listen up. Here's your orientation crash course." He crosses his arms over his chest, all business now. "Most ships dock between five and seven a.m. We open at eleven. Tables are full by eleven-oh-one and stay that way all day. We close at ten p.m., but since most of the ships reboard by eight, the last two hours of the day are quiet, and we don't need a dedicated bartender. Your hours will be twelve to eight. Sound good?"

"So far."

"You'll get one full-day and one half-day off every week. Week is defined as Sunday to Saturday. Your days off will change from week to week depending on the cruise schedule. Max of four ships in port per day, but sometimes we only get two or three in the beginning and end of the season. You're more likely to get a day off on a two- or three-ship day."

"Got it."

"Tips are yours to keep. You'll make more if you go along with the whole 1890s saloon theme. Take my word for it. We try to stay in character. Waitresses are saloon girls, mostly. Tour guides for the museum upstairs play-act as working girls. You'll meet Bear on Monday. He sits on a stool

84

in the front by the swinging doors and basically acts as security. I doubt you'll have an issue behind the bar, but believe it or not, cruisers can get handsy with the staff, especially when the drinks are flowing. Bear takes care of that for us."

"Someone touches you," says Tanner from behind me, his voice black as night, "let me know."

I glance at him over my shoulder and roll my eyes, even though I sort of like this testosterone-fueled, protective Tanner. It's sexy as hell.

"Don't worry about me, baby," I purr, running a hand down his arm. "You know I can take care of myself."

"Whoo!" Bruce exclaims, grinning at us. "Is it hot in here or is it me?"

"It's hot in here," says Tanner.

"It's really not," I tell Bruce.

"So I'll see you at noon on Monday?" he confirms, grinning at Tanner before winking at me.

"I'll be here," I tell him, letting Tanner take my hand and lead me back outside.

chapter seven

Tanner

As soon as the saloon doors shut behind us, I drop her hand like it's on fire.

What the fuck is going on with me?

Why did I want to kick Bruce's ass for calling McKenna "boyish"?

And why the fuck did I picture a naked McKenna riding my cock when she called me "baby"?

"You okay?" she asks from beside me, taking two steps to keep up with every one of mine.

"Fine," I grunt.

"Did I do something wrong?"

I stop walking and turn to face her. "Are you attracted to me?"

"Not..." Her eyes lock with mine. "I mean, not intentionally."

"But you are."

"Are *you* attracted to me?"

I feel my face twist into a grimace. "Not intentionally."

"You're not really my type," she says.

Ouch. That shouldn't hurt, but it does, and I have no idea why, but it stings.

"You're not mine either," I snap back.

"Well, good!" she cries, her eyes narrow like she doesn't think it's "good" at all. "Then we shouldn't have a problem."

"The problem still exists," I tell her. "Don't call me 'baby' anymore."

"Fine. Don't threaten to beat up any man who touches me."

"I didn't."

"You pretty much did."

"Well, you're *supposed* to be mine."

"I *am* yours!" I yell back at him.

"Young love!" exclaims Andi Jones, proprietor of the King Kone. She stands in front of her ice cream shop with a bottle of Windex and a rag. "Tempestuous! Passionate!"

I take a deep breath. It's really important to sell our relationship to Andi since she's Ramona's boss.

"Hey, Andi," I say, putting my arm around McKenna's waist and hauling her against my side. "Just a little spat."

"Lover's quarrel?" coos Andi.

"Something like that," I say. "Andi Jones, this is my fiancée, McKenna Cabot."

"Fiancée?" she asks. "Well, I heard a rumor from Brucie, but wouldn't've believed it if I hadn't seen it for myself!" She holds out her hand. "Welcome to Skagway, dear."

McKenna is rigid against me, but she takes Andi's hand. "Thanks so much."

"Aren't you two the mismatched pair?" titters Andi,

looking down at McKenna, then up at me, then back down at McKenna. "Love comes in all shapes and sizes, doesn't it?"

"I guess so," McKenna says, a little salt in her tone.

Andi looks up at me, a mean smile curling up the sides of her lips. "Tanner, you remember Ramona from last summer, don't you?"

I stare at her without answering; I'm not rising to Andi Jones's gossipy bait.

"Well, she's coming in tomorrow and staying for the season! Won't that be a hoot? For Ramona to meet McKenna?"

I'm about to snap from her taunting. "You know what, Andi—"

McKenna places her palm over my chest, then steps in front of me, placing herself between me and Andi. "You tell her I can't wait."

"Fireworks!" says Andi, a maniacal gleam in her eye.

"No, ma'am," says McKenna firmly. "There'll be none of that."

Andi raises her eyebrows at McKenna, then looks at me. "She's sensible, this one."

"She's the best," I say, placing my hands on her shoulders and feeling grateful.

"Well, la-di-da."

"We'd best be going," says McKenna, taking my hand. "Have a lovely day, Mrs. Jones."

"It's Andi!" she yells at our backs. "I'm not a hundred."

"Could've fooled me, you crazy old bat," mutters McKenna just loud enough for me to hear.

I snicker at her sass as we walk to the hardware store. "Needle and thread?"

"Yes, please."

"This is the only store in town open year-round. Their motto is: *If we don't have it, you don't need it.*"

"That's presumptuous."

"They do have a little of everything," I tell her.

"Tanner Stewart!" booms Jasper Fullerton, the store's owner. "How's the weather in Dyea?"

He's been asking me—and the rest of my brothers and sisters—this question since we were old enough to answer. For this reason, we call him "One Joke" Jasper to each other.

"Same as Skagway, Mr. F."

"But no better!" he follows up, as he always does. His eyes flit to McKenna. "And who's this?"

"McKenna Cabot, please meet Jasper Fullerton, a.k.a. Mr. F. Mr. F., McKenna's my fiancée."

"Tanner! You're getting hitched?"

"Yes, sir."

"Where're you from, little lady?"

"Seattle," she says, offering Mr. F. a small smile as she shakes his hand.

"Pretty as a picture, Tan!"

"Thanks, Mr. F."

"You fixing to move up here, McKenna?"

McKenna looks up at me, her eyes wide and uncertain. I smile at her, putting my arm around her waist and liking the way she folds against me.

"Still figuring it all out, Mr. F."

"When's the wedding, son?"

I can feel McKenna's eyes back on my face, but I don't look at her this time. I don't want for us to seem like we don't know what we're doing.

"Wintertime. When it's quiet. Probably down in Seattle," I tell him.

"Oh, sure, sure. Traditional for the bride's family to have the nuptials close by."

"Yes, sir."

"Well, McKenna, you're welcome here anytime," Mr. F. tells her. "If you kids need help with anything, let me know."

He strides away to help a customer choose a socket wrench, leaving us alone.

"I wasn't ready for those questions," she whispers as I steer her toward home goods. "We need to prepare a little better."

"We did fine," I tell her. "And you did great with Andi, by the way."

"Is it just me, or are there a lot of, um, *colorful* characters in Skagway?"

I chuckle softly, sliding my hand across her back to find hers. We touch palms softly, then thread our fingers together.

"You're not wrong," I say. "I read a blog post once where the writer called Skagway "beautiful, but baffling." I liked that. It made sense, you know? Because it's quirky here."

"It's hella quirky, all right."

"Is that okay?" I ask her, surprised to realize that her opinion matters to me. If she hates it here, it'll hurt me on some level because it's my home and I love it.

"It's growing on me," she says, pulling her hand away from mine and continuing toward a shelf filled with shampoo, conditioner, and other ladies' toiletries.

In point of fact, I think, fisting my abandoned fingers as I watch her walk away, *you're growing on me, too.*

***

McKenna

"Ken! Oh, my god! Tell me everything!" screeches Isabella.

I wince in pain, fumbling with my phone to turn down the volume on my earbuds. "Iz, you're going to make me deaf!"

"I'm just so glad to hear from you! How is it? How's he? What's your job like? Do you like Skagway? Hate it? Tell me!"

"Okay. First off, I live in Dyea, which is close to Skagway. I have an awesome cabin all to myself, and I love it. I've only been to Skagway twice—once when I flew in, and once earlier today—and I like it so far. My boss is eccentric but seems okay. Get this. I have to wear a long skirt and peasant blouse to work and adopt, like, a character from the 1890s."

"I thought you were bartending."

"I am."

"In a theater?"

"No. A historic bar."

I lie down on Tanner's massive bed, staring up at the pine trees through the skylight overhead.

"Okay. That's a little weird, Ken."

"Yeah," I admit. "A little. But the more you do the act,

the better the tips, apparently."

"Good thing you took those drama courses in college."

"I guess. I'm supposed to be a washerwoman-bartender or something. I don't know."

"You'll figure it out," she says. "What about the guy? I'm dying!"

I take a deep breath and let it go slowly as I think about the last couple of days. It's been an information and sensory overload.

"Honestly? I'm a little overwhelmed, I guess."

"Oh. Yeah?"

"Yeah. I mean, he's beautiful, you know? Over six feet tall, blonde and muscular and—"

"Yes, please, girl!"

I roll my eyes.

"Don't you roll your eyes at me, McKenna Diana Cabot!"

She knows me too well.

"Tell me more," she demands.

"But Iz…he's not what I'd usually look for if I walked into a bar or swiped left."

"And yet…"

"I don't know," I say, thinking about this morning. I didn't mind him touching me. That's for sure. "There's something about adopting a role, you know? You sort of *become* that role. I'm supposed to be his fiancée, and when we're walking around town holding hands or he's introducing me to someone with his arm around my waist, it's…confusing."

"Because you like him."

"Iz! Get real! I *barely* know him."

"But he's hot."

"In a giant, massive, intimidating, Viking god sort of way, yes. He's good-looking, I guess."

"Viking god?" she cries. "OMG, Ken! You think he's into you?"

You're not really my type.

You're not mine either.

"No," I sigh, recalling his words from this morning. "I don't think so."

"And yet…"

"Please stop 'and yetting' me, Iz."

"You're being indecisive, and you're rarely indecisive. It's making me wonder."

"Like I said, it's confusing. When we were in town this morning, we were holding hands, or he had his arm around me, and he's introducing me as his fiancée, and I'm calling him 'baby,' and—"

"You call him 'baby'? That's hot."

"It's not hot," I insist. "It's what dating people call each other. That's all."

"If you say so."

"I do." I sigh. "But now I'm back in my cottage, lying on my bed, and I don't feel confused at all. He hired me to do a job. He's paying me in transportation, room, and board. I'm doing this job to make money for Mimi. That's all there is to it, and there's definitely no room for a romantic entanglement that could fuck everything up."

I can feel Isabella rolling her eyes at me.

"Stop rolling your eyes at me, Isabella Maria Gonzalez."

"You're in a bad mood," she sulks.

"I am not."

"You need a man."

"I do not."

"How long's it been?" she asks, knowing full well that I haven't had a boyfriend since I lived in Montana. Between moving back to Seattle and getting Mimi situated, there hasn't been time for any extracurricular fun.

"What's your point?"

"I don't know," she singsongs to me.

"Can you quit it?"

"It's been months, right? How long can you go, Ken?" she asks. "Without sex?"

"As long as I need to," I snap. "Can we talk about something else, please?"

"Fine."

We talk about her mom, dad, and siblings, and the fact that Mimi's care center hasn't reached out to her with any issues yet. She tells me about her last few weeks of school—she teaches second grade at a private school—and how much she's looking forward to having her summer off. She sounds carefree, and it pinches a little because, in contrast, I feel like I have a world of responsibility on my shoulders. She makes me promise to call her in a few days with another update and tells me to behave myself.

We're about to hang up when she says, "Hey, Ken!"

"What?"

"Summer flings are fun."

"You'd know better than me."

"Give him a chance!"

"He's not my type, and I'm not his."

"Type schmype," she says. "You don't fall for a type. You fall for a person."

"He doesn't want a chance. He's not my type, and he's not my person," I tell her. "We're just helping each other out."

"Okay," she says softly. "I'll stay out of it."

"I love you, Iz," I tell her.

"Love you, too, boo," she says, hanging up the phone.

My hand falls by my side as I stare up at the pine boughs above and the bright blue sky beyond. I think of Isabella about to spend her whole summer boating and beaching and having fun. It's a beautiful day, and I only have two more before work starts full-time—I should make the most of my free time this weekend.

When I first arrived yesterday, Tanner mentioned a hot tub and river out back behind his cabin. I wonder what the river's like. The water's probably freezing cold, but it's warm and sunny today. I bet it would feel great.

I rummage through a bureau drawer for some running shorts and a tank top, pairing them with thick socks and hiking boots. I'll take off the socks and boots once I get there and go wading. Grabbing a towel and my phone, I head out the front door, down the porch steps and around the cabin.

In the back, there's the hot tub Tanner mentioned, and a rough-hewn wooden sign pointing down a wood-chip path reading: *To The River*. With a canopy of branches over my head, I walk in dappled sunshine, the sound of trickling water closer with every step I take. Birds chirp overhead, and a light breeze rustles the trees. *This is heavenly*, I think, taking a deep breath of cool, clean air. I could definitely get used to this.

At the river, which is shallow and clear with fresh water rushing over smooth rocks, I find a boulder to lean against while I take off my shoes and socks. I've always loved the water, which isn't surprising since Seattle's surrounded by bays, inlets, rivers, sounds, lakes, and to the west, the sea. Mimi and I used to spend every other weekend at Lake Sammamish when I was a kid. I still love it there more than anywhere else in the world.

I lean down to tuck my phone and socks into my shoes when I hear the unmistakable sound of a hammer being cocked.

"Don't move."

Still squatting, I freeze my body against the boulder behind me, raising my head slowly to find Tanner about twenty feet away from me…and a black bear directly between us.

He trains the rifle on the bear's head.

Seemingly oblivious to us, she sniffs a bush full of bright red berries, swiping at a full branch with her paw and drawing it to her mouth.

"D-Don't shoot it," I whisper, my voice thin with fear. "P-Please…don't…"

"Then don't move," he repeats softly. His voice is level and low, almost soothing. "They have a strong chase instinct. If you run, she'll run. And then she's toast."

"I won't move," I murmur, wishing my heart would slow down. Can she hear it? Will it draw her over to me? Will it make her—

"What the hell were you doing back here anyway?"

"It's a n-nice sunny day," I answer, my knees starting to ache from holding my squat. "I thought I'd go wading."

"What did you bring for protection?"

I glance at my shoes and socks. "Nothing. It didn't occur to me that—"

"You can't just go for a swim here like you're at the beach in Seattle."

"I know that now."

The bear looks up, as though just realizing we're sharing her space. She looks at Tanner, then at me, then at Tanner, then goes back to eating her berries. A long, sharp, fearsome claw snags a branch, and she sits back on her bottom to slurp the berries off. When one branch is picked clean, she grabs another.

"Remind me to get you some bear spray," murmurs Tanner, his eyes narrow, his gun still aimed at the bear's head.

"What's that?"

"Name says it all. You spray it in the bear's face, it burns their eyes, and they run the other way."

"Not necessary," I say. "I won't be wandering in the woods alone anymore."

Another branch licked clean, the bear moves on to the next bush and grabs the closest branch, pulling it to her mouth.

"She's not afraid of us," I whisper in wonder, adjusting

my squat just a touch. It doesn't help. My muscles are screaming in protest.

"Not if we stay still and quiet."

"Is she used to people?"

"Maybe. Or humans haven't been aggressive toward her, so she doesn't know to be scared. Plus, she's young and hungry. Black bears come out of torpor in the spring. She needs to bulk up now."

I watch in fascination as she finishes the last branch, then gets up on her hind legs, her snout sniffing the air for more bushes with berries. Since there aren't any more right here, she falls back down to four feet and heads for the water, wading in without looking back and wandering away upstream.

"Thank fuck," mutters Tanner after a few minutes, putting the safety back on, lowering the gun and slinging it onto his back.

I close my eyes, my whole body suddenly like jelly, and reach around for the rock I've been leaning against so I can pull myself up. Suddenly, I feel Tanner's hands under my arms, yanking me up and against him, then holding me tightly. He hugs me against his chest, his heart hammering into mine, his breath in hot puffs against the top of my head.

"Jesus, you're trouble," he mutters against my hair, his arms flexing to tighten around me. "If something had happened to you…"

"I'm okay," I murmur. "I'm okay now…"

After such a scare, it feels so reassuring to be safe, to be held. I should probably pull away, but I don't. I lean into him, fighting for a deep, clean breath, and seeing stars when I finally get one. I fill my lungs and diaphragm, resting my cheek against his T-shirt and breathing in the faint smells of pine-scented deodorant and laundry softener. I listen to the steady thrum of his heart and savor his life force, which feels so sure and strong around me.

With my eyes closed and my body safe, I indulge myself just for a moment—I let myself dream. What if we were a couple? What if I was his, and he was mine? What would it be like to love someone like Tanner and be loved by him in return?

My breath hitches. My heart swells with longing.

My brain hastens to remind me of the brutal facts of my life.

People don't stay.

Fathers get arrested.

Mothers leave the state.

Grandmothers get Alzheimer's.

People don't stay. They leave. They abandon you. Especially the ones who are supposed to love you. Maybe they leave because you're not lovable. Maybe they leave because they're not capable of love. But one fact is salient and clear: they *always* leave.

Love isn't for you, McKenna Cabot.

I pull away, pushing gently against his chest and standing up straight on my own two feet.

"Thank you."

The words aren't adequate, but I don't have any others. Not right now.

He drops his arms from around me, his eyes searching

mine like he wants something—needs something—from me. I guess he doesn't find it because he clears his throat and scuffs his boots on the ground, readjusting the rifle on his back. When he looks back at me, his face is composed, and his eyes are cool.

"You're my responsibility while you're here."

I lean down to pick up my shoes and socks, glad he can't see the confusion in my eyes. "Should we head back?"

When I look up, he's already walking away.

chapter eight

Tanner

I can't stop thinking about our encounter with the bear by the river yesterday afternoon.

Specifically, I can't stop thinking about the fact that I wanted to kiss McKenna like crazy as I held her in my arms. Her body had been weak as a kitten's when I pulled her up against mine, and every cell in my body had called out to protect her, to give her whatever strength I had to offer, to let her know that I'd never let anything hurt her if there was breath in my body.

And then she pushed me away.

Not gonna lie, it stung.

I mean, I'm used to women being into me. I'm in good shape, I'm good looking, I have a good job, a nice home, and yeah, I get grumpy sometimes, but I'm—generally speaking—not an asshole. It's not unusual for me to head into town during the high season, meet a hot tourist at one of the bars in town, and end up fucking her before she's on her way to Ketchikan.

McKenna and I are spending the entire summer together…it bothers me a lot that she isn't into me.

I get it that I'm not her type. She's this short, slight, college-educated chick from a big city. And I'm this big, shaggy mountain man from the wilds of Alaska who only finished high school.

I brood about this for a moment—about the differences in our educations and worldliness—but the reality is that she doesn't act superior or condescending to me. Honestly, she doesn't seem to care either way about my education, and I don't sense that she looks down on me for living in Dyea. She likes my cabin. I can tell. She seems to like Alaska. So I can't blame her lack of interest in me on education or location, even though it would be so much easier to paint her as a snob and hate her for it. But she's not a snob. And her childhood, in many ways, was a lot harder than mine. We both lost our mothers, but she also lost her father and grandfather at some point, and didn't have any siblings for support and camaraderie. What a lonely life for a little kid who'd seen too much heartache in such a short amount of time. I can't imagine what the first few years of her life must have been like.

And yet, here she is, all grown up with a college degree and decent job, looking after her grandmother.

I admire her.

I admire the hell out of her.

And suddenly my neanderthal brain wonders if admiring someone can turn into attraction and if that's what I'm experiencing now. Because when I met her at the airport a few days ago, I felt zero attraction to her. And now? After spending just a little bit of time with her, I can't stop thinking about her. And I guess I just wish that if *I* felt up for a summer fling with McKenna Cabot, she felt the same.

But she doesn't.

I humph with annoyance as I place another log on the chopping block and bring down my axe with a satisfying *thwack!* The log splits neatly, and I reposition one half, then the other, and split them again.

"You pissed at that log?"

I look over my shoulder to see Hunter standing behind me. Running my forearm over the dripping sweat on my forehead, I lean down and pick up the four log quarters, adding them to the massive pile of firewood we keep behind the lodge.

"Nope."

"Frustrated with something else?"

"Shut up, Hunter."

Hunter snickers like the asshole he is, then takes off his shirt, and wrangles the axe from where I buried it in the block. He reaches for a piece of log and lines it up, whacking once, twice, three times before it finally splits.

"Someone's out of practice," I note, arms crossed over my chest where my pecs are bulging.

"Shut up, Tanner," he says.

"Why're you here?" I ask him. "Don't you have a tour this morning?"

"Yep. One and done," he says, splitting one-half cleaner than the other. I pick up the uneven quarters as he lines up an especially thick log on the block and grabs a wedge to help split it. "We did the one-mile walking tour of old Dyea, then headed into Skagway for ninety minutes of Beers, Brawls and Brothels. They decided to stay in town for lunch and shopping. I'll go back for them at three."

"A rare afternoon off and you're spending it with me splitting wood?"

"It's early in the season," he says. "Got no one in town to cuddle up with...yet."

"Well, be careful. You know how well that went for me last year."

"Speaking of..." Hunter stops what he's doing and faces me. "She's here."

"Ramona," I say, my mouth going dry as my stomach flips over.

"Ramona," he confirms with a grim nod. "I saw her walking from the Fairway Market back to her apartment over the King Kone this morning."

"Did she see you?"

He shakes his head. "Don't think so."

"McKenna and I are headed into town tonight. Guess we'll see what happens."

"Hey. McKenna wasn't at dinner last night. Everything okay?"

He's right. She wasn't. It bugged me not to see her.

"There was an incident yesterday at the river," I mutter. "She wanted to go wading but didn't have the sense to bring bear spray with her."

Hunter tenses. "What happened?"

"Nothing, thank God. I saw her head out and decided to follow, just in case. There was a small black bear eating berries by the shore. Young."

"Did she charge you?"

"Nope. We stayed low and quiet, and she wasn't bothered by us…but you know the damage they can do if they're surprised or riled. Even the little ones."

"True enough. You're lucky nothing happened."

I think about McKenna's body melting into mine, the way she let me hold her, the way her hair smelled like wildflowers.

"Oh," Hunter murmurs. "Apparently something *did* happen."

My neck snaps up. "No. It didn't."

"Glad to hear it because I was sort of wondering…you mind if I make a move? She's really cute, and if you're not interested…"

"Don't make me hurt you, brother."

"Whoa. *Hurt me?* Is that where you're at with her?" Hunter stares at me curiously, hands on his hips, axe by his side. "I thought you said noth—"

"Nothing happened yesterday, but I don't know exactly where I'm at. I don't—I mean, she's not…I mean…I wouldn't be okay with you making a play for her. Clear?"

"Clear," says Hunter. "She's yours. I'll look elsewhere."

I nod, taking the axe from his hand and lining up another log.

She's yours. I like the way that sounds even though I know it's not true.

"You're shit at chopping wood, too."

Hunter chuckles as he shrugs back into his flannel shirt, not bothering to button it. "You want me and Harper to join you two in town tonight?"

"Why? You think I can't handle it?"

"Just offering moral support."

For a second, I consider having my older brother and sister tag along, my own little posse to show down Ramona De Alicante. But then I think about Hunter's question—*…you mind if I make a move?* —and I shake my head no. Best not to throw him together with McKenna while I'm still confused about my feelings for her.

"I've got it."

"Okay, then. Good luck."

Hunter heads back over to the lodge, while I get back to splitting logs, wondering if "I've got it" will turn out to be famous last words.

***

I show up at the door of my cabin at six o'clock to pick up McKenna, after having stopped by the dining room to tell my family I wouldn't be working tonight. I suspect Hunter already told them about Ramona's arrival in Skagway because no one pushed back or griped about losing a set of hands at tonight's campfire. They were pretty quiet all around, actually, until Reeve muttered something like, *"Good luck…you're gonna need it."*

It feels strange to knock on my own front door, but while McKenna's in Dyea, my house is hers, and that includes me not entering without knocking. What feels stranger still, however, is the zing of longing I feel when she answers the door. Dressed in a black leather jacket, a white blouse trimmed with lace, pencil-thin black jeans, and black boots, she looks like a different person—sophisticated and feminine and a little bit badass. For the first time since arriving in Skagway, she's done her hair with gel, and she's wearing makeup. Those dark-brown eyes, framed with a fringe of long, black lashes, are more Alice Cullen-y than ever.

"Whoa," I murmur.

"Too much?"

"Just right."

She takes a deep breath and cocks her head to the side. "Ready, my beloved?"

"Yeah," I say, still looking her up and down. She didn't suddenly grow curves overnight, but I find I'm not missing them. Her slim, spare body shape is growing on me. Fast. "You look good."

"Thanks," she says, but her smile doesn't reach her eyes.

"You say that like it's a surprise."

"Yeah," I murmur, feeling turned around by her transformation.

"It's a surprise that I look good? Gee, thanks, Tanner. You sure know how to spoil a girl."

"No! I didn't—I mean...okay, yeah, I'm a little surprised. I've never seen you all..." I gesture to my own eyes, then point at my lips. Hers are a dark maroon. Almost plum. And a little shiny. Totally hypnotic.

"Oh. Makeup? Yeah. I don't like it. I almost never wear it. But for tonight, I thought..." She shrugs, stepping past me on the porch and heading down the stairs. "Might as well pull out all the stops."

I follow her down the stairs feeling loutish and clumsy. She went to the trouble of looking her best, and the first thing I did was insult her. *Fucking idiot.*

"I'm an ass, McKenna," I say from behind her.

"Mm-hm," she hums. "Sometimes you are."

"You look amazing," I tell her, trying to make amends. "I'm grateful."

She stops at my car, turning to look at me. "You're welcome. Just holding up my end of the deal."

As we pull out of the parking lot, I find myself fumbling for words. I want to tell her that Ramona's back in town, but at the same time, I don't feel like bringing her up. The air feels crackly and alive between me and McKenna.

Tension, I think. *So much tension.*

Does she feel it, too? Or is it just dumb me, developing a crush on a woman who's only here to make money for her grandmother's care?

"How about some music?" she asks, leaning forward to fiddle with the radio dial.

"Sure. Whatever you want."

She stops at 70s on Seven, turning up the volume for the Eagles' *Desperado*.

"Great song. You like the Eagles?" she asks.

"I like most music from the seventies," I tell her. "Fleetwood Mac. Eagles. Elton John's early stuff. I grew up listening to it."

"Me, too," she says. "Probably because our

grandmothers raised us, right?"

"Yeah," I say. "Probably. My Gran still has all of her old vinyls and a working turntable from, like, fifty years ago. I'll show it to you."

"I'd love to see her collection!" says McKenna. "Bet it looks a lot like Mimi's."

"You like Simon & Garfunkel?" I ask her.

"Love them."

"Bread?"

"Of course."

"Jim Croce? Are you a *Bad, Bad Leroy Brown* fan or more of a *Time in a Bottle* girl?"

"*Time in a Bottle* always made Mimi sad. She'd change the station when it came on." She pauses for a second, in thought. "I think…"

"What?"

"I think it reminded her of her daughter. She blamed herself for Sheila's addiction." McKenna stares straight ahead, out the windshield, while the Eagles croon about letting someone love you before it's too late. "My grandfather served in Vietnam, and he wasn't okay when he got back. He hit the bottle hard, and I guess he was pretty abusive when he was on a bender. Mimi said she would have left if she hadn't gotten pregnant with Sheila, but she did, and it was the '70s, you know? She was scared of trying to raise a baby alone. My grandfather died of cirrhosis when Sheila was twelve, but the damage was already done. She was a child of addiction who became an addict. It's a cycle."

"I'm sorry," I say, because I can't think of anything else

to say. This is heavy stuff. Super heavy.

"Yeah. Me, too." She shakes her head. "Ugh. I'm so sorry I got into all of that. I never talk about this stuff really. But songs can take you back to a moment, you know?"

"Definitely," I agree. "And hey…for whatever it's worth, it seems like you and your Mimi figured out a way to break the cycle. With you."

"To some extent," she says, her tone guarded. "I don't do drugs, and I'm careful about my drinking. I don't have a lot of memories from the first four or five years of my life. That may sound weird, but it's true. I can't remember much. That said, a therapist I saw in college told me your brain starts making memories right around three-years old. They're in my head, whether I remember or not, which means the trauma's there, too. I have a hard time trusting people." She clears her throat and adds: "It makes me hard to love."

It's got to be one of the saddest sentences I've ever heard in my life.

"Hard to love? What do you mean?"

She squirms in her seat, reaching forward to turn off the radio, then roll down her window. Clean, fresh air rushes into the car as we trade the dirt road of Dyea for the paved one of Skagway.

After a few minutes of silence, I realize she's said all she's going to say, my question left unanswered.

***

McKenna

Damn it!

I could kick myself for going on and on about my personal bullshit when he's probably already anxious enough about having to see his psycho ex-girlfriend tonight.

Selfish, McKenna. So. Damn. Selfish.

I had put on the radio to try to lighten the mood—I could feel some lingering tension from yesterday's bear hug at the river, and it was making me nervous—and then I ended up swallowing all the oxygen in the car by yammering on about my hard-knocks' childhood.

I never do that. Never. I've made a concerted effort my entire life to rise above my shitty childhood and keep the sordid details to myself. I don't even talk to Isabella as freely about Sheila as I just did with Tanner. I don't know what's gotten into me, but I don't like it.

Disgusted with myself, I concentrate on getting my head in the game for tonight's showdown with Ramona, which is, after all, the entire reason I'm here.

"Um, uh…Ramona. Have you heard anything? Is she in town yet?"

"Yep. My brother saw her walking from the market this morning."

"So, what's the plan for tonight?"

"I thought we'd go to SBP for drinks and dinner. She'll show up there at some point."

"And then…?"

"I'll introduce you two, and—with any luck—that'll be the end of any Ramona drama."

Or the beginning, I think. If she's even half as nuts as he indicated, I'm not sure she'll give him up as quickly as he

111

hopes.

"Hey," he says, his face a little sheepish when I look over, "I know you're not actually, um, *into me*, but anything you can do to sell this tonight…I'd really appreciate it."

You know when someone says something *to* you, *about* you, that they *believe* is true—that maybe you've even *encouraged* them to believe is true—but it's *not* entirely true? It pings different in your head, and your first instinct is to correct them—to tell them what they're getting wrong…except I can't put my finger on exactly what Tanner's getting wrong.

I only know that his words don't sit well with me.

They don't feel true at all.

"Sure," I hear myself saying. "No problem."

"Great," he says, his voice soft and flat. "Thanks."

I sit back in my seat, staring out the open window and feeling annoyed. Nothing seems to be going right tonight—from the way Tanner greeted me, to my verbal diarrhea, to what he just said about my not being into him.

Even though I'm not.

I mean—I'm not, right?

I'm only here to make good money, quick, right?

Right.

And getting romantically involved with Tanner Stewart could be disastrous to that goal if things got messy.

Because Tanner has a messy track record.

Phew. So, good. I'm not into him. I'm—

Oh, you're into him.

No, I'm not.

Yes, you're definitely into him.

Fine!

Fine.

But getting involved with him—for real, romantically—wouldn't be smart.

Agreed.

So…where does that leave me?

Very much into a man who's posing as your fiancé, who would absolutely, positively not be a good idea for you romantically if making money to care for Mimi is the most important outcome for your summer.

I look up as Tanner parallel parks on Broadway, and end my internal dialogue determined not to allow my fledgling crush on Tanner go any further.

However, we're about to play make believe for the next couple of hours, which means I can indulge my attraction to him any way I want, as long as I can turn it off when we get back in the car to go home.

Tanner opens my door for me, and I take his hand as I get out of the car.

"Thanks, baby," I say, my voice soft and low.

His fingers entwine through mine.

"What did I say about calling me 'baby'?" he growls.

"What did you say about me selling it tonight?"

He grunts noncommittally as we walk up a side street toward the Skagway Brew Pub.

"Trust me, Tanner," I whisper. "Let me do this my way, and I promise you, she'll believe it."

Outside of the bar, he stops walking and turns to me, searching my face with bright blue eyes before resting his gaze on my lips. And me? A girl who's secretly crushing on him in

113

real life, but supposed to look like his devoted fiancée for the next few hours? I do what any other hot-blooded woman would do when her "beloved" gives her a look that would melt the glaciers outside town. I take his other hand in mine and lean up on my tiptoes as high as I can.

"Kiss me," I breathe. "And just in case she's watching, make it good."

His lips crash down on mine like he's been fasting for months, and I'm offering him a seven-course meal. There's no foreplay, no testing or tasting or butterfly kisses. He plunders my mouth, boldly swiping his tongue along the seam of my lips until they eagerly part, welcoming him inside with a whimper of relief. His arms tighten around me, flattening my breasts against the hard muscles of his chest. I cup the back of his neck with one hand and lay the other over his heart, which thunders with a racehorse gallop, raw and real and running away with me whether I like it or not.

But I do like it.

Too much.

So much that when he pulls away with a low, frustrated groan, I'm breathless but panting. My eyes open slowly, to find him staring down at me, his face registering the intense riot of emotions that I feel, too.

"Fuck," he murmurs, looking surprised.

"Yeah," I whisper.

It's been a while since I was kissed, but in my entire life, I don't ever remember a first kiss ever making me feel like I do right now.

"Good enough?" he asks me with one eyebrow raised.

"Mm-hm."

"Ready to go inside now?" He grins at me, looking very pleased with himself.

"Sure," I say, feeling jelly-legged.

His fingers find mine, braiding through them effortlessly as we step inside the lively bar and restaurant.

"Tanner!" calls one of the bartenders. "Good to see you, man!"

"Hey, Grady!" Tanner pulls me through a crowd of people waiting by the hostess station just inside the door. We stop at the bar where he reaches over to shake his friend's hand. "How's it going?"

"Fair enough. What can I get you?"

"Klondike IPA for me." He squeezes my hand, his eyes soft when they catch mine. "What do you want, babe?"

Babe. Sigh.

"Do you have a lager?" I ask Grady. "Or pilsner?"

He looks approvingly at me. "One of each. What do you prefer?"

"Lager, I guess, if it's not too hoppy."

"You know your beers?"

"The light ones," I tell him.

"She's a catch, Tanner." He offers me his hand. "I'm Grady. I can't believe you chose to work with Bruce at the Parsnip instead of here."

"Sorry," I say, with a surprised chuckle. "I'm an anthropologist. History always wins."

"I get it," he says, grabbing two clean pint glasses. "But if Bruce's theatrics don't work out for you, you're still welcome here. We could always use another bartender. Especially one who knows her hops."

He turns to grab the beers as Tanner puts his arm around me and pulls me close to his side. "Are you flirting with Grady?"

"Nope. I'm just talking to him," I say, biting my lower lip and watching Tanner's eyes rivet on the spot. "I'm here with you, baby. Only you."

"Damn straight," he says, his eyes darkening.

I can still feel the imprint of his lips on mine, and my cheeks flush, wanting them there again.

"Whew! I'd offer you two a room," says Grady, placing our beers on the bar in front of us, "but the inn upstairs is all booked."

"No need," I say, dragging my eyes away from Tanner's to smile at Grady and pick up my pint glass. "We're here to drink and eat." I wink at Tanner as I take a sip. "We'll get to the good stuff later."

"Damn, Tanner," says Grady. "I think I just got pregnant."

Tanner whoops with laughter, kissing the top of my head before downing half his pint in a single gulp.

Grady's eyes land on my ring. "When's the wedding, you two?"

"Wintertime," I tell him, remembering what Tanner told the hardware store guy a few days ago. "In Seattle."

"I'll be on the lookout for my invitation," says Grady.

"You know you'll get one," says Tanner.

As Grady moves down the bar to help another customer,

I look at Tanner, my face upturned. "So far, so good?" "*So* good," he says, leaning down to brush his lips against mine.

My heart flutters. My stomach flips. A *zing!* between my thighs makes me wish Tanner and I were alone. *He's not your fiancé*, my brain reminds me, like it's getting worried. *This is just an act, remember?*

I lean away, taking another sip of my beer to cool off when I hear a woman's voice break through the din of bar and restaurant white noise. Without quite reaching shrill, it's high and intense, and it makes the hairs on the back of my neck stand up.

"Tanner? Tanner!"

And I know—I know it in my bones before even looking up, that I'm about to come face to face with *her*, with Ramona De Alicante.

I turn around slowly, like I couldn't care less who was talking to my man, all the while itching to see her—to understand who captured his heart last summer, and how I compare with her.

"Tan-Tan!" she cries, plowing sloppily through the same crowd that Tanner sliced through cleanly a few minutes before. "I've missed you!"

And suddenly I feel like I'm in one of those old west movies. This woman—my nemesis, I guess—is about five-foot-ten with dark, wavy hair that cascades down her tan shoulders, and curves to spare. She's dressed in super short denim shorts, a way-too-tight fire engine red tank top, white cowgirl boots, and a white, rhinestone cowboy hat. In red,

117

white and blue, with giant boobs, pasted-on mega lashes, and a sultry glare, she slowly flicks her eyes from Tanner to me. Her smile—huge, perfect and white—fades. Her eyes widen. Her nostrils flare. I lean into Tanner, who tightens his grip around my waist.

This is when I notice that the activity and conversation in the bar has come to a halt. No one talks. No one breathes. Everyone—bartenders, waitstaff, and patrons alike—waits with bated breath to see what will happen next.

Like I said…it's a showdown.

She stares at me like she wants to murder me with her bare hands before zipping her disbelieving gaze back to Tanner.

"What the fuck?" she asks, staring at Tanner as she gestures to me with a flick of her chin. "Who the *fuck* is she?"

I know he's nervous. I know he's been dreading this moment since he heard she was coming back to Skagway. And I'm not about to let her push him—or me—around. I've already survived too much in this life of mine to let this cheap-ass rodeo Barbie intimidate me.

"*She* is McKenna," I say.

Here's the truth. If she'd been more polite and less of a bitch, I might have stepped forward and offered my hand to her. But her bad manners don't deserve my civility. Instead, I lean my head against Tanner's side and place my palm flat over his heart in a tried-and-true sign of possession. And yes. I use the hand that has my engagement ring shining from the fourth finger.

Ramona's eyes zero in on my opal, and she looks like her

head might explode. She puts her hands on her hips, throwing dagger eyes at Tanner.

"And who the *fuck* is McKenna?" she demands.

Tanner takes a moment to kiss the top of my head before responding.

"My fiancée."

At this point—and, yes, I know, I know...a better, smarter, kinder woman might try to diffuse the situation instead of adding fuel to the fire, but Ramona is a bully, and in my experience, bullies take advantage of kindness. Their behavior doesn't improve when it's offered.—I face Tanner.

Leaning against his body, up on tiptoes, I murmur, "And you're mine, baby," before letting him kiss me senseless in front of the whole bar.

Senseless.

That's me.

 chapter nine

Tanner

If I had any doubts that I was slipping and sliding down a steep hill, brakes broken, falling hard and fast for McKenna Cabot, they are now gone.

The way she handled Ramona? The way she leaned up for that kiss?

Fuck me.

I'm in trouble.

I'm smitten and good.

I'm vaguely aware of my friends whooping and hollering as we kiss, but with McKenna wrapped in my arms, and her sweet, soft lips moving hungrily under mine? It's just as likely I'm hearing the spark and boom of fireworks going off in my head.

When I finally draw away from her, feeling liquid and electric at once, I watch her eyes open slowly.

She mouths the words, "So good," and fuck, but she's right. It is. *She* is. *This is called chemistry*, I tell myself, and it's either there between two people or it's not. Well, it's between me and McKenna in spades.

She slides her gaze away from my face, and I realize that she's turning to face Ramona.

"Any more questions?" she asks, reaching up to backhand her slick lips.

Ramona whimpers softly, staring at McKenna for a long, furious moment.

"You're a bitch," she hisses.

"Watch your mouth," says McKenna.

"Fuck you," Ramona snarls.

"Absolutely. He will. Later."

Damn.

I ignore the way my blood surges to my cock because I'm a little worried that Ramona might lunge forward and attack us. I pull McKenna tightly against my side to keep her safe.

"I think you should go," I tell Ramona.

"You'll regret this," she says, her eyes narrowing to slits, and spittle collecting at the corner of her lips like a rabid dog. "I'll make your life a living hell. I promise you that, Tanner Stewart."

Then she turns on her white-booted heel and pushes her way back out of the bar.

If I wasn't so elated by what appeared to be a clean victory, I might have had the good sense to be scared of such a bold threat. Because Ramona, as I well know, pulls out all the stops when it comes to crazy—and she wasn't just facing rejection now. McKenna and I had just added public humiliation to her list of grievances.

But with my heart bursting with gratitude, and my body

thrumming from two knock-out kisses, I can't think of anything but the amazing woman by my side.

"Don't worry about her," I whisper close to her ear.

She grabs her beer and takes a big gulp. "Her eyes were crazy, Tanner."

"Yeah. I told you. She's nuts."

"I think she meant what she said," says McKenna. "About making your life hell. About making you regret this."

"Maybe," I say, gesturing to Grady for another round.

"At least she threatened you in front of a full restaurant," says McKenna. "That means plenty of witnesses. If she does anything insane, you can press charges. Or get a restraining order."

"I don't think that'll be necessary."

"What do you mean?"

"She's just mad."

"She's not 'just mad,'" McKenna insists. "She's *unhinged*."

No argument here about Ramona being psycho, but McKenna's suggestion of a restraining order feels way over the top. In little towns, we don't think like that. Maybe it sounds provincial, but we don't call the cops at the first sign of a beef with someone else. We give it time. We try to work it out. We hope that common sense eventually triumphs. Anyway, I don't feel like talking about Ramona anymore. I'm just glad this first meeting is out of the way, and Team Tanner came out unscathed.

"Hey," I say, grinning at McKenna, whose face is still tense, "you were amazing."

Her expression eases, and she offers me a little smile.

"Oh, really?"

"Have you done this before?"

"What? Been someone's fiancée for hire? Nope," she says. "You're my first."

My gaze skitters to her lips. I want to kiss her again. I want to kiss her all night. I want to kiss her all summer long. I want to kiss places on her body that I have no business, no right, to be thinking about. And then I want to kiss them all over again.

McKenna takes a step back from me, looking down at the floor.

"What's wrong?"

"Nothing," she says. "I'm just—where's the ladies room?"

"Back there."

"Thanks," she says, her eyes guarded. "I'll be back in a minute."

I watch her go, wondering about the sudden change in her mood. One second, we were flirting about her being my fake fiancée. The next, she looked like she wanted to run away.

"That was…interesting," says Grady, taking our empties and rinsing them in the bubbly sink under the counter. "She's a fiery one, that Ramona."

"She's a nutcase."

"Yeah," says Grady. "I was trying to be nice."

"Not on my account, I hope."

He shrugs. "You two were hot and heavy last summer, if memory serves."

"All in the past, my friend."

"Well, I like your new girl a lot better," he says. "Big step up."

"I agree."

"Hey, Tanner!" calls Rina, one of the hostesses working at the front of the restaurant.

I step away from the bar. "What's up?"

She gestures to some hikers who look trail worn and dusty. "These folks just walked in. Said they saw a RAV4 being keyed on the street. Don't you have a—"

Before she can finish her thought, I'm running out of the SBC toward my car. And sure enough, the word "DICK" has been sloppily scratched into the driver's door.

"Fuck!" I yell, snapping up my neck to find Ramona's apartment window over the King Kone. A curtain flutters back into position. "You fucking bitch!"

The lights in the apartment go dark as I stand there next to my car, hands on my head, my heart thudding with anger. Fixing this mess will cost $1000 or more. And in the meantime, I have to drive around with the word "dick" carved into my car. Fuck this!

If she does anything insane, you can press charges.

Maybe McKenna's right.

I stride back into the bar, looking for the people who witnessed the vandalism. Maybe they'd be willing to give the police Ramona's description so Joe can arrest her ass.

"Where'd they go?" I ask Rina. "The two hikers?"

"Oh, sorry. They left."

Shit.

"Where to?"

She shrugs. "I didn't ask. Sorry."

So, no witnesses. Great.

I see McKenna making her way through the crowd back toward the bar. She looks for me, and I wave her over to the door.

"Everything okay?"

"Ramona keyed my car," I tell her.

"What? When?"

"Just now."

"Did anyone see?"

"Two hikers came in to report it, but they're already gone."

"You have to tell the police," she says. "Let's go file a report. Right now."

I take a deep breath and huff angrily, all of my glee about kissing McKenna and besting Ramona long gone.

"What's the point? Without witnesses, it'd be her word against mine."

"She threatened you less than fifteen minutes ago. Everyone heard her."

"It would *still* be her word against mine about the keying."

"Okay, fine, but it would put her on the police's radar."

"So what?"

"You're not hearing me," McKenna says, her forehead creasing. "I'm saying—"

"I get what you're saying!" I bark at her. "But fuck it. I just want to go home."

She puts her hands on her hips and stares at me intently

for a second before shrugging. "Fine. Let's go home."

**

We drive back to the campground without any music or chit chat, me feeling furious and pig-headed, her shifted away from me in her seat, doing something on her phone. After a few minutes of silence, she shares what she's been up to.

"Intentional vandalism in excess of $850 damage is a class C felony in Alaska," she announces. "Maybe there are traffic cameras on the street, or—"

"Stop," I mutter. I don't want to hear it. I want to go home, go to bed, and wake up tomorrow ready to research how to buff out key marks on YouTube.

"I don't get you," she says, putting her phone back in her purse and rolling down her window.

"What's to get?"

"This woman has harassed you for a year. To the extent that you moved away last summer and looked for a fake fiancée online just to get rid of her. Why won't you go to the police? Why won't you report her behavior? Why won't you ask for help?"

I dig my heels in. "Because I don't need help. I can handle it."

"Yeah," she scoffs. "You're handling it really well."

"I didn't notice you complaining when I paid your airfare to come up here and offered you a free place to live."

"Wow," she murmurs. "You're being a total jerk."

I know I am. I know it. But damn it, I don't want to go whining to the police like a scared little bitch. I want to handle this myself. And maybe, with any luck, Ramona got her anger out of her system by keying my car. We humiliated her. She destroyed my car door. Even Steven. Maybe it's over now.

"Just because I don't want to do things your way doesn't make me a jerk," I mutter.

We roll into the campground, and I pull in front of my cabin, but before I can even say "goodnight," McKenna's slamming her door closed and hopping up the stairs without a glance back at me. I blink as the front door slams shut.

"Fuck," I shout, banging on my steering wheel, which does nothing but pop a blister I got chopping wood earlier today.

I consider knocking on my door to apologize to her, or at least thank her again for everything she did for me tonight but think better of it. She'll cool off by tomorrow.

I hope.

***

McKenna

I spend Sunday altering my work costume and avoiding Tanner, which isn't that hard. His cabin has all the sustenance I need: eggs for breakfast, ham and cheese for lunch and a microwave to heat up a plate of frozen lasagna for dinner.

I catch up on my Netflix favorites while I hem my skirt and tuck my blouse and call Mimi's care home in the afternoon to get an update on how she's doing. I'm glad to hear that she's been watching movies in the rec room and attending yoga classes. Apparently, she and another resident got into a shoving match over who owned Mimi's red embroidered slippers, but they ended up forgetting the argument twenty minutes later when the other woman walked away wearing them. The nurse assured me that this behavior is standard and not to be concerned, but I made a mental note to send her some new slippers.

As evening turns into night, I'm about to watch the next episode of my favorite reality show, "Love at First Sight," when there's a knock on my door. I open it, bracing myself to continue my spat with Tanner, so I'm surprised to find Harper, Parker, and Reeve standing on the porch instead.

"Hi," says Parker, holding up a bottle of Prosecco.

"We thought you could use a girl's night," says Harper, cradling a basket of nail files, buffers, and polishes.

Reeve thrusts a carton of Oreos at me. "There's never a bad time for cookies."

"Come on in," I say, stepping aside so they can enter their brother's cabin.

Since I've been camped out on the couch all day, there's only space for one to sit. Harper plops down there, while Parker opts for a pillow on the floor and Reeve pulls a little stool out from under the coffee table. I gather up the costume I finished hemming and take it to the bedroom to make a spot for myself while the girls pour the wine and break out the cookies.

When I join them, Parker hands me a glass of wine.

"Should we toast my jackass brother?" she asks, a twinkle in her eye.

I'm surprised. I thought they might be here for an intervention on his behalf, but it looks like I was wrong. We clink our plastic cups together and gulp down the sweet wine.

"He's so bullheaded," says Harper.

"And bossy," adds Reeve.

I have this weird impulse to defend him—to tell them that he's not that bad, which is strange, because all day I've been having imaginary conversations with him, complaining about the same things they find annoying, too.

"Can't get out of his own way," says Harper. "That's a fact."

"Remember the school bus?" asks Parker. "What a nightmare."

"Tell the story!" begs Reeve.

"I'll do it," says Harper, finishing an Oreo and dusting her hands off on her cut-off shorts. "When our mom died, Reeve was a baby, Sawyer was four and Parker was five. Hunter and I were already in high school, and that September was supposed to be Tanner's freshman year. First day of school rolls around, Hunt and I get on the bus to Skagway as usual, but Tanner? Nope. Wouldn't do it. He refused to get on. Wouldn't get out of the car even when Daddy drove him all the way there. Daddy tried to drag him out of the car, but Tanner was already pretty big at thirteen. The Principal—who must've seen the melee outside—headed out to the car and said that Tanner shouldn't come into the building until he was ready, but that if they didn't figure it out within three days, he'd be truant. Daddy tried to reason with Tanner, tried to bargain with him. Nope. Nothing worked. He wouldn't go to school, so our father gave up and took him back home."

"Stubborn," mutters Reeve.

"That's for sure," says Harper.

"So Gran started homeschooling him," says Parker. "Next year, it was my turn to get on the bus. What did I do? I refused. Tanner didn't go. I figured…why should I?"

"Even Hunter and Harper couldn't get her on that bus," says Reeve, grabbing another cookie. "She kept saying, "If Tanner don't go, I don't go." over and over again."

"But then, out of nowhere, here comes Tanner, walking over to the bus stop with a backpack on his back and a paper lunch sack in his hand. And he puts his arm around me, and he tells me he'll be with me every step of the way. So, we get on that bus together," says Parker. "Even though he's fifteen and I'm six, we sit side by side in the front seat, and he holds my hand the whole time. Bus stops at the high school, Hunt and Harp get off, but Tanner stays on. When we get to the grade school, he gets off with me and drops me off at my classroom. Tells me at the end of the day, he'll be saving me a seat next to him on the bus. Then he walks over to the high school and enrolls himself in tenth grade. And you know what? When I got on that bus at the end of the day, there he was, waiting for me. We did that every day for a year."

I'm entranced by this story of teenaged Tanner, who couldn't be persuaded to do something for his own good but went out of his way to do it willingly for the good of someone he loved.

"He's ornery, for sure," says Harper with a little eye roll. "No one on earth can get him to do something he doesn't want to do."

"But," I say, feeling a little defensive on Tanner's behalf, "he went on the bus…for *you*."

"Yep. Every day," says Parker, pouring herself a little more wine. "Weirdo."

"The weirdest," says Reeve. "Harp, will you paint my toes hot pink?"

Harper nods, patting her knee. "Put your dogs up here, babycakes."

As Reeve moves her stool closer to her oldest sister, I tilt my head to the side, looking at Parker. The sun rises on my thoughts, and I have a stark aha moment in its glare.

"If I want him to file a police report about his car, it needs to be for *me*, not for *him*."

"Bingo, smartypants." Parker winks at me. "He'll do just about anything for someone he cares about."

"Then maybe *you* should ask him instead," I say with a scoff.

Parker's eyebrows furrow. "Me? Why?"

"Wait! Do you think Tanner *doesn't* like you?" asks Reeve, her eyes incredulous.

"Boy is smitten," murmurs Harper, concentrating on Reeve's little toe.

"No! No, he's not. It's just an act, I promise," I say, curling up tighter into the corner of the couch. "You guys have *seen* Ramona. We all know what his type is. Gorgeous. Tall. Sexy. With huge boobs and long hair and long eyelashes and …I'm not his type. Not at all. I'm little and short and just—"

"Can't get out of his own way!" cries Parker. "It's crazy-making."

"Agree," mutters Reeve.

"You're wrong," says Harper gently but firmly, looking up from Reeve's feet. "He's *super* into you."

"He's not," I insist, but my words lack conviction as my mind segues back to our kisses last night. Those were just for show, right? One, to get us into the act, and the other to prove our "love" to Ramona. It wasn't real. It was just the deal we agreed on. That's all.

"He *is*," says Parker, scooting closer to me. She grabs a tube of red polish from her sister's basket of supplies. "Want me to paint your nails?"

I'm eager to get off the topic of me and Tanner and grateful for the change in subject.

I scrunch up my nose. "What would Bruce say?"

"Oh, lawdy! Nothing good." She pretends to twirl a mustache corner as she waggles a finger at me. "'Nail varnish is not authentic to the Gold Rush era, young lady!'"

We all laugh, and Reeve asks me to turn on some music, which I do. When the Stewart girls leave two hours later, the wine and cookies are gone, and I'm left alone with my thoughts as I stare up at the stars through the skylight in Tanner's ceiling.

He'll do just about anything for someone he cares about...Boy is smitten...He's super *into you...*

His sisters' words go round and round and round in my head, making sleep hard to come by, and weaving dreams of little Tanner and little me holding hands on a school bus bound for Skagway.

***

I look ridiculous.

132

The prairie skirt fits comfortably around my waist, but the hem is a little crooked from my meager seamstress skills, and the peasant blouse dips way too low, showing off assets I don't have. Hm. I pull my push-up bra out of hiding and belt the shirt around the waist, which helps give me a little more definition on top. Then, I sit on Tanner's bed and pull on the boots Bruce gave me, wishing flip flops were authentic to the "Gold Rush era" and chuckling to myself about Parker's spot-on impersonation of him last night.

I'm not exactly excited for my first day at work, but I'm here to make money, and my goal today will be to charm the pants off of any tourists who come wandering into the Purple Parsnip in search of sarsaparillas. If I bust my ass over the next three months, I should be flush by the time I go home.

I hear Tanner beep the horn outside and grab my bag, hurrying out of the cabin and down the steps to join him in the car. My heart leaps when I sit down next to him. He smells like he just jumped out of the shower, and his stubble is freshly shaved. I didn't realize how much I missed him yesterday.

"Morning!" I chirp.

"It's almost noon."

"Until then, it's still morning."

"Okay," he says. "Good morning, even though some of us have been up since the crack of dawn."

"And some of us will be working until dark," I remind him.

"Buckle up," he says, reaching for my seat belt and pulling it over my chest.

His forearm brushes against my breasts and small though

they are, they feel it like a caress, my nipples swelling like pebbles under my padded bra.

"I've got it," I say, taking the buckle out of his hand and shoving it into the latch. Our fingers brush against each other, and a frizzle of electricity shoots up my arm.

As he pulls away from the cabin, he clears his throat and glances at me. "I, um, I wanted to say sorry about the way I acted on Saturday night. I was…jerky. You've been great, McKenna. The last thing you need is for me to be difficult."

"You were stressed," I say. "And it was pretty terrible what she did."

"I watched a YouTube video this morning and ordered some supplies on Amazon. I think I can fix it."

"You know…speaking of Saturday night, I don't think I was very clear with you," I say, my tone even and measured, "but Ramona *frightens* me."

He jerks his head to the right to look at me, letting his car idle at the exit to Dyea Road. Staring at me intently, he reaches out to take my hand.

"You don't have to be scared of her," he says. "She threatened me, not you. She won't go after you. I won't let her."

His thumb strokes the pillow of soft skin at the base of my thumb, and I try to ignore the butterflies fluttering in my tummy.

"I appreciate that. I do. But you can't be with me all the time. What if she tries something while I'm at work or while I'm taking a break or something? I know you don't want to file a police report, Tanner, but I think I'd feel a lot better if I knew they had their eyes on her."

He takes a deep breath and nods. "I understand. We can go to the PD tomorrow before I drive you to work, okay?"

Wow. That was easy. His sisters were right.

"Okay. Thanks."

Without thinking, I lean over the console between us and kiss his cheek. His skin is warm and smooth beneath my lips, and my eyes flutter shut for a second. His fingers curl into the back of my hand, tightening until my eyes flick open, and I pull away.

His sisters may have been right about other things, too.

He clears his throat again, his jaw flexing and releasing twice before he shifts the car into drive and turns toward Skagway.

"I have a new type," he says softly.

"A what?"

"A new type," he says a little louder.

My heart gallops. Goosebumps rise up on my arms.

"Really?"

"Uh-huh."

"Well," I say, "let's see...your old type was tall—"

"I like short now."

"—with lots of curves."

"Curves are overrated."

"Is that right?"

"Yep."

"You like long, wavy hair, right?" I ask, my lips twitching, dying to smile.

"Short is cuter."

I cup my ear and lean closer. "You said short is…*sexier*?"

He chuckles. "Yep. You heard me right. *Sexier.*"

"Because puppies are cute. Short is sexy."

"Amen," he says, glancing at me with a raised eyebrow. "But for the record, cute can be sexy, too."

I can live with that. "What else?"

"I like college girls now," he says. "Smart is *super* sexy. So is anthropology."

I giggle with delight. This is a new side to Tanner, playful and flirty. And I like it. God, I like it so much.

"Let me get this straight," I say, as downtown Skagway comes into view too soon. "You're looking for a small, not too curvy, short-haired, cute, sexy, college-educated anthropologist. Have I got that right?"

"Exactly," he says, parallel parking in front of the Purple Parsnip, and turning to grin at me. "Know anyone who fits that description?"

Oh, my heart.

If I'm not careful, I'm going to fall for him. And if I do, it's going to hurt.

Be careful, warns my heart, but my brain tells my heart to shut up. *Just have a summer fling!* it suggests. *Nothing too serious. Something casual and fun.*

Isn't that exactly what Isabella suggested? Maybe it's exactly what I need. Besides, he is way too delicious—and way too available—to ignore.

"I might," I tell him, wondering if his heart is beating as fast and furious as mine. "How about I let you know when you pick me up?"

He nods slowly, sliding his hungry eyes to my lips and then back to my gaze.

"Sounds good to me."

 chapter ten

Tanner

After I drop off McKenna, and still buzzing from my proposition, I spend the afternoon taking a family of five on an afternoon hike up the Chilkoot Trail.

I've probably walked this route a hundred times or more in my life, but I still find it fascinating—I like seeing the history of my home through fresh eyes, and it occurs to me that this deep love of history and place is something that McKenna and I have in common. *Maybe it's something that could draw us closer together this summer*, I think.

At its height in 1898, Dyea was six blocks long by nine blocks wide and had over a hundred and fifty businesses, including saloons, restaurants, hotels and mercantiles, but also doctors, a dentist, drug stores, a brewery, two newspapers, a church, two hospitals, and an undertaker. By 1903, only five years later, less than ten people still lived there, most of them my kin.

All that's left today is the remains of the once 2-mile-long wharf, the metal shell of a rowboat, one last standing false storefront, and three cemeteries, which are the final resting place of the stampeders caught in the 1898 avalanche on Palm Sunday.

From Dyea, we follow the Taiya River through the cool coastal rainforest to Saintly Hill, named for its quick and dirty 300-foot ascent, which would get the blood pumping for Gold Rush stampeders, who were carrying hundreds of pounds of supplies and equipment for their long journey north. Even seasoned hikers consider Saintly Hill one of the most arduous parts of the Chilkoot Trail. Luckily, however, it's followed by narrow, level ground along an old logging road, which includes the ruins of two structures by an abandoned 1940s sawmill.

Not long after, we reach Finnegan's Point, where the National Park Service maintains several warming huts with wood stoves, bear lockers, and a latrine. It's a convenient place for me to rest and refuel my hikers and to fill them in on the short, but significant, history of Finnegan's Point.

Gold was discovered in Dawson City, Yukon territory, Canada, in August 1896. The news reached the west coast of the United States by the spring of 1897, and the first ship of stampeders docked in Skagway in August 1897. They stocked up on the supplies they needed to make the trip north, and quickly made their way to the trailhead of the Chilkoot Trail in Dyea.

By late August 1897, Finnegan's Point, five miles from the Chilkoot trailhead, was the first significant resting point on the 300-mile Chilkoot Trail, and included a blacksmith shop, a saloon, and a restaurant. The following spring, it also included ferry service across the Taiya River.

But by April 1898, one stampeder described it as no more than a convenient stop for "hot donuts and coffee." And by the spring of 1899, with the gold "rush" winding down, the once-lively rest area had been completely abandoned.

In honor of that lost stampeder's account of Finnegan's Point, we typically start lunch with hot coffee brought up in a thermos on my back and homemade donuts that Reeve fried and powdered last night.

Sitting around a campfire with the Daniels family—mother, father, teenage daughter, and twin sons—I boil hotdogs, reheat baked beans, and answer questions about the Yukon Gold Rush as best I can.

But I'm not on point today.

My mind keeps slipping back to McKenna and our drive into Skagway this morning.

I wonder if I'm growing on her the way she's growing on me. I wonder what she'll say when I pick her up tonight. I wonder how she'll feel when I finally slide inside of her, hard and hot, for the first—

"Mr. Stewart," asks one of the Daniels twins, shattering my fantasy, "why did fewer than half of the prospectors who came to Skagway make it to Dawson City?"

I clear my throat, shooing away images of a naked McKenna, and turn to the youngster.

"Great question. Remember what I said about the Canadian government requiring that every prospector coming from Alaska brought a year's worth of gold mining equipment, supplies, and food with them? That was a ton of supplies, which they carried on their backs in stages. Let's say a miner was partnering with a friend. He'd bring a hundred pounds of supplies up a mountain, leave it with his partner, and then go back down for another hundred pounds. They'd do that twenty times—ten times each—before they'd start moving everything in stages again. One mile at a time. For three hundred miles."

"Many of them died during the journey," says Mrs. Daniels.

"Or gave up," mutters the daughter, who's been complaining about tight boots for most of today's hike.

"It was a hellish journey," adds Mr. Daniels. "Some died of disease. Others were murdered or froze to death. Remember what Mr. Stewart said about dozens of prospectors dying in an avalanche?"

"What was the point?" asks the other twin, tucking into a second donut. "Money? That's it?"

"Yep. To be rich," I say. "That's it, really."

"Was it worth it?" asks Mrs. Daniels, waiting patiently as each of her children answers the question.

I get some hot dog buns out of the bear locker we rent from the NPS and make plates of food for the family as I consider Mrs. Daniels's question myself.

Over a hundred thousand men left the Lower 48 in search of Yukon gold. Tens of thousands died. Others *spent* a fortune *seeking* a fortune they never found and left Alaska destitute. Only a few hundred actually left Alaska with life-changing amounts of money. One percent. Only one percent found what they were looking for.

Was it worth it?

My mind slides back to McKenna and reframes her as a modern-day prospector of sorts, here in Alaska to make quick money to care for her aging grandmother. Here we are, over a hundred and thirty years later, and Americans still view Alaska as a land of quick riches, albeit in a far less dangerous way…berry-picking bears notwithstanding.

How many 1890s stampeders traveled north to make money for their families? I wonder. *How many, like McKenna, came here out of need, not folly? When McKenna looks back on her life, will she think that her summer in Skagway was worth it?*

I hope so.

I hope she makes all the money she needs, and when her grandmother is long gone, and McKenna is old and gray, living in a cottage near a college in Seattle, she knows that she did what she had to do to care for someone she loved. I hope she lives a life without regrets.

As the family eats their dogs and beans before turning back to Dyea, I fleetingly wonder if McKenna's memories will hold any place for me in the great someday of her forever. When her summer in Alaska plays like a movie in her mind, will I co-star, or feature, or even be remembered?

It pinches my heart to think that she will forget me.

As we head back into the forest, I rub my chest, wondering if this summer could somehow turn out to be more dangerous than the last. How smart is a summer fling if you grow attached, only to be left behind?

I'm filled with doubt as I guide the Daniels back down

to the once-vibrant, now-ghost town of Dyea. Because those who come to Alaska seeking fortune rarely stay. And we who remember them are the forgotten few left behind.

***

It's still light when I leave to pick up McKenna in town, but hours have passed since my deep thoughts at Finnegan's Point.

Unfortunately, I'm still troubled by them.

Mostly because I've only come up with one way to have a physical relationship with McKenna, and it's this: I can't fall for her.

I can be attracted to her.

I can spend time with her.

I can like her all I want.

And if she's willing, I can fuck her to my heart's content.

But I can't fall in love with her. If I do, I could end up hurt when she leaves. And I really don't want to lose eight months of lonely off-season in Dyea mooning over a woman from Seattle who didn't come to Alaska to fall in love and left without a second glance.

So, don't fall for her, I tell myself. *Keep feelings out of it.*

Bearing in mind the already-transactional nature of our relationship, I think that maybe it's possible for McKenna and me to add a physical element to our agreement without jeopardizing our hearts. It's just a matter of her wanting the same thing I want: a no-strings-attached fling.

By the time I get to Skagway, I'm still feeling conflicted but better. I'm convinced I've hacked the problem, and that "friends with benefits" is the only solution.

***

McKenna

I've spent all day in a romantic haze.

You're looking for a small, not too curvy, short-haired, cute, sexy, college-educated anthropologist. Have I got that right?

Even now, pulling my hundredth beer of the day into a frosty glass stein, I glance at the antique clock on the wall and grin. He'll be here soon.

I never expected to get involved with someone this summer, and almost as soon as Tanner was on my radar, I convinced myself he'd be a poor choice for romance. I was determined to concentrate on my reason for being in Alaska in the first place—to make money for Mimi's care. Done and done.

Except...

He's beautiful.

And interesting.

And protective.

And funny.

And when we kiss, the whole world disappears, and my heart—oh, my stupid heart—beats furiously for more. There's this, too: I *like* posing as his fiancée. I wouldn't mind pretending to be his fiancée in private, too.

Every reason I had for *not* getting involved with him has evaporated over the last few hours, leaving me wanting him. Wanting us. Even if only for the summer. *Ideally* only for the summer. I've never been in love before, and I have no interest in falling in love with Tanner Stewart. But a fling? A sweet fling with wet kisses and hot sex and more of that megawatt lightbulb turned-on-ness? Bring it on.

"Miss McKenna!"

I look up to see Bruce standing at the end of the bar.

"I'm ready, Bruce! Whaddaya need?"

"Two Mule Skinners and two root beers. And then..." With a flourish, he puts on his monocle, takes out his pocket watch, opens it up, inspects it thoroughly then snaps it shut. "You're off the clock, young lady!"

Bruce, I've learned today, does nothing in half measures, and it's fascinating and exhausting at once. But he was also right: the thicker I lay on the bar wench act, the bigger the payout.

"Thank you, kind sir," I say, with a demure curtsy.

He winks at me as I turn around and start mixing the skinners.

I've made some killer tips today—over a hundred dollars in cash, and even more once the credit card gratuities are processed. Vacationing cruisers are damn good tippers, and that's a fact. Financially speaking, it's going to be a very good summer.

I place the four drinks on a tray and briefly consider sliding them down the shiny bar to Bruce, but I'll need some time and practice to perfect moves like that. Instead, I walk them down to him.

"Your order, sir."

He nods deferentially. "An excellent first day, Miss McKenna."

"Thanks, boss," I say. "See you tomorrow."

I untie my apron and throw it in a bin of dirty linen behind the bar. Closing out the register takes a minute. I rolled up my cash tips half an hour ago during a five-minute lull, and Bruce will tally up my credit card tips and add them to my paycheck at the end of my shift.

I sling my purse over my shoulder and head outside, letting the saloon doors swing closed behind me. Stepping onto the boardwalk in cold, damp Skagway, I marvel at the light. What a wonder! It's four hours from midnight, and barely fifty degrees, but the sun's still out.

"What're you smiling at?"

I was so distracted by Skagway's strange beauty, I didn't notice Tanner standing against his car to my left. But my body reacts instantly—my heart beats faster, my cheeks flush, and I catch my bottom lip between my teeth.

He grins at me, his blue eyes crinkling.

"Howdy, ma'am," he drawls, tipping an imaginary hat.

"Good evening, kind sir."

"Good first day behind the bar?"

"*Great* first day. You were right, the tips are spectacular."

"Yes!" he cries, lifting a hand for me to high-five.

I step forward and smack my palm against his, letting him lace his fingers through mine as he lowers our hands together.

"Fancy a walk, Miss McKenna?" he asks, glancing at the mostly quiet boardwalk, then back at me.

"Sure," I say, falling into step beside him.

We cross the street, away from the line that snakes out from the still-open King Kone. I'm not in the mood to deal with a potential Ramona confrontation after a long day at work, so I'm relieved to avoid her shop. "So, fiancé, tell me about your day. What trouble did you get into?"

"Took a family of five up the Chilkoot to Finnegan's Point. Had lunch. Walked back." He pauses for a second. "Thought a lot about you."

A frisson of heat darts up my arm from where our hands are joined. "What did you think?"

"I thought that we've got three months of summer ahead of us, and I get to spend them with you."

My stomach flips over the same way it does on the first drop of a roller coaster. Falling. Flying. Full steam ahead.

"But," he continues, his voice softer and lower. "I don't want for either of us to get hurt."

"Neither do I."

"I was thinking that some ground rules might be a good idea?"

His tone isn't as confident as usual, and if I'm not mistaken, there's a slight bit of sheepishness to his suggestion. I wonder why. *Is he uncertain of my reaction? Does he think my feelings will be hurt if we agree to keep feelings out of our physical relationship?*

"Tanner," I say, "there's so much you don't know about me."

"Sure, but I don't want to—"

"I'm *not* going to fall in love with you," I tell him firmly, stopping us in our walk so I can face him. "You don't have to worry about that."

He blinks at me. "Oh."

"I don't do that."

"You don't—"

"Put it this way, I'm the *opposite* of Ramona." I take a step closer to him, so that when he inhales, his chest brushes against me. "But I agree we should have some ground rules. Here are mine: One, don't sleep around if you're sleeping with me. I don't want to catch anything. And two, if what we're doing runs its course for you, just be upfront, okay? Let me know you're not into it anymore, and we can go our separate ways. That's it." I shrug like I believe everything I'm saying. Like I'm as casual about my feelings as I claim to be. And mostly, I am, not because that's who I *want* to be, but because I know it's for the best. "I don't get serious, so if that's what you're worried about, you don't need to be."

He scans my eyes, then flinches. Like, actually flinches like something just bit him, and it stung. When he looks down at our feet, his eyebrows are still knitted together.

"Tanner? You okay?"

"So what will this be?" he asks me, raising his head to look into my eyes. His eyebrows stay furrowed.

"What do you want it to be?"

"I guess I thought we could…" He takes a deep breath and lets it go slowly. "Hook up? For the summer?"

"Cool."

"And keep it casual," he says.

Didn't I just say that?

"Mm-hm. Exactly."

"And you don't…mind?"

Mind? Hasn't he been listening?

"I'm leaving at the end of August. You live here. What good would it be for us to *actually* fall for each other? That would be stupid."

"Yeah," he says. "I guess so."

"So, we're on the same page?"

"I mean, yeah, but, you'll be...what? My girlfriend?"

I wink at him. "Your fiancée."

"No," he says, "I mean...for *real*. What will you be to me? What will I be to you?"

Nothing. Not really.

"Consider it an extension of our original agreement," I tell him. "We'll pretend to be engaged this summer. We'll do everything an engaged couple does...except plan a wedding. And at the end of the summer, we'll"—she uses air quotes—"'break up,' and I'll go home."

"So it'll *all* be fake?" he asks.

"Yeah," I say. "We're posing as an engaged couple hooking up when we want to and keeping romantic feelings out of it. When it's done, it's done."

"And you're okay with that?" he asks, pulling me closer. His arms lock around me. The hard muscles of his body—his biceps, his pecs, his abs, his cock—push against me, into me, and I'm reminded of how big he is, and how small I am, and *Oh, my god*, of how I want every inch of him all to myself. "You're sure?"

"Mm-hm."

"I've never met a girl like you," he says softly, and I almost get the feeling he doesn't know he's spoken aloud.

"Do "ground rules" turn you on?" My heart is racing. I

want him. Fuck. I want him so badly. "Once they're in place, we can do whatever we want, Tanner."

"What do you want, McKenna?" he asks me, his voice gravelly.

"You," I murmur, leaning up on tiptoes. "I want you."

"I'm yours," he says, his lips crashing down on mine.

***

The ride back to his cabin is quiet, but the car is filled with electricity. It sizzles between us, powerful and thrilling, a promise of what lies ahead.

His bed is like a ginormous pillow, and if I was rested, shaved and showered, I'd insist he share it with me tonight. But I've just worked an eight-hour shift in a peasant blouse, prairie skirt and boots. Despite the chill in the air, I sweated through a good portion of today. I'm smelly in places I'd prefer to be fresh, my feet hurt, and I need a good night's sleep.

"Hey," I say, turning to him. "Not tonight, okay?"

He whips his head to the right to glance at me. "What?"

"Not tonight," I repeat, my cheeks flushing, which is ridiculous after our frank conversation and steamy kiss on the boardwalk. "I've been working all day, you know? I need a shower. And I'm beat."

"Oh!" he says, nodding. "Yeah. Of course. I get it. Yeah. Not tonight."

The electricity in the car takes a hit, and I miss it, which is why I open my big mouth without thinking.

"But we could…" I'm about to suggest that he lets me take a shower and then comes over to watch a movie, but I stop myself, and here's why…

We never addressed the matter of friendship, and frankly, that's a much more serious conversation for me. Relationships aren't risky, but friendship? Friendship has the power to *really* hurt me. If we start doing things that friends do—hanging out, watching movies, talking, sharing, spending time together—a friendship could develop between us. And for me, friendship is a *big deal*, second only to my relationship with Mimi. My friendship with Isabella, for example, is completely familial; it's a relationship I'd go to the mats for. I'd guard it and protect it with everything I have, with everything I am. I might even die for it. In contrast, I'm pretty sure I could sleep with Tanner all summer long and keep it casual.

Relationships are fleeting.

But friendship? It's sacred. It's real.

Do I want to be friends with him?

Do I have room in my life to be friends with him?

I have no idea, I think, squirming in my seat. I really don't want to consider these questions, let alone answer them. They're too big. Too important.

"We could…what? Tell me."

"I don't know if it's a good idea."

"Tell me anyway."

"I don't know what your plans are for tonight," I say, feeling real risk and uncertainty for the first time since he picked me up tonight, "but I need to wind down for a couple of hours after work. I was thinking about watching a movie, and I was wondering if—"

"Yeah. Sounds good."

"It doesn't mean anything," I'm quick to add.

"What do you mean?"

"It's just a movie," I say, stopping short of adding, *We don't have to talk or anything. It doesn't mean we're friends.*

"Yeah," he says, unbothered. "I get it. We're not sleeping together tonight."

I'm about to say, *You don't get it at all,* but I decide to leave it alone.

I can control myself. I can sit next to him on the couch or the bed and watch a movie beside him without making it a bonding experience. I mean, we're not going to start braiding each other's hair and telling each other our deepest secrets, right?

Except there's something about Tanner that makes you say too much, I think, remembering our car ride into Skagway on Saturday night. One minute we were talking about music, and the next, I found myself telling him all about my Granddad's drinking and Sheila's addiction.

Don't do that again, I tell myself. *Promise you won't do that again.*

"Great," I hear myself saying. "Come over in an hour."

"I'll bring the popcorn," he says, grinning at me as he turns into the campground.

And I'll bring the self-control, I promise myself.

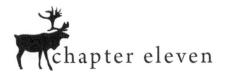

chapter eleven

Tanner

I drop her off at my cabin, parking the car in my usual spot and telling her I'll be back in an hour with snacks to watch the movie.

Then I grab a rifle from my brothers' cabin and go for a walk in the woods while I still have an hour of light because I need to process the most unexpected conversation I've ever had with a woman.

I got exactly what I wanted.

I got an exclusive, but super casual, fuck-buddy for the summer.

Perfect, right?

Except, no. Not perfect.

Not perfect at all.

I think I wanted to be in control of the situation in a way I wasn't with Ramona, so I thought "ground rules," that included my right to refuse any feelings she might develop, would make me feel safe. What I didn't expect was that she'd be the first to take feelings out of the equation entirely. And once they were gone? I felt…sad. I felt like I'd made a bad deal. I felt like I'd lost something. I felt like I wasn't getting what I wanted at all.

Turns out I'm not quite as cool as I thought.

Turns out I like the prospect—or at least the option—of developing feelings for someone I'm fucking. And I mean, no, I'm not going to turn down a summer of sex because she doesn't "do" love, but I'm not sure how I feel about none of it being "real" either.

Honestly, it kind of sucks.

But it's also a challenge I never saw coming. Something inside of me wants to convince her that not only is she lovable, but with the right guy, she's *capable* of loving, too.

"I'm a mess," I mutter, a great horned owl *hoo hoo hoo*ing in agreement overhead.

"Truer words were never spoken," pipes up a voice from behind me.

I turn on my heel to find my older sister, Harper, standing behind me.

"Are you following me?"

"Saw you head into the woods."

"And…"

"And yeah. Decided to follow you."

"What do you want?"

"Why are you a mess?" she asks, repositioning her own rifle higher on her shoulder as we keep walking toward the river.

"McKenna and I decided to—"

"Get together? Cool. I knew you liked her." She raises her eyebrows. "So, what's the problem?"

"That I like her."

"Um. I don't understand," says Harper. "You and your fake fiancée, who you happen to actually like, have decided to get together for real, right?"

"Yes and no."

"Tanner, you're being extremely annoying. Spell it out for me, please."

I sit on the same boulder that McKenna was leaning against a few days ago. Harper stands in front of me, arms crossed over her chest. Of all my siblings, Harper and I, who are only thirteen months apart in age, look the most alike. When when she glowers, I get an idea of how I look doing the same, which is to say: terrifying.

"Yes, she's my fake fiancée. Yes, we decided to hook up when we want to. Yes, I like her. But we decided to keep feelings out of it, and when the summer's over, so are we."

"So, basically, every dude's dream."

"Yeah," I mutter, looking out at the water.

"Of all my brothers," says Harper softly, "you're the one I worry about the most and the least."

"That makes no sense," I tell her.

"I worry about you because under all that grumpiness, you're sweet, which means you can get hurt. And I *don't* worry about you, because yeah, that sweetness might get you hurt, but God made you resilient, too." I stare at her, waiting for her to say more. "You can't help how you feel. You like her? That's good. Go ahead and like her. And if she leaves, sure it'll

hurt, but you'll get over it. You'll be okay. So just do you, Tan"
She grins. "Or better yet…just do her."

"You're ridiculous," I say, chuckling in spite of myself.

"Yeah. Maybe." She shrugs. "I can live with that."

"I'm watching a movie with her tonight."

"Then what the hell are you doing here with me?"

I slide down from the boulder, turning back toward my cabin.

"Hey, Harp," I say, remembering that McKenna wants to talk to a police officer about Ramona. "Is Joe still working Tuesdays?"

"How am I supposed to know?" she snaps.

"Thought you might."

"Why would I?"

"Everyone in Skagway suspects how he feels about you."

"That's on *him*. There's nothing between me and Joe Raven."

I tilt my head to the side. "Used to be, if memory serves."

"Shut up, Tanner," she says, breaking into a sudden sprint back to camp.

My sister is literally *running away from her feelings,* I think, watching her go.

She and Joe dated in high school, and they seemed pretty crazy about each other, too. I remember him being around all the time—Hunter and I would catch them kissing, that sort of thing. But something—I don't know what—happened to make them go their separate ways, and as far I know, she's never talked about it with any of us. I wonder about it sometimes, but she refuses to discuss it, and I guess I need to respect that.

While Harper's screwed up about her own love life, however, her advice was good. I'm going to enjoy myself with McKenna this summer, and whatever happens, happens. And if it hurts, it hurts. I'll pick up the pieces after she goes.

I'm at peace with my intentions when I knock on my door. I'll live in the moment for as long as the moment lasts and deal with the fallout later.

"Hey," says McKenna, opening the door for me.

"Hey," I answer, unable to keep myself from smiling at her. I hold up two pouches of microwave popcorn, and she takes them.

Her hair's damp, and her face is shiny and clean from the shower. She's wearing light pink sweatpants low on her hips and a matching cropped sweatshirt that teases her flat stomach when she moves and shows off the gentle slopes of her neck, collarbone, and shoulders. I know they're probably just pajamas to her, but to every guy on the face of the earth, there's something insanely sexy about a barefooted woman in loose sweats.

"Come in," she says, her smile shy.

As I toe off my shoes, I realize that the TV and lights in the living room are off.

"I thought we'd watch in the bedroom," she says, heading into the kitchen to pop the popcorn. "More comfortable, right?"

Fuck. The bedroom? I mean, yes, my bed's more comfortable than the living room couch, and the TV's bigger in there, but...*fuck.* It's the *bedroom.* It has a *bed.* A bed where

I want to fuck her until the sun sets and comes back up again.

"Y-Yeah. Comfortable," I say, leaning against the back of the couch and watching her move around my kitchen. It's incredibly intimate, actually, to see her so comfortable in my space. She programs the microwave, then grabs a large bowl from a cabinet next to the fridge.

"I moved everything down from the upper cabinets," she says with a self-deprecating chuckle, "so I wouldn't have to drag a chair over every time I needed something."

"It's your place for the summer. Do what you want."

We stand in awkward silence for a minute or two, occasionally trading glances, hyper-aware of each other, the attraction between us sucking its fair share of oxygen from the room and making me a little light-headed.

"So, we're both sci-fi nerds, right?" she asks. "Did you ever see *Equals*? With Kristen Stewart and Nicholas Hoult?"

"I don't think so."

"It's one of my favorites. A little sci-fi, a lot dystopian. You game?"

"Sure."

She pours the two bags of popcorn into the bowl and leads the way into my room, where she's lit a dozen candles on the desk, bedside table, and bureau. It bathes the room in a soft, warm light that screams "SEX" in my head and makes blood sluice south of my hips.

How the fuck am I supposed to get through a movie with her?

She slides onto the far side of the bed, tucking her legs under her. It's the most innocent pose ever, but all I can think about is how much I want to touch her. My fingers twitch with longing. I wet my lips because my mouth keeps watering.

"You ready?" she asks, all big brown eyes and bare shoulders.

"I don't know if I can do this," I murmur, opting for honesty. My cock is semi-hard and throbbing behind the zipper of my jeans. It's been weeks since I had sex, and I want this woman something fierce.

"You can't..." She looks confused. "...watch a movie?"

I rub the back of my neck, still standing in the doorway of the room.

"Yeah. I'm not sure—" *Can she hear the frustration in my voice?* "—if I can watch a movie. On my bed. By candlelight. With you."

She blinks at me, the corners of her lips tilting up just slightly. "Ohhh. You're not sure you can control yourself?"

"I want you, McKenna," I say, crossing my arms over my chest. "I mean, I respect the fact that you're tired tonight, or not ready yet, or—"

"I'm ready," she whispers, holding my gaze.

"But you said—"

"—that I wanted a shower," she says, standing up. "And I got one."

"I don't want to force you."

"Force me?" She steps in front of me, slipping her hands under my T-shirt and sliding them up my chest, her palms exploring the ripples of my muscles on their leisurely ascent. "Does it feel like you're forcing me to do anything I don't want to do?"

I reach for the back of the T-shirt and pull it over my

head. She does the same with her sweatshirt, revealing small, pert breasts, creamy and smooth with pebbled pink nipples. I cup her jaw and lean forward to kiss her, gasping softly when her chest presses into mine for the first time. Skin on skin. Man, I love it.

I reach for her hips and pick her up easily, thrilled when she spreads her legs to straddle my waist. My cock is thick and throbbing, and I know she can feel it pressing against her when she moans into my mouth. Her fingers curl into my cheeks as she opens her mouth to mine, her tongue warm and wet as it slides inside.

I lay her down on the bed and settle my body on top of hers, bracing most of my weight on my elbows so I don't crush her. Her fingers slide down my arms to my hips where they skim inward to my belt buckle. She looks up at me with a grin as she grips the leather hard and jerks the prong from its hole.

"Take these off," she murmurs, opening the metal button with one hand and tugging on the zipper with the other. "I want to see you. *All* of you."

Her words feed the raging fire inside of me, and I leap up, standing by the side of the bed and pulling down my jeans and boxers in one quick yank.

She sits up, wearing nothing but sweatpants, and places her palms on my hips as she stares at my erect cock, which is so close to her lips, I can feel her breath when she exhales. She looks up at me, her eyes owning mine as she leans forward and takes me in her mouth.

***

McKenna

I knew exactly what I was doing when I decided to invite him into the bedroom. The truth is that I got a little nervous in the car. But I had a little time to think in the shower, and by the time I got out, I knew I wanted him just as badly as he wants me.

As I work him into my mouth, easing my lips down his pulsing length, I'm certain I've never been with anyone as big as Tanner. His cock is longer and wider than average, which doesn't really surprise me since every other part of him is Viking-sized, too. A shudder moves through me when I realize he's going to be inside of me in a few minutes, but I'm so wet, I'm hoping he'll slide right in.

His hands land on the sides of my face, and for one terrible second, I think he's trying to hold me in place so he can thrust his dick down my throat. I brace myself, but it doesn't happen, and when I look up at him, it appears he's in actual pain. I lean back, slowly sliding my lips along his length as I let him go. I swirl my tongue around the ruby knob before looking back up at him.

"Is everything okay?"

"Fuck, yeah," he groans. "I just don't want to come yet, but I keep getting close. It's been a while…I wasn't expecting this…I'm…"

"I get it," I tell him. "It's been a while for me, too."

"Then it's your turn, baby."

He places his hands on the bed, on either side of my hips, then drops to his knees. Looking up at me, his blue eyes direct and clear, he reaches for the waistband of my sweats.

His fingers slip beneath the elastic, touching down on my skin and possibly looking for underwear, but I'm not wearing any. I scoot forward for a second so he can pull the pants over my hips. Then, I sit back down on the bed, as naked as he is.

Placing his palms on the insides of my knees, he spreads my legs gently, and though I expect to feel a moment of self-consciousness as he exposes me so completely, I don't. I stare up at him, holding his eyes with a mix of trust and exhilaration until my legs are spread wide. Marveling at the intimacy of our eye contact as he puts my body in such a vulnerable position, I grin at him just before he bends his head forward. He places his hand softly on my stomach, pressing gently, urging me to lie back.

I whimper as he nuzzles my close-cropped strip of damp curls, spreading my lips with his tongue and sliding forward. My last boyfriend didn't love eating pussy, so it's been a while, which only increases my excitement. Blood races to my clit, making it even more sensitive. I close my eyes and try to breathe as he licks and sucks, nips then soothes. I can feel my orgasm growing, that delicious swirling making my hips lift off the bed and my fists twist the fabric of the comforter between my fingers.

"Do you want to come?" he asks, his voice breathy and deep.

Yes. Yes. It feels so good. Yes. Yes—

No! Wait. Not yet.

"I want you inside me," I moan, forcing my eyes to open as I lean up on my elbows.

"Me, too."

He stands up, opening the bedside table drawer. I already know there are condoms in there, but I don't want him to use one. I want to feel him—his heat, his hardness, the throbbing of his heartbeat through his veins, the ridges of his swollen flesh.

"No condom," I tell him.

"Yes, condom," he answers, taking out a silver packet and ripping it open with his teeth.

"No," I say. "I don't like them."

"I won't do it without one."

"But I'm on the pill."

He stares at me for a long second, like he really wants to believe me. Then he shakes his head and proceeds to roll the condom onto his cock.

"Tanner, I haven't been with anyone since my ex-boyfriend in Montana," I say, sitting up. My bare feet touch the sheepskin rug on the floor by the side of the bed. "And I had a physical in April. I'm clean. I'm healthy. I promise. My pills are in that drawer. Check. I take one every morning."

He glances at the drawer, then back at me. "How do you know *I'm* clean?"

"Because you said it's been a while."

"Who knows what that means? 'A while' could mean a week to me. Maybe I'm not clean. Maybe I'm—"

"You wouldn't do that. You wouldn't even touch me if you thought you could hurt me." I reach for his hands, threading my fingers through his and tugging him closer to me. I think of him standing guard over the bear with the

163

berries. "You wouldn't put me in danger, Tanner. I know you well enough to be certain of that."

His eyes are still conflicted, but his face softens, and it gives me the courage to reach forward with one hand and gently unroll the condom from his cock.

"Please," I say, dropping the limp rubber on the bedside table. "I promise it'll be okay."

I lie back on the bed, bending my knees and spreading my legs in invitation. I'm still holding one of his hands, which I squeeze. "Tanner, I want you."

His resolve seems to waver as he joins me on the bed, kneeling between my legs, his cock aimed at my pussy. He unlaces our fingers, but holds my hand, bending his head to press his lips to the center of my palm. His breathing is shallow and quick. His eyes averted.

"I've never..." he murmurs.

"Never what?" I tease. "Are you a virgin, Tanner Stewart?"

I'm positive he's not, but I have a moment of uncertainty when he hesitates.

"No, but..." He lifts his head, his eyes slamming into mine. "The truth is that I've only done it once like this."

"Like what?"

"Bareback."

As soon as he blurts out the word, he looks away, leaning back to sit on his haunches.

Oh. Oh, my god.

I do some quick math in my head and realize that in twenty-nine years, and likely with multiple partners, Tanner has *always* worn a condom, with one exception. I wonder what happened. I wonder why he'd deprive himself of feeling everything when there's nothing in the world that feels so good.

I've been half-reclining against the pillows, but now I lean forward, scooting closer to him so I can cup his jaw in my hands. As gently as I can, with only a little pressure, I make him look at me.

"Why only once?"

"It was in high school," he says softly.

"What happened?" I ask.

"Pregnancy scare."

"Was she…?"

"No, but—"

"It was enough to make an impression."

He gulps softly, resting his heavy head in my hands, and I have the distinct impression that we're doing work here, Tanner and me. We're facing something together. And it may be *his* issue—*his* bad memory—but I won't let him tackle it alone.

"Hey," I whisper, trying to lift his head. He resists me. He doesn't want to look at me. He's not ready. "Tanner. It's okay."

"I wrecked the moment," he gripes.

He doesn't see me smile, but I do. Grumpy is good. Grumpy is better than sad or scared.

"We'll have plenty of moments," I tell him. "All summer long."

Finally he looks up at me. "You don't use condoms at

all?"

"I don't like them," I say. "You can't feel as much. And—this is a little gross, but we're sitting here naked, so I've got nothing to hide—they make me itchy."

"Itchy? Do you have an allergy? To latex?"

"Maybe," I say, shrugging.

He sits back, sitting cross-legged, and maybe this sounds weird, but I can feel a shift in him, and it reminds me of something I heard on Sunday night. *He'll do just about anything for someone he cares about.*

"Show me your pill pack?" he asks, a new resolve in his voice.

"Sure," I say, jumping up to open the bedside table and take out the aqua plastic case inside. I open it before handing it to him. "I took today's this morning."

He stares down at the pills for a second, his eyes tracking them day by day, until he gets to today. Finally, he snaps it shut and holds it out to me. I take it from him and pop it back in the drawer.

"Now what?" I ask, standing by the bed, arms crossed under my breasts.

"You tell me," he says.

We're buck naked in his bedroom, bathed in candlelight…and the foreplay we shared ten minutes ago? It was top notch. But something bigger than sex happened while we weren't having sex, and I feel like I want to respect that, too.

"Are you okay?"

He nods. "Yeah. Thanks for showing me your pills. Sorry

if I freaked out."

"It's okay. I get it." I tilt my head to the side, grinning at him. "Do you still want to have sex?"

"Yes, please," he says, and it's so earnest and so adorable, I giggle. He frowns. "You're laughing."

"It's only because I like you," I hear myself say, but *Oh, my God, where did those words come from, and why did I just say them aloud?*

"I like you, too," he says, holding out his hand to me.

As I take it, he uncrosses his legs, spreading them out in a v, and I realize his erection, which could have softened during our intense conversation, hasn't shrunk at all. It stands tall and proud, a blue vein winding around it like a vine, and makes a delicious shiver of anticipation run down my spine.

"Is that for me?" I flirt, kneeling on the bed.

"If you want it."

"I want it," I breathe, placing my hands on his shoulders as I straddle his lap.

I position myself over his cock, my breasts flush against his chest and our noses brushing. As I sink down onto his massive thickness, I wind my arms around his neck and let my head fall forward onto his shoulder. Gravity and desire do the rest. I'm not saying it doesn't hurt—it does, a little—but it also feels…amazing.

He groans this guttural, primordial sound which makes my muscles clench in protest as I lift a little, then sink down again. It's easier this time. We're slippery.

His hands land on my hips, and he holds on tight, forcing me to bear him with every magnificent thrust. I rest my cheek on his shoulder, my eyes closed, my body his, my orgasm from before building higher and higher as he drives into me, as his skin forges a bond with mine, as his heart pounds against my chest, and his breath falls quick and fast against my neck.

Maybe it's because we've gotten to know each other beyond a Tinder meetup, or maybe it's because we just shared a pretty intense conversation, but I feel *close* to him, and not just physically. *Emotionally.* And it's new for me. New and scary and kind of wonderful, too. Everything feels heightened: his hands on my hips, his lips on my throat, the sounds he makes, the way we fit together. It *feels* different. *I* feel different.

Tears slide from my eyes as my orgasm peaks, and waves of pleasure rip through me like a tsunami. I throw back my head and cry out just as he floods my womb and calls my name.

"McKenna!" Harsh and breathless.

He holds me so tightly, I might feel crushed if I didn't need and want his arms around me. But we are marooned together in a sea of intense pleasure; we hold on to each other and ride out the waves together.

He murmurs my name in softer and softer pants. "McKenna. McKenna. McKenna. McKenna…"

A litany. A blessing.

He kisses my neck, then rests his damp forehead on my shoulder. My head is tucked under his chin, my heart slowing down in tandem with his.

Nothing—not anything, ever in my life—has ever felt so right, so safe, so complete, so…perfect.

Oh, my God, I'm in trouble.

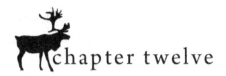

chapter twelve

Tanner

Happiness makes time fly.

Over the next two weeks, McKenna and I fall into a routine: I wake up beside her at dawn, careful not to disturb her sleep, drive her to work at eleven-thirty, then head back to Skagway to pick her up at eight.

She's a regular at our evening campfires now, and after just a few days of hooking up, she invited me to move back into my cabin, so we're living together. I've never lived with anyone who wasn't family, but it's strangely organic to share my space with McKenna. It doesn't feel crowded; it just feels comfortable. No. Better than comfortable. It feels right.

Especially the nights.

Our nights together blow my mind. Every time I'm inside of her, I'm convinced it's the best time. Until the next. And the next. And so on.

It's good.

It's so fucking good, and I'm so fucking happy, it scares me. Because with every day that passes, I'm closer to the day she'll leave. And honestly, I'm starting to wonder how I'll survive it.

I try not to think about it at all. I try to live in the moment and enjoy this intense fucking happiness because I know it's fleeting. I know that it's for now, not forever. And I can't blame her if I end up hurt. I walked into this relationship with my eyes wide open.

"Is it morning?" she murmurs, still half asleep even though the six a.m. sun is bright through the skylight overhead.

"Shhhh," I whisper, kissing the top of her head. "Go back to sleep."

She sighs, nestling into my side and resting her head over my heart. "Stay with me."

Tempting. So tempting. But I'm already taking off two hours a day to drive her back and forth to work. I need to get up early to make up for that time.

"Can't," I say, stroking the soft, bare skin of her back. "Wish I could."

"Mmm," she hums, pressing her lips to my chest.

"Kenna," I groan. "Don't. Please."

"Later?" she asks, raising her head to look at me.

"Later," I promise, leaning forward to kiss her.

"Have a good day, baby," she murmurs, letting her head fall back on the pillow.

She's asleep again thirty seconds later. My woman is not a morning person.

My woman.

Mine.

More and more, I think of McKenna as my girlfriend, my fiancée, my woman, my person. More and more, that's who she is to me. And the belonging to each other feels amazing. It's the inevitable separating from one another that feels terrifying.

Don't think about it, Tanner. Live in the moment.

I head into the bathroom to shower and shave, getting dressed in jeans and a T-shirt before grabbing a cup of coffee from the kitchen.

Our cabins are completely full this week, and I wave at a family having coffee in Adirondack chairs by the campfire as I head to the lodge to help with breakfast.

"Tanner! Thank God!" says Reeve, who's placing baskets of muffins on each table. "Will you get the coffee set up?"

"Where's Parker?" I ask. "It's her job."

"Stayed in town last night. Should be here soon."

I raise my eyebrows at my youngest sister. "Is that right?"

"Yessir."

"Do we know the identity of the special someone with whom she stayed?"

"We do not," says Reeve with a shrug.

In the kitchen, Gran and Harper are making eggs and bacon, while my Dad mans the toaster and Sawyer sits at a computer terminal in the corner.

"Dad, we're overbooked on Saturday," he says.

"Nope."

"Yes. You've got me and Harp in Whitehorse with one family, Hunter taking another family for an overnight up the Chilkoot, while you and Tanner do Beers, Brawls and Brothels for cruise groups at ten a.m., noon, two p.m., four p.m., and six p.m. There's no one left to do the Kayak Tour to Haines."

"If memory serves," says my dad, "I have another adult daughter. Pretty sure her name is Parker? She can do Haines."

"Parker's going to the tourism convention in Sitka."

My Dad's face falls. "Shit."

"Yeah," says Sawyer. "Shit."

"I can do the Haines trip," says Reeve, who takes another tray of muffins out of the oven.

"No, miss, you cannot. You're not eighteen yet," says Gran, shaking her head. She looks at her son. "Garrison, you need to figure this out."

"Dad," I say, "can you handle the Skagway city tours alone?"

"Long day, but yeah, I guess I could." He looks at my little sister. "Since you're so eager to help, you can come along with me. I'll send you back to the cruise terminal to corral the next group while I finish with the one before. We'll work in tandem."

"Sweet!" crows Reeve.

"McKenna and I will take the group to Haines," I tell my Dad. "She's got Saturday off."

"McKenna doesn't work for us, son."

"I'll take the group to Haines and bring McKenna along with me," I amend.

"I like McKenna plenty," says my Dad, "but I think she'll be a distraction."

"You got no other options, Gary," says Gran.

"Fine," says my Dad. "Take McKenna. But no

canoodling in front of the guests."

"I don't canoodle," I say, filling a carafe with hot coffee and screwing the lid on. It takes me a second to realize the hum of activity in the kitchen has stopped completely. When I turn around, five pairs of Stewart eyes are focused on me. "What?"

"You canoodle," says Harper.

"You canoodle *big time*," says Reeve.

"Gran," I say, "help me out."

"Can't," she says, scooping scrambled eggs onto a platter. "The girls speak the truth. You canoodle because you're smitten."

"You're all over each other is what you are," says Sawyer. "Not that it's a bad thing."

"What's not a bad thing?" asks Parker, who breezes into the kitchen.

"Where have *you* been?" I ask.

"Good question!" chirps Reeve.

"Didn't you wear that sweatshirt yesterday?" asks Sawyer.

As they give Parker the third degree instead of me, I fill my arms with coffee and slip back to the dining room unnoticed.

***

When we filed the police report against Ramona two weeks ago, Joe promised to stop by the Kozy Kone and have a word with her about giving me and McKenna space. To my surprise and relief, she hasn't bothered us since. Yes, she shoots us dirty looks whenever we run into her, but she hasn't made

173

another scene, threatened us, or destroyed any more of my property.

I think my sisters were right; Ramona finally understands that I've moved on, and she's decided to move on, too…which is why I'm startled to see her standing in front of the Purple Parsnip when I drop off McKenna for her shift.

"What's going on here?" asks McKenna as I parallel park.

"No clue." I lean over to kiss her goodbye. "Have a good day, huh?"

"Yeah," she says, staring at Ramona, who stares back with narrowed eyes. "Text me an update about whatever this is, huh?"

"I will," I promise, kissing her again.

McKenna jumps out of the car and heads into work, and I pause for a second. I don't want to talk to Ramona, but she obviously wants to talk to me. If I ignore her and drive away, I'll just be delaying the inevitable. I roll down my window, and she saunters over.

"What do you want?" I ask.

"Hi, Tanner. Hi, Ramona. It's great to see you. How're you doing?" She's trying to be cute, but it comes across as passive aggressive and creeps me out.

"Hi, Ramona."

"That's better, isn't it? More civil. More polite."

I check my watch. "I need to get going. Did you need something?"

"*Need* is such a funny word, isn't it? I mean, there are plenty of things I *want*…but need? That's different."

"I don't have time for games," I say, reaching for the gear

174

shift.

"Wait. Wait. Wait!" she cries, leaping forward and putting her talons on the windowsill.

"Get to the point, Ramona."

"I just want to be friends," she whines. "With you..." She gestures loosely to the Purple Parsnip and grimaces. "...and her. I guess."

"I don't think so."

"Wow," she says, her bright red fingernails curling into the leather of my car door. "That's hurtful, Tanner. I'm offering you friendship, and you're throwing it back in my face."

I look up at her. "Are you kidding me right now? You pretended to kill yourself. You pretended you were pregnant. You tried to set me up for battery. You keyed my fucking car."

"I *was* pregnant," she says. "I lost the baby."

"Yeah. Right."

"And I was mad that you wanted to break things off."

"No shit."

"And you have no proof I even touched your car."

"I know it was you, Ramona. Just leave us alone."

"Fine!" she shrieks, stepping back up on the boardwalk. She puts her hands on her hips and screeches, "Fuck you, Tanner! You broke my fucking heart, and I tried to be the bigger person, but—"

"Stop screaming," I snarl. "You're making a fucking scene!"

Town is jam-packed with tourists, many of whom stop in their tracks to gawk at our confrontation. A flush creeps up my cheeks, and my palms, which grip the steering wheel like they wish it was her neck, start to sweat.

"I'll make a fucking scene if I want to!" she screams, putting on a show for some younger tourists who take out smartphones to film her outburst. "Fuck you, Tanner Stewart! Fuck your stupid, fucking, second-rate campground! Fuck your fucking family! And fuck your ugly, fucking, boy-bodied fiancée!" She leans closer to my window, lowers her voice and purrs: "I didn't know you liked little boys."

Anger strikes me like lightning, white hot and furious, especially when I look at the double doors of the Purple Parsnip and see McKenna standing there next to Bruce. She couldn't have heard Ramona's whispered words, but she definitely heard Ramona scream "ugly, fucking, boy-bodied fiancée."

McKenna lifts her chin, swipes at her eyes, and then heads back inside with Bruce at her heels. I want to run after her—to tell her she's beautiful and perfect just the way she is, but she's already gone, and anyway, Ramona stands between me and the restaurant.

Stay in your car.

Don't do something you'll regret.

"Shut your fucking mouth!" I growl at her.

"Oooo! Big man!" She cackles, and it's this insane, shrill noise that chills me to the bone. "Or what? What're you going to do, Tanner?"

I have a sudden fantasy of jumping out of my car and punching her in the face. I imagine her nose exploding in blood as she falls backward to the ground, and it's so satisfying, I reach for the door handle, like I just might get out of the car and do it.

My phone buzzes loudly beside me, snapping me out of my trance.

I grab it like a lifeline.

> **McKenna**
> **Listen to me, baby... She's insane. She's just baiting you. She wants you to do something crazy. Don't fall for it. Go home. I'm okay. I'll see you later. xo**

Staring at the words, I can feel my heart slow down. I remind myself that McKenna and I are a team, and I thank God to have her on my side. I read her text over and over again as Ramona continues her one-woman show, ranting and raving like a goddamned lunatic about her "broken heart" and "broken dreams." And then, staring straight ahead, I push the window-up button, shift the car into drive, and pull away.

On the way home, I stop by the police station.

"Joe here?" I ask Vera, who sits up front and answers the

phones.

"Joe!" she yells. "Tanner Stewart's here."

A second later, Joe appears at his office doorway, a paper napkin stuck into his collar.

"I'm interrupting your lunch," I say. "Sorry."

"That's okay," says Joe. "Come on in. We can talk while I finish."

I sit down in front of his desk, where I sat with McKenna just a couple of weeks ago. My knee bounces nervously. I'm calmer than I was a few minutes ago, but my blood's still boiling.

"Ramona again?" asks Joe.

"Yeah."

"What now?"

"She made a scene in town. Screaming and carrying on."

"Did she use profanity?"

"Yessir."

"Well, that's a delight for the tourists, huh? But cursing in public ain't illegal, per se, unless she was disturbing the peace." Joe takes another bite of his sandwich. "Did she slander you?"

"What do you mean?"

"Did she scream anything that wasn't true?"

"She called McKenna 'ugly.'"

"Well," says Joe, "that's unkind, but it ain't illegal."

"Can I file a restraining order?" I blurt out. I never thought it'd come to this, but damn it, I've had enough.

"It's possible, yes, especially if you could get a few witnesses who saw the whole thing. Alaska Statute 11.61.120

prohibits harassment, and that includes some forms of verbal street harassment. If a street harasser exhibits the intent to harass or annoy you or insults, taunts, or challenges you 'in a manner likely to provoke an immediate violent response,' you can report him or her."

"Why didn't you go to law school, Joe?"

He stares at me hard for a minute, then rips the napkin from his neck and throws away the rest of his sandwich. "Wasn't in the cards."

Interesting. I know he got into law school in California. I remember the day he was accepted…and I remember how proud Harper was. I lean forward in my seat, about to say as much, when he warns me, low and firm, "Leave it, Tanner."

You don't mess with Joe Raven when he tells you to back off.

"Fine. Give me the form," I tell him. "For the restraining order."

Joe pushes a button on his desk phone. "Vera, get me a DV-150 form."

"Protective order?" she confirms.

"Yes, ma'am."

He presses the button again, and I squirm in my seat. The words "protective order" make me feel like a pussy. I don't need *protection* from Ramona.

"No shame in this, Tanner," says Joe, like he's reading my mind. "She's tested the patience of a saint, and you're no saint."

"I'm not doing it for me."

If it was just me? I would never have gotten the police

involved. But I remember what she said two weeks ago about being scared of Ramona, and I picture her face today when Ramona called her "ugly." Maybe I can't get Ramona arrested for her behavior today, but I'd like to make life a lot harder for her any way I can with whatever tools I can find, and that includes using the law.

"I'm doing it for McKenna."

***

McKenna

All things equal, it wasn't one of the best days of my life.

Bruce did his part to try to make me feel better after Ramona's outburst, but the other girls looked at me with pity for the rest of the day, and it didn't just make me uncomfortable, it made me angry. Yes, I signed on to be Tanner's fake fiancée, and yes, I knew his ex-girlfriend was crazy, but I definitely didn't think I'd be called "ugly" and "boy-bodied" to my actual boyfriend in the middle of a crowded street.

So fucking humiliating.

Not to mention, one of my coworkers was kind enough to share with me that a video of the incident was already uploaded to TikTok. No, Ramona didn't call me out by name, but she mentioned Tanner, his family, and his campground. Anyone from Skagway or Dyea could easily figure out she's talking about me.

When Tanner picked me up, there was a beautiful bouquet of wildflowers in the front seat waiting for me, and I was glad to hear that he got the ball rolling on a restraining order, but for the first night since we got together, I really want to be alone. I'm in too bad a mood to join him and the other Stewarts at the campfire tonight. Instead, I slip into my comfiest sweats and pop myself a bowl of pity popcorn like Mimi used to do.

You know what we need, duckling? Pity popcorn and a good movie.

She always knew how to make things better.

In honor of Mimi, I cuddle up on Tanner's bed and stream one of her favorite movies: *The Boy Friend*, a little-known musical shot in 1971, and starring Twiggy, a then-popular model from England.

Like me, Twiggy was thin and flat-chested with big eyes and short hair, but she was also a style and beauty icon, which was probably the point of Mimi showing me the movie in the first place. I still remember the first time we watched it together—I'd come home from seventh grade in tears because Michelle McCauley had barred me from the girl's locker room and told me to "get changed with the other boys." Mimi assured me that I was just as feminine as any other girl, and that beauty came in all shapes, sizes and forms. That afternoon, we ate pity popcorn, watched *The Boy Friend*, and I went to school the next day with my eyes lined and mascaraed like Twiggy's.

Ramona's nasty description of me wasn't the first time my body had been compared to a boy's, and it probably won't be the last. That doesn't mean it didn't hurt, though. Especially in front of Tanner.

Even *The Boy Friend* doesn't help me feel better tonight, so I turn it off, put on my bathing suit, and go outside to sit in the hot tub under the stars. Tanner keeps it warm all the time, so it's always ready to be used. But when I pull off the cover, something stinks. Like, really bad. And the water's a rusty red color instead of its normal crystal clear. I climb up the three steps to get a better look inside, and scream.

As I stumble back down the stairs, I fall against Tanner, who grabs me around the waist and hauls me up against him.

"What's wrong?" he demands through harsh, panted breaths.

I turn around in his arms and look up at him. "I—I think something's dead in there."

A second later, Hunter, Sawyer, and Reeve round the corner of the cabin.

"Everything okay?"

"What happened?"

"Hand me the skimmer, Reeve?" asks Tanner, who's standing on the landing over the tub.

He maneuvers the pole around, finally raising it with a full basket. Some kind of mangled animal lies dead in the rope mesh. He flips it over, and the carcass falls onto the ground.

Hunter squats down over it. "It's a hare."

"Snowshoe hare," agrees Sawyer.

"Water's fucked," says Tanner. "Can't shock it. I'll have to dump it, scrub the tub, then refill it."

"Poor thing," coos Reeve. "How'd you get stuck in there, little one?"

"They can wiggle into anything," says Hunter. "You know that."

Sawyer stands up. "Drowned, got bloated, and started

decaying. I'll get a shovel and bury it. Reeve, give me a hand, huh?"

As Sawyer and Reeve head back around the cabin to get a shovel from the barn, Hunter puts his hand on my arm. "You okay?"

Tanner suddenly appears beside me. He takes my hand and squeezes it. "I've got her, Hunter."

Hunter looks at his brother, rolls his eyes, then drops his hand from my arm. "If you need help tomorrow, let me know."

"Will do."

Hunter walks away from us, and Tanner pulls me back into his arms. "You okay?"

"It hasn't been a great day," I confess, "and this is the rotten cherry on a shit sundae."

"Want to talk about it?"

"No. Not really." I wrinkle my nose. "And definitely not here. It stinks."

He lets me go, turns off the heater, then uncorks the bottom of the tub so it can drain. Rusty-colored water flows out of the tub with a whoosh.

"I'll clean it tomorrow."

"No rush," I say, looking over at the rabbit's little body on the cold ground. I'm not sure I'll want to go back in the hot tub for the rest of the summer. "You think it hopped in there on its own, huh?"

Tanner nods. "Wouldn't be the first time. Tub's warm, you know? Probably feels like a good idea on a really cold night. He got trapped and couldn't get out."

I guess it makes sense, and certainly the Stewarts know more about local wildlife than I do. Come to think of it, I'm feeling pretty cold myself, now that the shock of finding a dead body is wearing off. I cross my arms over my chest.

"I guess I'll take a hot bath instead."

"Want some company?" asks Tanner, his eyes hopeful.

I'm still embarrassed about what Ramona said. I feel a little fragile, to be honest, which is why I'm surprised that spending time with Tanner sounds good to me.

"Only if we can forget the rest of today ever happened."

"Agreed. But before we wipe our memories, can I say one thing?"

"Okay."

He puts his arms around my small body, looking down at me, holding my eyes with his. "I think you're beautiful, Kenna. All of you."

"Tanner, you don't have to—"

"Let me be really clear: I'm crazy about you, woman. Whatever you are is exactly what I want. The way you think. The way you feel. The way you look. It's all good. It's all perfect. You hear me?"

Tears brighten my eyes. I try to swallow over the lump in my throat, but I can't, so I decide to thank him another way instead. I lean up on tiptoes and kiss him, channeling everything I feel for him into that kiss—everything I feel, but will never, ever say.

I'm crazy about you, too.

Whatever you are is exactly what I want, too.

I'm falling for you so hard, Tanner Stewart.

Breathless and desperate for more, we hold hands as we race inside the cabin.

***

Saturday morning dawns bright and sunny for our day trip to Haines.

Though I'm not a morning person, I wake up at the crack of dawn with Tanner, excited for the ferry ride, lake kayaking, and visiting a new town. I mean, I've been in Alaska for a month now, and all I've seen is Skagway!

Back in Washington, kayaking was something I did every so often, and I'd call myself competent if not intermediate. I'm certainly not a newbie, which is how Tanner wants to treat me.

"We *all* wear life jackets," he says, turning onto Dyea Road, headed for the Skagway Cruise Terminal. "Even me."

"We're going to be on a lake!"

"So what?"

"If you fall into a lake, you swim to shore," I say. "There's no current. No undertow. No sharks—"

"You're wearing a life jacket," he says. "If you don't, you can't come with me, and I'm not kidding."

I frown at him before nodding. "Fine. You're the tour guide. You're in charge. But if you make me wear a kid's life jacket, we're breaking up."

He chuckles, taking my hand and kissing the back of it. "We're not breaking up."

"Tell me the itinerary for today," I say, even though he already told me once last night.

"We pick up our group at the cruise terminal, then we

185

lead them over to the ferry terminal where we have a forty-five-minute ride over to Haines. Keep your eyes open for humpbacks and harbor seals on the ride over."

What an awesome life to go on tours every day, I think. *Your whole life is essentially one big, cool vacation.*

"What's there to do in Haines?"

"Not a lot, actually. It's really different from Skagway."

"How?"

"So, Haines is a 45-minute ferry ride or a 20-min seaplane ride away from Skagway, but it's like a different world over there. Where Skagway gets a ton of cruise traffic in the summer, Haines is more of a regular, year-round town. More people live there, but it's quieter, for sure. To be honest, it's a lot more Alaskan. There's even a Tlingit Village half an hour northwest of Haines called Klukwan. That's where PawPaw grew up."

"I'd love to see it!"

"Not this trip, but maybe another time. They have a great cultural center open to the public."

I'm sorry to miss it, but as he says, we'll go another time. Alaska is so culturally rich, I feel like I could spend a lifetime trying to understand its history.

"So, after the ferry ride, then what?"

"In Haines, we're picked up by one of our partners, who drives us over to Chilkoot Lake where life jackets and kayaks are waiting. We explore the lake for about an hour in two-man kayaks, and then we head back into Haines for lunch."

"Wood-fired pizza."

He nods. "At Alpenglow."

"Alpenglow. That's such a pretty word."

"It is, isn't it?" He grins at me. "And such delicious pizza."

"Then what?"

"Then we take the ferry back to Skagway and drop off our group at the cruise terminal."

"Our group," I repeat, looking down at the aqua polo shirt I borrowed from Reeve. It says STEWART TOURS over my left breast with a bear and pine tree embroidered underneath. It matches the shirt Tanner's wearing. "You love this, don't you?"

"Alaska? Yep. I do."

"And leading tours. Hiking the Chilkoot. Kayaking. Looking for whales. Doing what you do. You're happy."

"Yeah. I guess I am."

"Do you know how rare that is?" I ask him. "To love what you do?"

"Aren't you happy teaching?"

I barely have to think before answering. "No. Not really. I was happier working at the museum in Montana than I am teaching at a community college in Seattle."

"Why is that?"

"I grew up in Seattle, but I don't love the city. Never really did. I only went back because Mimi needed me. But I *loved* the wilds of Montana; I could've stayed there forever."

"We have wilds here, too," he says, glancing over at me with a sweet smile.

"But no Mimi."

"No," he says gently. "No Mimi."

My heart clenches as it does whenever I think of leaving him. I refuse to put a name on the feeling that makes me ache. I don't want to inspect it any further. If I name it aloud, it will become a thing that exists. And if it exists, he will reject it because that's what happens when I care about someone. Almost without exception, they leave me behind.

Better to be the one that leaves, I remind myself. *Don't fall in love with him. Don't let it happen.*

"How's she doing?" Tanner asks. "Your Mimi?"

"Good," I say. "Isabella visited her on Thursday and said she seemed content."

"I'm glad." He turns into the lot for the Skagway Cruise Terminal and parks in the shadow of a massive ship. "Ready to roll?"

"Sure," I say, relieved to stop thinking about hard things and get on with our day.

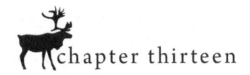

chapter thirteen

Tanner

Alaska has a fiercely independent spirit, so it surprises a lot of tourists that the Fourth of July is such a big deal here.

Maybe it's because Skagway is already such a historic town, or because it was that fiercely independent, intrepid spirit that led so many prospectors to our shores, maybe it's because—like our Arctic brothers and sisters in Scandinavia who celebrate Midsommar—the days are so long, we may as well make the most of them. I don't know the exact reason, but Skagway, like the rest of Alaska, pulls out the stops on Independence Day, and I have always loved it.

There's a 5K fun run at eight a.m., and the kiddie parade starts at nine thirty a.m., followed by the big July Fourth parade at ten a.m.

Afterward, there's a picnic basket auction, pork sliders and frozen margaritas in front of the Parsnip, and a German-style Biergarten in front of SBC. There are Victorian games in front of the historical society, axe throwing at Smuggler's Cove, a block party near the depot, and troubadours at every location, singing country songs and old favorites. Skagway holds the Guinness World Record for longest throw at our egg toss on Broadway, which attracts kids and adults alike, and there's a tug of war just after. And that's all before noon!

The afternoon gets *really* competitive. You'll find a hot dog eating contest, a log splitting contest, and horseshoe and cornhole competitions at different venues around town. As still-sunny nighttime approaches, you find a spot to eat, drink and listen to music, and at midnight, there are fireworks over the harbor.

It's good, old-fashioned, American fun from early dawn to late dusk, and I challenge any town in the Lower 48 or Hawaii to do it up bigger than Skagway. And even if they do? I'm staying here.

"So…you're saying you like the Fourth of July?" asks McKenna, totally deadpan.

I jump on her half-naked body, tickling her under the arms until she's giggly and breathless.

"Stop! S-Stop it, Tanner!"

"You are so sassy," I tell her, bracing my weight on my elbows as I settle my cock over her pussy and thrust forward, my boxers rubbing against her panties.

"You love it," she says, rotating her hips.

Yeah, I think. *I sure do.*

I lean down and kiss her, reaching under her tank top to fondle her pert little breasts, which I've become a little obsessed with. The way her nipples harden when I suck on them? Holy shit, it's crazy sexy.

She sighs into my mouth, which I take as a cue to

continue. I skim my lips over her chin, and slowly down her throat, kissing the hollow between her collarbones before sliding her tank top over her head. Sucking one of her nipples into my mouth, I lave it with my tongue until she whimpers, then slide to the other, circling it with my tongue before sucking it between my lips. Her fingers, buried in my hair, curl into my scalp, and I slide lower on the bed, kissing a trail from her breasts to her hips. She parts her legs, and I kneel between them under the covers, sliding her panties to her knees and burying my face in her pussy.

When she orgasms, I lap up her wet heat before tugging my boxers off over my erection and lining up my cock at the entrance of her sex. With my face hovering over hers, I urge her to open her eyes.

"Kenna, baby, look at me."

Her eyelids are sluggish and slow as they uncover her brown beauties.

"You good?" I whisper.

I don't expect to see tears flood her eyes, but I've noticed that it happens more and more often lately, and I've decided to take it as a quiet sign that something real and raw and extraordinary is growing between us, all the more breathtaking because neither of us expected it. I welcome those tears—they tell me more than McKenna's able or willing to tell me in words. I'm grateful for them.

She nods, sliding her palms down my back. When she gets to my butt, she pushes me forward and lifts her hips.

Come into me.

I'm lost as I slide forward. I'm found as my eyes close.

I'm one with her as I move inside of her, two parts of one whole, two mismatched parts that just happen to fit together perfectly.

At the same time I feel my orgasm peak, I feel the words "I love you" form on my lips. I groan in half-pleasure and half-pain as I squelch the words but feel my cock explode inside of her.

"Kenna!" I cry out, grasping at her body, trying to get as close to her as I possibly can. "Kenna, Kenna, Kenna…"

Saying her name is as close as I can get to telling her how I feel.

I'm falling in love with her.

It's undeniable, and it's ridiculous, and it's the most simple and true thing I've ever known. I'm going to love her like I love my family. Like I love Alaska. Like I love the changing seasons or the midnight sun. I'm going to love her because she's a part of what makes the world a place for life and heartache and perfection. And the moment she leaves me, the colors all around me will dull to gray and the heartbeat of the entire earth will fall into torpor. And I will wonder how I'm still alive.

She clutches my neck, her fingers laced and tight. Her hips are flush with mine, keeping my cock deep within her as the walls of her sex grab and relax, milking me dry and leaving me spent.

With a shuddering breath, I roll to my side, bringing her with me.

I slip from within her with a slight twist of my hips but hold her close as she nestles in my arms.

"Baby," I say, "you good?"

"So good," she murmurs, kissing my chest.

"Every time's better than the last time."

"I know."

"What if—"

Shut up, Tanner.

I catch myself just before I ask her about extending the summer to forever.

"What if...what?" she asks.

I roll onto my back, and she leans on my chest, grinning at me in this post-sex way that makes me want to fuck her all over again.

"Nothing," I say, lifting one of her hands and kissing her palm. "So, I told you that we don't have to work today, right? Even though we have guests in the cabins, they know that we don't do any meals today. No housekeeping. No campfire. Nothing. We offer a shuttle into Skagway in the morning and one back in the evening, but that's it. Other than that, they're on their own."

"I love it that your family doesn't work today."

"Never have. Never will. Fourth of July, Thanksgiving, and Christmas. Those are Stewart family holidays." I chuckle softly, but it's a rueful sound. "My Mom used to say that."

"How did your parents meet?"

"My Mom was from Oregon," I tell her. "Came up here one summer to make money."

"Like me," she says.

"Uh-huh."

"Then what?"

"Fell in love with my dad and stayed."

"And had six kids." She grins at me. "Why'd she name you all after workers?"

I shrug. "I don't know. I wish I could ask her."

"What did she study?"

I rub my forehead. "I think, uh, English. But she quit. She had just finished her junior year in college when she came up here. Never went home. Got pregnant with Hunter and stayed."

"God, that's so romantic."

"You think?"

She gives me a look. "Tanner, it's *empirically* romantic. It might even be the definition."

I grin at her, sliding my hand down to her ass and squeezing. "I love it when you use big words, Professor Cabot."

"Shut up, Tanner," she says all sassy, hopping out of bed and stretching her arms over her head. She's so naked and comfortable and beautiful, I take a mental picture of her even though it will ache to look at it later.

"Come back to bed," I say, even though we need to get up if we're going to make it into town in time for the kiddie parade.

"No," she says, grinning at me. Her breasts are pink from my beard, her nipples still rosy from my lips—seeing the evidence of our lovemaking on her body makes me hard all over again.

"Come on."

"Forget it. I'm not missing the best Fourth of July

celebration in America," she tells me, standing in the bathroom doorway. "I'm taking a shower, then you're taking a shower, and then we're both getting dressed."

"Cruel woman," I mutter.

She winks at me, then disappears. A moment later the shower is on. I roll back onto the bed, staring up at the bright blue sky. I'm happy. *God, she makes me so happy.* This must have been how my Dad felt that summer—flush with the newness of love and drunk on its possibilities. How did he get my Mom to stay? I'll have to ask him sometime.

Huh. My eyes refocus, then squint again. Is the skylight scratched? But it's glass.

I stand up on the bed to get a better look, and shoot, it is. It's scratched pretty badly. Shit. A branch must have fallen on the roof and done a number on it. I'll have to figure out how to polish it out.

Now that I'm up, I throw on some boxers and grab a cup of coffee from the kitchen, making one for McKenna, too. She takes it with cream, no sugar.

"Your turn!" she calls from the bedroom.

I hand off her coffee on my way to the shower, kissing her shiny nose and marveling at how much I love our shared domesticity.

If only it didn't have to end.

And then I remember something that almost stops me in my track. On Saturday, as we were driving to the cruise terminal for the Haines tour, I said there was plenty of wildlife in Alaska, and she answered, "but no Mimi."

As I turn on the shower, letting the warm water pelt my

skin, I turn those words over and over in my head. What if her Mimi *could* somehow be moved to Alaska? Surely it isn't out of the realm of possibility for someone with Alzheimer's to be cared for here instead of in Yakima, right? Not to mention, McKenna doesn't seem to have a strong bond with Washington, and she appears to be building one with Alaska.

Convinced that I could be onto something good, I wash my hair, scrub my butt, and resolve to look into memory care centers in southeastern Alaska.

***

The Stewart family doesn't work on the Fourth of July, but every other business in Skagway makes a killing today, and McKenna's bartending two extra hours of overtime tonight. I'll pick her up before the fireworks at ten.

But for the next two hours we're free to enjoy the festivities together.

We get to town in time to catch both parades, then head over the footbridge by the airport, where McKenna stops us for a second to look for salmon. From there, we cross the river to Smuggler's Cove for the annual axe-throwing competition. My brothers and I participate every year, and once in a while, one of us even wins.

McKenna finds my sisters on the sidelines as I join Hunter and Sawyer at the sign-in table. Hunter's two years older than me and shit at log splitting, so I should be able to beat him. But Sawyer, who's a decade younger than me, has already got his shirt off, and the kid is ripped like crazy. Hell, I'm even a little jealous.

"Fuck, Sawyer! What you been eating?"

He grins at me, puffing out his chest, only twenty-years-old, but crazy cocky. "Ha! Not much of a 'kid' anymore, huh?"

"You'll always be a kid to me," I say, ruffling his hair before taking off my own shirt, and tying the flannel sleeves around my waist.

I look over at McKenna with my sisters, and my heart beats faster. She sticks out—short and dark-haired surrounded by my almost-six-foot tall, blonde, blue-eyed sisters—but I love that she looks different. She's easy to find. She's impossible to miss. And for now, anyway, she's all mine.

"Tanner Stewart," says Miss Clearwater, my second-grade teacher, "I don't have all day, do I?"

"No, ma'am," I say.

"That's thirty dollars for one entry, young man."

I take a fifty-dollar bill out of my wallet. "Keep the change."

"Thank you, kindly," she says.

Half of the entry fees will be given to the winner as a prize, but the other half goes to the Skagway Traditional Council, a local organization that provides services to our tribal citizens.

She hands me a printed number and a safety pin, and I pin it to my jeans, then head over to the bleachers to sit with my brothers.

"Is McKenna bartending today?" asks Hunter.

I nod. "She's gotta be at the Parsnip by noon."

"How's it working out for her there?"

"Good, I guess. She's making bank on tips."

Sawyer waves to someone in the crowd, and my eyes

197

follow his gaze, but I don't see anyone smiling back at him.

"Someone here to cheer you on?" I ask him.

"Maybe," he hedges.

"Sawyer's got a secret girlfriend," says Hunter, knocking his shoulder into Sawyer's.

"Shut up, Hunt," mutters Sawyer, but his cheeks flush, which means Hunter's right.

"Be careful," I say. "Some of the seasonal girls are nuts."

"Just because things didn't work out for you last year doesn't mean they won't work out for me."

"I'm just saying be careful."

"Hey, Tan," says Hunter. "We have honeymooners coming in next week, and Dad put me on an overnight trip to Whitehorse, but I thought it might be more fun for you and McKenna to take 'em. Maybe more comfortable for them, too. You know, going up with a couple instead of a single dude."

"Yeah, definitely. Been wanting to take her north," I tell him. "I'll ask McKenna which day she's off, and we'll see if we can make it happen."

"Cool." Hunter leans back against the bleachers, staring at her. "Hey...does she have any sisters?"

I elbow him in the side. "Dream on, brother."

He's quiet for a second, then says: "It'd be nice to meet someone like her."

"Stop crushing on my girl."

"I'm not," he says, looking away from her. "Ooof. Danger at three o'clock."

I shift my eyes to where he's looking, and see Ramona

standing on the sidelines, smiling and waving at someone in the bleachers. Hunter and I follow her gaze to…

Fuck. No.

"Sawyer!"

He's grinning at her, but stops and turns to me, his expression landing somewhere between belligerent and guilty.

"You cannot be fucking serious," I growl.

"Sawyer, what the hell are you doing?" Hunter demands.

"Being nice. It's nothing," says Sawyer, shrugging.

"*Nothing?*" Hunter bellows.

"She's only messing with you to get to me!" I say.

Sawyer's eyes narrow. "I know this'll come as a shock, but not everything's about you, Tanner!"

"True," says Hunter, "but this is."

Sawyer rolls his eyes at Hunter. "It's no big deal. I waved hello. You guys are freaking out for no reason."

"She's dangerous! Don't be stupid," I say. "Stay away from her. Promise me."

"I'm barely ever around her. I'm in Whitehorse or on the Chilkoot five days a week."

"Promise, Sawyer," says Hunter, his tone deadly. "Do *not* get involved with her."

"I fucking promise." He gets up and switches seats, joining two guys he knows from high school.

"What the fuck?" mutters Hunter.

I shake my head. I don't know. Sawyer knows how crazy she is; why the fuck is he going near her?

Miss Clearwater steps up to the microphone to announce the rules and kick off the competition, but my excitement for the Fourth has taken a huge hit. If Ramona hurts Sawyer, I'll never forgive myself. I'll need to keep an eye on him.

***

McKenna

This week I get Friday off, and I'm especially excited because Tanner and I are taking a newlywed couple, Lauren and Jeff Friedman, up to Whitehorse, Canada, somewhere I've heard a lot about. It'll be my first trip north to the Yukon, and Tanner promises that the wildlife and scenery along the one-hundred-mile journey are amazing.

We sat with Lauren and Jeff for a little while after last night's campfire, and they seemed really cool. They're from somewhere outside of Philadelphia and just got married last week. They chose Alaska for their honeymoon because they're super outdoorsy, and they've already visited Ketchikan, Sitka, and Juneau on a cruise. Now they're on the land portion of their trip which includes Skagway, Anchorage and Fairbanks. What an awesome trip.

I pack lightly for our overnight—just a change of clothes, a windbreaker, some toiletries and an extra sweatshirt. Whitehorse is the capital of Canada's smallest and westernmost territory, Yukon, and the largest city I will visit since leaving Seattle six weeks ago. Now, don't get me wrong, I *really* don't miss city life, but the promise of several museums, a 4-star hotel, dozens of restaurants, and the convenience of a Wal-Mart, has its appeal. I'll enjoy an afternoon and evening filled with creature comforts (and hot hotel sex!), and then we can return to beautiful Skagway.

"So," says Lauren from the back seat, "I never asked last night: how long have you two been together?" I glance at Tanner and grin. We're wearing matching polo shirts again.

"About, um…five weeks," he says.

"Wait!" says Jeff. "Five *weeks?*"

"Yep."

"You seem like you've been together a lot longer," says Lauren. "We were thinking you were just behind us." She chuckles. "I guess the first few weeks of dating and the honeymoon stage have a lot in common."

"Agree," says Jeff. "During both, you're all blissed out and sexed up and happy. I know I am."

"Me too," says Lauren, and kissing noises follow.

I look over at Tanner, who winks at me and mouths, *Me too.*

And because he's so adorable and I like him so much, I mouth, *Me too,* too.

About thirty-five minutes into the ride, we make a stop at Bridal Veil Falls, along the Klondike Highway, and take some pictures.

Lauren and Jeff take selfies first, and then I offer to take a few photos for them. It's a beautiful location, and when I'm done, Lauren insists on returning the favor.

Tanner and I stand together smiling with his arm around my waist, and then suddenly, when I'm not expecting it, he swoops me into his arms and kisses me. I'm giggling and laughing, with my legs flailing, but when I look at that picture in the car a few minutes later, all I can see is happiness…

And it scares the shit out of me.

You're getting too close. You've got to slow down.

In another forty-five minutes, we stop at Emerald Lake, so called for the vivid green of the water, which is almost other-worldly. I try to capture it on my iPhone, but I can't. It's too vibrant. Too spectacular. I put my phone back in my pocket and soak it up with my eyes instead.

While I'm admiring its beauty, Tanner comes up behind me and puts his arms around me. "I can't decide which is prettier...you or the lake. Or you standing by the lake. That covers both, huh?"

"Why is it so green?" I ask.

"There's a layer of marl on the lakebed. When the sun reflects off of it, it appears green."

"What's marl?

"Um. I think it's some sort of calcium clay."

"Can you swim in it?"

"Sure," he says. "But it's freezing."

"Always? Even in summer?"

"Always," he confirms.

I close my eyes and lean back against him. With the sun on my face and his arms around me, life almost feels...perfect. And yet it's that very feeling that makes me pull away from him.

"We should probably get going, huh?"

He lets me go, stepping over to the Friedmans and taking a few more pictures of them before loading us all up in the car.

Why can't you trust him? Why can't you let yourself love him and

202

let him love you?

I glance at him as we continue our drive north: the strong line of his jaw, dusted with blonde whiskers, and the aqua blue shirt that shows off his eyes. He's beautiful and sweet and he cares about me—genuinely. And yet, anytime I feel like I might be letting my guard down, alarm bells sound in my head and I push him away.

It makes me sad.

And it's exhausting.

By the time we get to Whitehorse and check into our hotel, I've got a splitting headache and I'm feeling grouchy.

"What can I do?" asks Tanner, who was looking forward to a romantic dinner. "I've got Advil and Tylenol. Would that help?"

I take two Advil, put on a clean T-shirt and get under the covers.

"I think I'll just call it an early night," I say. "Sorry."

"Mind if I go out and get something to eat?" he asks.

"Nope."

"Can I bring you back anything?"

A new brain. A new heart. A mother who wasn't an addict. A father who didn't spend my childhood in jail. The guts to love you. The courage to believe you could love me back.

"Nothing," I say, closing my weary eyes.

***

I get a good night's sleep and when I wake up in the morning, my headache is gone, but my worries remain. If anything, they're worse than they were last night. They're heavy and annoying and make me feel jittery and anxious.

While Tanner takes the Friedmans out to breakfast, I take a long shower and try to get to the root of my immediate unease.

Maybe it's hearing Tanner say that we've been together for five weeks and knowing that my time with him has flown, or because hearing him say "five weeks" forced me to realize that we only have six weeks left together. My summer in Skagway is already half gone, and despite my best efforts, it's going to hurt like hell to leave.

Maybe it's the weird pressure of spending time with newlyweds, who have their shit all figured out—they made the ultimate commitment to each other and couldn't be happier. I'm jealous of them, and at the same time, what they have scares me. Isn't it just a matter of time until Jeff realizes he doesn't really love Lauren, or Lauren realizes she's made a terrible mistake and leaves?

Or maybe it's being back in a city, albeit a such smaller one than Seattle. It reminds me of what's waiting for me when summer is over and fills me with such melancholy, it aches.

I can't pinpoint exactly what's souring my mood, but it lingers all morning, making me listless and quiet. Hugs and kisses from Tanner don't help. Visiting museums and cultural centers in Whitehorse doesn't help. Food doesn't help. I'm just going to have to sit in this anxiety until it passes.

The only thing that eases my anxiety is the thought of going to work later for the night shift. Getting back to the Parnsip will be a good distraction. It won't lift my mood, per se, but the thought of mindlessly slinging drinks for a few hours will be a relief from too much deep thinking.

As we get closer to Skagway, my phone starts buzzing like crazy, reminding me that I haven't had a cell signal since leaving the United States yesterday.

It's probably just Bruce reminding me that I'm working from four until ten tonight.

I'll be there, Bruce! I think. *Geez!*

I pull the phone from my bag, and my stomach instantly starts flipping over when I see that I've missed four calls from Mimi's care center in Yakima, at least three from an unknown caller, and a dozen calls and texts from Isabella.

My hand is shaking as I hold the phone up to my face to unlock it and Tanner, sitting in the driver's seat beside me, notices.

"Everything okay?"

"I don't think so," I whisper, a terrible chill making my throat and jaw feel like pins and needles. I glance over my shoulder, relieved to see that Lauren and Jeff are nestled together, asleep in the back seat, but I still keep my voice down. "I don't have an international plan, so I missed a bunch of calls and texts. I think—I think something may have happened to Mimi."

"What? Is she okay?"

"I'm trying to—"

"What does Isabella say?"

My heart is racing, making me feel light-headed and cold. My fingers skitter clumsily across the phone screen.

"I don't know!" I half-cry, half-whisper. "You're stressing me out! Give me a second!"

I scroll to Isabella's first message, which basically just tells me to call her. After six identical messages sent a few minutes apart, she writes more:

Isabella

Your Mimi fell this morning. They took her to the hospital, and I'm headed there now. I'll keep you updated, but please call me, Ken. I don't want to make any decisions for her without talking to you first.

My blood chills as I note that three more texts, begging me to call her, follow. Iz never, ever texts while driving, but she sent all three of these between Seattle and Yakima, which speaks to her panic.

There's another, more detailed, message that follows:

<u>Isabella</u>

OK. I'm at the hospital in Yakima. Mimi's in surgery. They can't get a hold of you. She slipped in her shower, fractured her ankle, broke her wrist, and knocked out some teeth. They already set her wrist and they're setting her ankle now. I don't know if you should come home. Maybe.

OMG. YOU
HAVE TO
CALL ME,
KEN.
WHERE
ARE YOU?

I can't see the screen anymore because my eyes have flooded with tears. I blink like crazy, which makes them fall, but new ones fill my eyes before I can see the screen clearly. I use my sleeve to rub my eyes.

I press Isabella's number to call her, but the signal's not strong enough to make a call yet.

"Damn it!" I cry through clenched teeth.

"What's going on?"

I sniffle, trying to draw a deep breath, but I can't. "Mimi f-fell. She b-broke her wrist and h-her ankle and sh-she's in s-surgery, and...and..."

He reaches over and puts his hand on my thigh. "Is Isabella there with her?"

"Y-Yeah. B-But...b-but..." *I'm not. Mimi needs me, and I'm not there. I wasn't even reachable.* I stare at my phone, willing the signal to get stronger, but it stays at one paltry bar. "When the fuck does the signal come back?"

"Not until Skagway," he says, squeezing my leg. "Just breathe. She'll be okay, Kenna."

"You don't know that!" I snap, knocking his hand off my leg. I don't want him to touch me right now. I need to think. "I should go home. I need to go home."

"Hey. Wait. She's in the hospital, right?" he says calmly.

"And Isabella's there."

"She has b-broken bones, Tanner! She's hurt and I'm f-far away! I'm *here*. I'm fucking here!"

I'm full-on crying now. When I feel a hand land on my shoulder, I know I've woken up the honeymooners with my drama.

"McKenna," asks Lauren, "is everything okay?"

"My grandmother's in the hospital," I mumble, feeling embarrassed and annoyed, frightened and terrible.

"What do you need?" asks Jeff.

"Just to call my friend, Isabella. And the hospital. And...and..."

Out of the corner of my eye, I see Tanner's hand start to slide over to me, but I flinch, tilting my body away from him. It's not fair to blame him. Rationally I know that. But fear has a strange way of making us irrational, and I *do* blame him. I blame him for suggesting the trip to Whitehorse, and driving the car that took us there, and inviting me to go along.

"Tanner," says Jeff, "signal's strongest in Skagway, right? Don't take us to Dyea. Stop in Skagway. Lauren and I can find something to do there while McKenna calls whoever she needs to."

"Th-thanks, Jeff," I murmur.

I write a quick text to Isabella, hoping that even if I can't make a call yet, maybe a text can get through.

McKenna

I'm so sorry, Iz! We were in   Canada

**for a night
and just
getting back
to Skagway
now. I'm
going to call
you in—**

"How far are we from Skagway?" I ask Tanner.

"Fifteen minutes. Twenty tops."

**—15-20 min.
Thank you
so much for
being there.
I don't know
what I'd do
without you.**

The text takes a while to load, but finally appears to send. I stare at the screen, praying that Isabella will respond quickly.

"What happened?" asks Lauren gently.

"She fell in the show-er," I say, the word "shower" cut in two by a soft sob. "She broke her ankle and her wr-rist and kn-nocked out some t-teeth."

"Oh, my god. I'm so sorry."

"She has dementia."

"That's rough," says Jeff. "Sorry, McKenna."

Clutching my phone like a lifeline, I turn toward the window, everything outside a blur of browns and greens and blues through my tears. If I lose Mimi like this, I'll never forgive myself. My phone buzzes.

<u>Isabella</u>

Thank God! She's out of surgery and all went well. Ankle and wrist in casts. Dental surgeon coming tomorrow morning. They'll make a mold to make false teeth. She's sedated and comfortable. They don't think there was any organ damage. She'll be here for two or three days and

then   go
home.
***

<u>McKenna</u>
I'm coming
home tonight.
***

<u>Isabella</u>
Don't. She's
comfortable
. The worst
has passed.
I'll stay until
tomorrow
just to be
sure she's
okay.   But
she's going
to need PT
over   the
next   few
weeks, Ken,
and   that's
going   to
cost $$. You
need   that
money.
Stay. Work.
I've got this.

***

<u>McKenna</u>

I owe you big time.

***

<u>Isabella</u>

No, you don't. We're ride or die, Ken. No in-between. I love you, girl. I'll keep you updated.

***

<u>McKenna</u>

I love you, too.

With a sob, I let my phone fall in my lap, covering my face with my hands and weeping with a mixture of relief and gratitude, guilt and worry.

"Baby," says Tanner softly. "You okay?"

"We can g-go home," I say. "She's g-going to b-be okay."

"You sure? You don't want to call anyone?"

Doesn't he get it? I *have* no one. There's no one to call. There's only Iz, and she's got everything under control.

"We don't mind, McKenna," says Lauren.

"No," I say, sniffling as I finally manage to get a full, deep breath into my lungs. A hiccup escapes my throat. "It's okay. The wi-fi's good at the campground. I can text Isabella more once we get back."

It's silent in the car for the remaining fifteen-minute drive back to Dyea. When we get there, Tanner parks the car in front of Jeff and Lauren's cabin, and Lauren gives me a hug.

"You're an amazing granddaughter," she says. "And your friend, Isabella, sounds amazing, too."

"Thanks, Lauren," I say, managing a small smile. "Sorry you had to deal with this on your honeymoon."

"No," she says. "You don't apologize for this."

Her kindness makes my tears start up all over again. "I'm g-going to go c-call Iz now."

"If you need me," she says, "I'm here. Knock on my door, okay? Anytime."

"Thanks, Lauren," I mumble.

I turn around and head to Tanner's cabin, walking by the campfire without saying hello to the Stewarts and other guests sitting there. I just want to get to my cabin, cry my eyes out, and then get the whole story of what happened to Mimi. I don't know what kind of dental coverage she has, so that could be an additional expense, and Isabella mentioned PT—

"McKenna!"

I'm about to open the cabin door when I hear Tanner's voice behind me. I turn around to find him standing at the foot of the porch stairs, his hand on the carved newel post, his eyes concerned.

"What?" I snap.

"How can I help? What can I do? What do you need?"

"Nothing," I say, clenching my jaw until it hurts. My eyes burn. My heart races. And I realize that I want to be mean. I want to lash out at him. It would be a relief to take my hurt and hurt someone else, and Tanner's the only one here. "I shouldn't have been up in Whitehorse with you. I shouldn't have been out of cell range for that long. I came up here to work and make money for Mimi's care, and I've gotten too distracted."

"Hey, wait a sec—"

"No," I say, lifting my chin as my heart screams and sobs for me to stop. "I can't let it happen again." I take a deep breath, gathering my courage to destroy this beautiful thing between us. "This is over, Tanner. We're over."

He winces, blinking his eyes in disbelief.

"I'm sorry," I say, opening the cabin door.

"Wait!" he cries. "Stop! No, baby. No. You're upset. You just need—"

I whirl on him in fury. "What I *need*, is to take care of the only person in the world who was there for me when no one else gave a shit! I need to put *her* first. Not *me*. And certainly not *you*."

"Kenna. Don't do this. Please."

The agony in his voice guts me. I blink my eyes like crazy as more tears burn my eyes.

"Leave me alone," I say. "I mean it."

Then I turn around, step inside the cabin, and pull the door shut behind me.

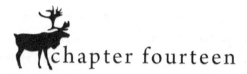

chapter fourteen

Tanner

If happiness makes time fly, misery makes it move like molasses. And hands down, this ranks as one of the worst weeks of my life.

As much as it hurts, I know I have to give McKenna space when we return from Whitehorse, so I ask Reeve to be McKenna's chauffeur to and from town. Then, I blow up the air mattress so I can bunk with my brothers. At some point, a small pile of my things is waiting for me on the porch of my cabin, and though that pile rips my heart to shreds, I collect it without a word.

I try to go about my business; help with meals, chop wood, build campfires, lead tours—but in the dark of night, with my brothers softly snoring nearby, I torture myself by remembering how she felt in my arms, and when I finally fall asleep, I sleep for shit.

After three days, I'm going out of my mind not being able to talk to her, and I stop by the cabin mid-morning to see how she's doing. She answers the door with red, bloodshot eyes, and I find some measure of satisfaction in the fact that she looks as bad as I feel.

"Hi," I say.

"Hi."

"How are you? How's Mimi?"

"What do you want, Tanner?"

"I want to know how you're doing; how she's doing." I reach for her, but she pulls away. "Please. Just give me a quick update. I'm worried."

She sighs, staring at her bare feet and crossing her arms. For a minute, I think she's going to ask me to leave, so I'm relieved when she starts talking.

"Mimi's back at the care home. She's confused about the bandages and keeps asking why she's wearing casts. It doesn't seem like she remembers what happened, which is a blessing, I guess. She's having partial dentures made for the four teeth that got knocked out when she fell. I have no idea how they'll get her to wear them regularly."

"I'm sorry, baby."

She looks up at me through watery eyes. "Yeah. It sucks."

It takes all of my strength not to reach for her and pull her into my arms.

"What can I do?"

"Nothing, Tanner."

"Please. Anything."

She shakes her head. "You're making it harder just being here right now."

She wants you to go. That's what you can do for her.

217

"Okay. I'll go."

I turn around and head down the stairs, fighting my longing to run back. I keep walking. I don't look back. I give her the space she needs, no matter how much I hate it. But I hope she doesn't mistake me giving her space for giving up on us. If anything, I'm more convinced than ever of my feelings for her and the rightness of us together.

Which gives me an idea: she might not need *me* right now, but she definitely needs *someone*…and I know exactly the person she needs.

***

"You're coming out with us," says Hunter on Friday night at ten.

"No," I say, lying down on my pathetic air mattress, my hair and shirt smelling strongly of the campfire that just wrapped up. Reeve just left to pick up McKenna, and I want to be here when she gets home. Sometimes it's the only glimpse I get of her all day. "I'm not."

"Yes, you are," says Sawyer, preening in front of the mirror. "No arguments."

"Fuck off, Sawyer."

"Shut up, Tanner," says Hunter. "You're coming."

"I smell like shit."

"Who cares? You got no one to impress, brother."

"Thanks for the reminder."

"C'mon, you know what I mean."

"I'm not in the mood," I grouse.

Sawyer rips the plug out of my bed on the way out the door, and it instantly starts to deflate.

"You little fucker!" I yell, throwing my pillow at the door as it slams shut behind him.

Hunter squats down beside me as I slowly lower to the floor. "What if we run into Ramona, huh? You gotta keep an eye on him with me."

There is, literally, no incentive in the universe that could get me to go out tonight, but somehow this one works. Damn Hunter for knowing me so well.

"Fuck!" I yell. "Fine."

"Change your jeans and put on a clean T-shirt. We'll be outside."

Lying on my limp air mattress on the hard floor, I'm the picture of pitiful, but Hunter's right: we can't let Ramona get her gnarled talons into our little brother. I stand up and change, not bothering to wash my face or comb my hair, and join my brothers outside.

"The Stewart Brothers Take Skagway!" howls Sawyer, who's technically not twenty-one yet, but has been charming his way into pint glasses for years now.

"More like…The Older Stewart Brothers Make Sure The Younger Stewart Brother Doesn't Get Himself In Trouble," I mutter, sitting shotgun next to Hunter.

"I promised I wouldn't get involved with Ramona. What else do you guys need?"

For her to move the fuck back to California.

"Where are we headed?" I ask Hunter.

"SBC? Parsnip?"

"Neither," I say. SBC is Ramona's favorite, and frankly, I'm not sure I can bear being at the Parsnip tonight.

"Happy Endings?" suggests Sawyer.

"Whatever," I say.

The Happy Endings Saloon is a bar attached to the Morning Wood Hotel and frequented more by locals than cruisers. Plus, they have darts and pool tables, which is a plus.

We park at the gas station next door and find an open high-top table. Hunter orders a pitcher and challenges Sawyer to a game of darts while I pour us three beers. When I look up, Joe Raven is standing by the side of the table.

"Can I join you guys?"

"Why not?"

Joe pulls over an extra stool, waving to my brothers before sitting down. "Girls coming in tonight?"

"No," I say, "*Harper's* not coming into town tonight."

"Cut it out with that," says Joe. "That's old news."

"And here's you, wishing it was still on the front page."

Joe rolls his eyes, finishing his beer. "Any more trouble with Ramona?"

"Nothing to speak of. Haven't seen her since the Fourth…although, she was giving Sawyer the eye at the axe-throwing contest, which pissed me off."

"Hope you and Hunter had a word with him."

"Why do you think we're out with him tonight?"

Joe nods. "Smart."

I plant my elbows on the table. "Tell me, for real, Joe. Why did you and Harp break up?"

He stares at me for a long second, then takes a deep breath and leans closer to me. "She ever talk about it?"

"Not a peep."

"Then that's the way it's gotta be, Tanner." He slides away from the table, challenging Hunter to the next game of darts.

Sawyer joins me at the table, glued to his phone as he gulps down half his beer. My hackles go up.

"Who you talking to?" I ask.

"None of your business," says Sawyer, pocketing his phone. "What happened with McKenna? We're all getting sick of walking on eggshells."

"Her grandmother's sick. She needs to concentrate on her family."

"That doesn't really make sense," he says. "When things are going bad, you need your people around you more than ever."

"She doesn't see it that way."

"I don't get it. You two are good together."

He's digging around an open wound with a knife. "I know."

"Is it over?"

"I don't know."

"Aren't you going to fight for it? If it was me, I'd fight for her."

"Knowing when to back off and give someone space can be a better strategy than fighting," I tell him. "I know what I'm doing."

The door to the bar opens, and four women enter: the Sutter girls, Ella and Millie, from Homer, followed by Mr. Caswell's niece, Ivy, and—*fuck me*—Ramona. The Kozy Kone girls. All four of them. Exactly thirty seconds after my brother was furiously texting someone.

"Are you fucking kidding me, Sawyer?"

"It isn't what you think," he whispers, heading over to the door to greet them.

Ella and Millie, twins who've been Skagway regulars for the past three summers, sidle up to the bar and order shots. I don't know them that well, but they've always been nice enough. They're attending the University of Alaska in Anchorage, and summers in Skagway pay their tuition. I'm guessing this'll be the last one. If my math's right, they'll graduate next June.

Ivy Caswell's the niece of Mr. Caswell, the high school guidance counselor, football, soccer, hockey and softball coach. She lives in Fairbanks, I think, but used to spend a few weeks with her aunt and uncle every summer. A bit younger than me, I think she's around Parker's age.

As Sawyer beelines to Ivy and Ramona, his body language tells me everything I need to know, and relief almost weakens my knees: he's not into Ramona at all. He's into Ivy. *Phew.*

As Sawyer and Ivy edge over to the bar to join the Sutters, Ramona looks over at me, a catlike grin spreading her garish red lips. As she saunters over, I think about running to the bathroom, but I'm not a fucking coward. I can handle her.

"Hey, Tanner. Where's the Mrs.?" She looks around dramatically. "Not here, I see. And Reeve's been driving her scrawny ass into town all week. Trouble in paradise?"

"Fuck you," I say, taking a sip of my beer and tilting my body away from her. Hunter and Joe are concentrating on their game and haven't noticed that Ramona's here.

"Tsk. Tsk. Where are your manners?"

"Where are *yours*? I obviously have no interest in talking to you, and yet you persist in seeking me out."

She pouts. "Maybe I miss you."

"The feeling isn't mutual."

Over at the bar, my brother talks to Ivy, who looks up at him with a sweet grin.

"Ivy's cute, isn't she?" asks Ramona.

"I don't really know her at all."

"Oh, I do! She's my roommate."

"Poor thing."

"I could say anything to her, you know? She'd believe anything I said. I'm like a big sister to her. I could tell her that Sawyer's a good guy…or a suspected rapist."

I whip my eyes to face her, disgusted and angry. "That's a lie. It's fucking slander."

"Well, I could *certainly* say your family's full of men who can't be trusted. That's a fact."

"What the fuck is wrong with you?"

"Don't swear at me, Tanner Stewart," she snaps. "Don't you dare swear at me."

"Leave me and my family alone, you crazy, psycho, stalker-bitch!"

"Hey, hey, hey," says Joe, who's suddenly standing behind me. "Let's watch the language, huh?"

"Officer Raven," says Ramona, placing a palm over her chest. "I'm so glad you heard that. It made me feel unsafe."

"Why are you over here bothering Tanner while your

friends are at the bar, Ramona?" asks Hunter, standing beside me.

"It's a free country," she says. "I'm just trying to be civil."

"Why don't you join your posse?" suggests Joe. "And stay away from the Stewarts?"

"Hard to do that when one of the Stewart boys is chasing my roommate all over town."

"You leave Sawyer *the fuck* alone!" I shout.

"Tanner," says Joe, putting his hand on my shoulder, "calm down. Hunter, get him out of here."

"Come on, Tan," says Hunter, "now. Come on."

"Thanks, Hunter," says Ramona, batting her eyelashes at my brother, "for protecting a lady."

"No lady here," mumbles Hunter.

"Fuck you, Ramona!" I yell over my shoulder.

"Stop it." Hunter grabs my arm. Hard. "Keep moving."

We leave Joe talking to Ramona and Sawyer at the bar talking to Ivy, and stand outside in the half-light of the gas station pumps.

"Fuck!" I scream to the sky. "Everything's fucked!"

"You gotta cool it," says Hunter. "You can't let her get to you."

"She's got a vile, nasty, fucking mouth!"

"What did she say that got you so riled?"

I face Hunter with my hands on my hips. "Sawyer's not into Ramona. He's into Ivy."

"Yeah, I just clocked that. It's good news, isn't it?"

"I mean, I guess, but Ramona's her roommate. She threatened to tell Ivy lies about Sawyer. Disgusting stuff."

"If Ivy believes shit like that, she's not worthy of Sawyer."

Hunter's words are so simple and true, my eyes flood with tears. Fucking tears. Embarrassing. Humiliating. But not without cause.

My little brother's happiness might be jeopardized by a woman I scorned.

I can't seem to escape her no matter what I do.

And I've fallen head over heels in love with McKenna, who wants nothing to do with me.

And it's Fucking. Killing. Me.

I swipe at my eyes with the sleeve of my flannel shirt, ashamed to meet my big brother's eyes.

But Hunter, roughly and without compromise, pulls me up against his chest and clasps his arms around me. I'm a grown man being bear-hugged by his big brother, and I'm so defeated and so tired, I can't even push him away. Even worse, I'm grateful. Because I know he loves me, and I love him back. So I hold on as worthless fucking tears slide out of the corners of my eyes, and my heart twists with sorrow.

And then, without a word, we get into the car, turn on the radio, and wait for Sawyer to join us so we can go home.

***

McKenna

Life sucks.

My eyes burn from crying.

My tips are down because I can't get into the whole "frontier bartender" schtick.

And my cellphone bill is going to be through the roof because it's not even the end of July yet and I've already gone way over my texting minutes.

I miss Tanner much more than I ever could have guessed. I miss the simple sweetness of our time together, the comfort of his arms around me while I fall asleep, the way he looked at me and touched me and put my safety and happiness over his own.

I didn't mean to fall in love with him, but I did, and with a little over four weeks until I go back to my life in Seattle, I can't let myself fall any deeper. I've got to let him go. I've got to put distance between us, or I won't survive leaving.

I cry for Mimi, too.

I cry because—reading through the lines of Isabella's reports—she's failing wildly and quickly, and I'm so far away from her. We don't Facetime because it upsets her, and flying down to see her would only eat into the money I need to care for her. Especially now.

Would it have been better to keep her at the VA Hospital in Seattle, where I could have seen her a few times a week? Was gardening and yoga classes worth the extra money? I wanted the best for her—I wanted to keep her stimulated because I read how important that was for dementia patients, but I haven't seen her in two months, and I didn't go back and see her when she got hurt, because every penny counts more than ever.

I feel so confused and lost and alone.

I don't know what's right.

I don't know what's best.

And in the absence of Iz, there's only one person whose council could have helped or mattered, but I can't spend time with him because it's breaking my own heart to be close to him.

It's raining today—overcast and gray through the skylight overhead—which checks out. It's my day off, and the weather reflects my mood perfectly.

Grabbing my phone off the bedside table, I read a message from Parker, inviting me to a Girl's Night at her cabin next week. I'm surprised because I've been avoiding the Stewart women lately. Reeve and I make our rides into Skagway in silence, for the most part, which has been fine with me. On some level, I'm sure they hate my guts for hurting their brother. Honestly, I hate me for it, too.

There's a morning update from one of the nurses on Mimi's floor; she didn't sleep well last night, and they had to give her a shot to sedate her. Isabella writes that she's headed out of town for two days and may not be reachable until she gets to where she's going. God, I've overburdened my best friend so much, I'm glad she's taking a break from me. I write back, telling her that I hope she's doing something fun and to forget about me and Mimi and everything else.

<u>McKenna</u>:
Be   careful.
Get laid. I love
you.

***

<u>Isabella</u>:
I'd love to

227

get laid, but I
could use a hand.

***

<u>McKenna</u>:
Okay,
weirdo.   From
me?

***

<u>Isabella</u>:
Yeah.   Is
Hunter single?

I stare at my phone for a second, blinking at the screen. *Wait. What? Hunter? Hunter who?* Of course I think of Hunter Stewart first, but that makes no sense. She's never met him.

<u>McKenna</u>:
#confused
What   are   you
talking about?

***

<u>Isabella</u>:
Hunter
Stewart.
Is he single?
Because he
picked me up at
the   airport and
I'm thinking

I jerk my head up because there's a knock on my door. A loud one.

Before I can totally process what I'm reading, I jump out of bed and race to the front door of my cabin where Isabella—*my Iz, my bestie, my family*—stands on the front porch, her phone in one hand and the handle of a rolling suitcase in the other. And right behind her? Hunter Stewart, hand raised, ready to lean forward and knock again.

"Morning, McKenna," he says.

Worlds are colliding wildly, and it's too early in the morning for me to get up to speed.

"Wha…What is—"

"Hey, Ken," says Isabella, giving me one of her trademark megawatt grins.

"ISABELLA!" I cry, tears flooding my eyes as my best friend opens her arms and pulls me close. "What—I can't! What are you doing here?"

"Tanner called me. Said you needed a friend. Sent me a ticket." Her lips are close to my ear, but she lowers her voice. "And sent his hot older brother to pick me up at the airport, thank you very much."

"Wait. What?" I still can't believe this is happening. "How—?"

She leans away to look at me, her face so welcome and so familiar—and so fucking needed—more tears start sliding down my cheeks.

"Tanner," she says. "I'm here because of Tanner." She looks over her shoulder at Hunter. "Thanks for the ride, hot stuff."

"A hundred percent my pleasure," says Hunter, smiling like the Cheshire cat. Jesus. I didn't know he had so many teeth. "Hopefully I'll see you around."

"Count on it," she purrs, turning back to me. "Girl! He is *scorching* hot."

I pull Isabella into the cabin, parking her rolling suitcase by the front door as I bump it shut with my butt. I run my hands through my hair and stand against the door, staring at my best friend like she's an apparition.

"How long are you here?"

"Two nights," she says, shrugging out of her jacket and putting it over the back of the couch.

"I need details. How did this happen?"

"I already told you how. Tanner. He arranged everything," says Isabella, looking around the living room sitting area. "This is cute, Ken! Very rustic chic."

"Tanner did this?" I whisper, my heart swelling with so much love for him, I feel like the Grinch on Christmas morning. While I was being a total and complete bitch to him, he was planning this surprise for me? It makes me want to cry my eyes out and run to him at the same time.

"Yes," says Isabella. "Called me. Planned everything. Paid for everything even though I tried to tell him it wasn't necessary. He insisted." She puts her hands on my shoulders. "For the record, I approve of him, girl. I approve of him very, very much."

"He's pretty amazing, huh?"

"Ken," she says gently because she knows me so well, "not everyone leaves. I'm here. I'll *always* be here. If you give him a chance, he may surprise you: he may stick around, too."

I hug her again, feeling lighter than I have all week. "I

have to, um…I have to do something. Put your stuff in the bedroom. I'll be right back."

I'm still wearing pajamas, and my feet are bare, but I rush out of the front door and down the porch steps, running blindly toward the wood pile behind the main lodge where Tanner often kills time on wet or quiet days.

When I get there, he's holding an axe by his side, bare-chested and crazy gorgeous as he talks to Hunter, who's no doubt filling him in on Isabella's arrival.

"Tanner!"

He looks up, and I can see that his lips want to tilt up in a smile when sees me, but he remembers that we broke up and frowns instead. His face is guarded, but his beautiful blue eyes, those mesmerizing windows to the soul, can't completely hide his hope.

"Hunter, give us a minute?"

Hunter nods, rounding the corner of the lodge to leave us alone.

There are several feet between us, but I don't close the space immediately.

"You invited Iz here."

He lifts his chin, his expression wary. "Yeah."

"Why'd you do that?"

"Because you needed someone. And it couldn't be me."

"You called her."

"Yeah."

"You convinced her to come."

"Didn't take much."

"But you paid for her ticket."

He shrugs, rubbing the back of his neck with his hand.

"Tanner," I say, holding his eyes as I walk toward him. "Why'd you do that?"

"I told you. You were sad. You needed—"

"Tanner," I half-sob, half-whimper, stopping close to him. "Why?"

He slams his eyes into mine, taking a deep breath and letting it go slowly. "You know why."

"Tell me," I say. "I need to hear you say it."

"Because I love you, Kenna. Because there's nothing I wouldn't do for you."

I'm standing on jagged wood chips, which is hurting my feet, so I take one last step forward onto his sneakered feet. His arms clasp around me, holding me steady, pulling me close.

"I love you," he whispers fiercely, his lips skimming the hot skin of my neck. He rests his forehead on my shoulder. "I know you didn't want us to fall in love, but I couldn't help it. It just—"

"Shut up, Tanner," I whisper. "Look at me."

He lifts his head.

"I'm sorry I hurt you," I tell him.

"Let me love you, Kenna," he says softly.

"Okay," I murmur with relief and in surrender, standing up on tip toes to kiss him.

 chapter fifteen

Tanner

For the record, I didn't invite Isabella to Skagway to get back together with McKenna. I invited her because I was worried about McKenna and hoped that a visit from her best friend would help. And it did. It really did.

Aside from the fact that it looks like we've reconciled, McKenna has finally come out of her shell again—she joined us for dinner in the lodge last night and for the campfire with Isabella. I watch her face when she's not looking at me, and there are cracks in her façade; a fragility that wasn't there before. It kills me that her Mimi's failing health is breaking her heart, but it reconfirms my intentions to be there for her— however she needs me and long beyond this summer.

I arranged with Bruce for her to have Saturday and Sunday off while Isabella visited, but I'm positive that Sunday comes too soon for my girl. I knock on the cabin door at eleven. Isabella's puddle jumper to Juneau leaves at twelve, and from there, another flight will take her back home to Seattle.

McKenna opens the door in leggings and a t-shirt, a little butterfly pin sweeping her hair off her forehead and making her look younger than she is. My heart pounds recklessly. My love for her feels boundless.

"Morning," I say, reaching for her hips to pull her closer.

Since Isabella's been sharing her bedroom since Friday, our moments alone have been quick and fleeting. I'm hoping that changes later today, but I've been telling myself that I won't put any pressure on her. She knows how I feel; and she's accepted, if not reciprocated, my feelings. That's enough for now. Whatever happens next, it'll be at her speed.

She wraps her arms around my waist and lays her cheek on my chest.

"I wish she could stay longer."

"I know," I say. "She's pretty awesome."

"It was so amazing to have her here."

I rub her back gently. "She can come back. Anytime."

"I know. But school starts the Tuesday after Labor Day. She'll be working."

So will you, I almost say, but it occurs to me—whether she realized it or not—that she just thought of herself as *here* on Labor Day, not in Seattle. I hold my breath, waiting for her to realize her mistake, but she just takes a deep breath and lets it go slowly. Maybe she's distracted by Isabella leaving, but I take it as a good sign for a possible future together. She may not realize it, but on some level, she thinks of herself as staying.

"Hey, we gotta get her to the airport if she's going to make her flight," I say.

"She'll be ready in a second. Iz doesn't go anywhere until

she looks perfect."

"Iz always looks perfect," says a voice from behind me.

I look over my shoulder to see Hunter standing at the foot of my porch steps.

"You come to say goodbye?" I ask my brother, who's been acting like a smitten idiot all weekend.

"I'm driving Isabella to the airport," he says. "Her request."

Isabella appears in the doorway.

"Ken," she says, "I know you want to drive me, but I can't stand a soppy scene at the airport, and you know it."

McKenna stiffens against me. "Please, Iz…it'd give us a few more minutes."

"And like I told you a million and one times, girl, goodbye isn't goodbye when it's us. We don't need more minutes now. We had the best weekend ever, and we have a whole lifetime of awesome minutes ahead."

McKenna lurches from my arms into Isabella's, holding on to her friend tightly. "I'll miss you."

"I'll miss you, too."

"Thank you for everything."

"Ride or die, *chica*," she says. "And we're not dyin' anytime soon."

"Kiss Mimi for me?"

"Absolutely."

"And travel safe?"

"Of course."

"And text me when you get home?"

"Always."

McKenna swipes at her eyes as she draws away from her friend, and I put my arm around her shoulders, encouraged when she leans into me.

"Thanks for coming, Isabella," I tell her.

"Thanks for inviting me, Tanner." She grins at me first, and then at us. "You're good for her."

"I love her," I say.

"I heard," says Isabella, flicking a glance at McKenna. "And by some miracle, she's still standing next to you. That's a first, *hermano*."

And hopefully a last, I think. I want to be the last man standing next to McKenna. The only man, from this day until the end of days.

"Come on," says Hunter, grabbing Isabella's suitcase and carrying it down the steps. "There's a plane waiting with your name on it."

Isabella grins at my brother, and wowza, I can feel the heat between these two. I haven't seen Hunter crush this hard in years.

Isabella leans her forehead against McKenna's.

"Love you."

"Love y-you," murmurs McKenna, her voice breaking on a soft sob.

"Take care of her," Isabella tells me, her deep brown eyes terrifying in their intensity.

"Don't worry."

Hunter waves goodbye to us as they speed away.

"What now?" McKenna asks, looking up at me with watery eyes.

"It sucks to say goodbye."

"So much."

"I wish I could think of something," I say, "to distract you."

She half-sniffles, half-giggles. "Are guys *always* thinking about sex?"

"Not always. Sometimes we sleep."

"I have to straighten up and change the bed sheets," she says. "Give me a hand?"

Honestly? I'd rather roll around in the bed sheets with her, but I promised myself we'd move at her pace, so I nod, following her back inside.

We pull the old sheets off the bed and McKenna takes them to the laundry room adjacent to the barn while I get the fitted sheet started. She's back right around the time I'm straightening the comforter and putting on the fresh pillowcases.

When the bed's remade, I lie down on top, gesturing for her to join me. She rolls her eyes at me before lying down, her head on my shoulder and my arm anchoring her to my side.

"So," I say, "are we back together?"

"I hope so," she says. "Yes. Absolutely. Last week was awful."

"Miserable," I agree. "I missed you."

She leans up on her elbow, grinning at me. "I missed you, too."

"You got scared, huh?"

"Mm-hm. My brain keeps warning me that I like you too much, but my heart's tired of fighting it."

"So don't," I tell her. *Please don't fight it.*

"I won't. But…but I'm not ready to say it back yet," she tells me, and I know she's talking about *I love you.* "I've only said it to two people in my entire life: Mimi and Iz."

"I get it."

"But Tanner, that doesn't mean it's not growing inside of me," she says, gazing at me tenderly. She touches each of my eyebrows with her index finger, then traces the line of my jaw. She runs the back of her fingers over my cheekbone and nods. "It is."

Bearing in mind how much this scares her, how she warned me that she doesn't "do love," I don't expect her to tell me something this wonderful. The sweetness and generosity of her words leaves me breathless and excited. I can't help the reaction of my body. It's been a terrible week without her; I've longed for her so desperately. And now that we're lying on a bed together, I want to consummate the strong feelings that exist between us.

"Kiss me," I say.

She leans down, brushing her lips against mine. At first, our kiss is slow and sweet, but it quickly deepens. She eases up, straddling my lap and holding my cheeks. Our tongues glide against each other as she grinds her hips into mine. When we're panting and breathless, I slide my lips away from our kiss and open my eyes.

"Do you want to…?"

"Yes," she murmurs. "Please."

"Sure?"

"Tanner," she says, her eyes wide and dilated. "Now."

I reach for the waistband of her sweats, pulling at them. She rises up on her knees so I can pull them down, then reaches for my shorts. I hook my thumbs in the waistbands of my boxers and shorts, buck my hips off the bed, and pull them down in one swift yank.

Holding my eyes, she squats over my erection and guides it inside her body, letting her head fall back as I fill her completely. And for just a second, we are still—one being, one soul, two humans who've found their person in this cold, crazy world we share.

I slide her sweatshirt over her head as she rides me, her hips sliding back and forth over my pelvis. Her moans and whimpers of pleasure make it hard for me not to come after being away from her for a week, but I don't want to orgasm right away. I need this closeness. *Slow down.* I reach for her hips, taking control of our lovemaking, forcing her to take all of me with every thrust, and holding myself in place, deep and still, before letting her slide away.

Her breathing shudders every time I impale her. Mine is shallow, too.

I love her. My god, I love this woman so much.

"Kenna," I say, the swirling inside of me making it harder to hold on to control. "I love you."

"Kiss me, Tanner." She leans forward at the waist so that her face is close to mine. "Kiss me while we come."

At the exact second that I burst inside of her, our tongues collide, our lips moving desperately, feverishly against each other.

When we're sated but still shaking, I roll us to our sides,

still grasping her body against mine, still deeply embedded within her as the aftershocks of our orgasm rock us both.

Our foreheads touch. I press my lips to the tip of her nose.

"I love you so much, baby."

"Keep saying it," she says, her voice low and soft. "Keep telling me."

"I love you," I whisper again, rolling onto my back but keeping her close to my side. "I'm not going to stop. I'm *never* going to stop."

She hums softly, a nonsensical post-orgasm *mmmm*, and I take that as a sign that my feelings are accepted and that somewhere inside of her, a like response is growing.

"Thank you, again," she says, rolling onto her back, "for bringing Iz here. It was the best surprise ever."

"She's a great friend," I say, kissing the top of her head.

"Hey," she says, pointing up at the skylight, "you fixed those scratches last week, didn't you?"

"Yeah. I thought I did." Huh. They're back...and worse this time. "I thought it was a branch, but once I got up there, I realized the gouges were pretty deep."

"What do you think? A bird?"

"Hawk or eagle talons could do it, for sure. Their rear talons are the same size as Grizzly claws, so, yeah, they can do some damage...but this would be weird behavior."

"Targeting your skylight?"

"Yeah. There are plenty of trees for nesting. We don't keep food on the roof. I don't know why it'd keep coming back here and scratching."

"Maybe it likes watching us," she says, grinning up at me.

"Can't blame it there," I tell her, brushing my lips on her forehead. "I could watch you all day, every day, for the rest of my life."

Her smile fades just a touch.

"No," I say. "Don't do that. Don't get scared. Don't back away."

"I'm still getting used to 'I love you.'" She takes a deep breath. "It's hard."

"To trust me."

"To trust anyone. I want to. I'm trying, Tanner, but forever's a long time. It scares me."

"I know," I say, holding her close. *Change the subject.* I look up at the scratches again. "You know what? I'm going to get two of those motion-activated cameras from the hardware store and set one up on the side of the cabin and another right near the skylight. We'll see what's been visiting us."

"Oh, that would be so cool! I see those videos on Instagram and TikTok. Once I saw a fox that kept getting through a dog door. The homeowners couldn't figure out who was eating their dog's leftover food every night while he slept in their room."

"Our own little mystery," I tell her, glancing at the clock on my bedside table. "As much as I hate to say it, I have to get up and get moving."

"It's Sunday! And you have the day off," she says. "Where're you headed?"

I'm headed to Haines. But I'm not ready to tell her why. Not yet.

241

"*You've* got the day off," I say. "I have an errand to do in Haines."

"Can I come?"

It kills me to say no, but the reality is that even though my errand is for her, I need to do this on my own. That said? I'm no fool. I planned for the possibility that she'd ask to go with me, and I found the perfect distraction.

"Well," I say, "you could. You definitely could. But if you do, you'll miss out on the massage I planned for you."

Her eyes widen to saucers. "The...the what, now?"

"Massage," I say with a chuckle. "Isabella told me they're your weakness."

"There's a spa in Skagway?"

"Nope. But there are a couple of damn good masseuses."

She leans up on my chest, smiling at me. "Have I told you how amazing you are, Tanner Stewart?"

"Yes," I say, "but I'm happy to hear it again."

"You're amazing," she says softly, and if I'm not mistaken, I think I might see love shining from her eyes. "Thank you."

"I love you," I tell her. "And you're welcome."

***

McKenna

"Miss McKenna!" calls Bruce from the upstairs balcony. "The dreaded gunslinger Soapy Smith has been seen approaching this establishment!"

I grab a plastic rifle from under the bar and pretend to cock it. "I'm ready, boss!"

Two "working girls," a.k.a. waitresses, pretend to swoon, and two other waitresses grab them under the arms and drag them to safety.

The patrons clap and chuckle with glee, waiting to see what happens next.

One of the busboys, dressed in denim and black leather with a bandit's bandana, pushes through the double doors into the saloon and shoots two cap guns into the air, making a couple of little smoke puffs over his head.

"Hand over all your loot!" he yells to me, throwing me a burlap bag.

Bruce rushes down the stairs. "Good sir! Take what you will but *please*, spare our lives!"

I put a bunch of Monopoly money in the bag and hand it back to the busboy, who slings it over his shoulder. As he leaves, I take a toy rifle from under the bar, point and shoot. *Pop!* He falls to the ground, Monopoly money scattering everywhere.

"Saved again by the bravest lady bartender in the west!" cries Bruce.

The crowd whoops and claps, the four waitresses grab the money and stuff it back into the bag, the busboy jumps up, takes a bow and heads back to the kitchen, and Bruce and I nod to the applause.

In through the double doors walk four members of the Stewart gang: Tanner, Hunter, Harper, and Sawyer, in town for drinks on a rare night off. I wave at them, gesturing to the table I saved for them hours ago.

Tanner comes over to the bar and leans over to kiss me.

"Bruce is still doing the old Soapy Smith bandit bit, huh?"

"You know Bruce."

Tanner rolls his eyes. "When do you get off?"

I check my watch. "Now."

"Come join us?"

"Absolutely. Give me a few minutes to change."

Five minutes later, I'm sitting with the Stewart crew at a table in the corner, the pitcher of beer on the table already halfway finished.

Hunter, who sits across from me, looks up from his phone as I sit down. "Isabella says hi."

"Say hi back," I tell him with a wink.

Since my bestie went back to Seattle last weekend, she and Hunter have been talking a lot, and from what I understand, he's already planning a weekend trip south to see her again. Grinning at his phone, Hunter's looking pretty satisfied.

Harper, on the other hand, stares at her beer, despondent.

"Harper," I say, nudging her. "You okay?"

She brightens for my benefit, but her smile doesn't crinkle her eyes. It's forced, not genuine. "Sure. Fine."

On her other side, Sawyer stares at his phone, not looking half as happy as Hunter. He flips his phone over and slams it down on the table, then chugs his beer and refills the glass to the top.

"Slow down, Sawyer," says Tanner.

"Shut up, Tanner."

"The energy at this table is whackadoo," I whisper to

Tanner.

"Yeah. I know. Hunter's like a pig in a shit bath, Sawyer wants to kill someone, and Harper's about to volunteer to be his victim."

"Stewarts!" I say, commanding four pairs of bright blue eyes. "What's going on with you three?"

"Ivy can't make it," mutters Sawyer. "Second time she's canceled on me this week."

Beside me, Tanner flinches. "Ramona's poisoning your well, Sawyer."

"Well, thanks for that, Tanner."

"It's not his fault," says Hunter. "Ramona's crazy. If Ivy can't see that…"

Sawyer's hands fist on the table. "Then what?"

"I'm not fighting with you," says Hunter dismissively, looking down at his phone. "You're pissed and sad. You're spoiling for a brawl."

"The girl you like lives fifteen hundred miles away," grunts Sawyer, still baiting Hunter. "I don't know what you've got to be happy about."

"Yours lives ten yards from here and won't come down the street for a beer. Distance doesn't mean shit. I got plenty to be happy about."

Sawyer chugs his second beer, then slams the pint glass on the table, stands up and stalks out of the saloon.

"You don't have to be an asshole, Hunter," says Harper.

"*I'm* the asshole? He was coming for *me*."

"Whatever."

"Why are *you* in a bad mood?" Tanner asks Harper.

"What's going on?"

She looks over at the saloon's double doors, her eyes widening. When I follow her gaze, I see Joe Raven standing there in plain clothes. He scans the bar, stopping when he finds Harper. He stares back at her, his expression bleak, almost angry. She shifts in her seat, picking up her beer and taking a tiny sip.

Joe beelines to our table, taking Sawyer's empty seat without asking, without saying hello to the rest of us. His eyes are focused like lasers on Harper, who stares at her drink.

"No," he bites out.

"Don't tell me what to do," she snaps, finally looking at him, two bright red patches of color appearing high on her cheeks. "I can do—"

"Harper! Stop!"

She flinches, blinking at him, and I realize her eyes are filled with tears.

"Sh-shut up, Joe," she mutters, standing up and stalking out of the saloon.

Joe watches her go, his expression stricken.

"Hey, Joe," says Hunter, looking shaken. "Is everything—"

"Shut up, Hunter," says Joe, leaping up to follow Harper.

"What the fuck?" mutters Hunter, wide eyes looking at Tanner for answers.

"No clue!"

Hunter's phone buzzes, and he jumps up. "Woot! She wants to FaceTime. Bye, guys!" He's the third Stewart to jump ship in five minutes.

"And then there were two," I say to Tanner, looking at the three empty seats across from us. "What just happened?"

"I'm thinking Ivy was supposed to show and didn't...Joe and Harper, um, your guess is as good as mine...and Isabella wants to Facetime with Hunter."

"You think Ramona said something to Ivy?"

"Yep," says Tanner, pouring the rest of the beer into our glasses. "She said she would."

I play with my opal ring, as I often do when the topic of Ramona comes up.

"I just wish she'd leave us all alone," he says. "I don't know how to escape her."

"Only three more weeks. Then the season's over and she'll be gone."

He looks at me, tilting his head to the side. "About that..."

"About what?"

"The season ending," he says. "Can we open a conversation about the possibility of you staying?"
"In Skagway?"

He nods. "With me."

"It's not that I haven't thought about it," I tell him honestly. "But I have no idea how to make it happen. Mimi's settled in Yakima."

"Right." Tanner reaches for my hand, threading his fingers through mine. "Remember when I went to Haines last weekend?"

"While I was having the best massage ever?"

He chuckles. "Yeah."

"Thanks, again, for that."

"My pleasure," he says, squeezing my hand. "So, the reason I went to Haines was because Gran told me about a place called St. Anne's. It's an Assisted Living and Memory Care center in Haines, a subsidiary of the Haines Assisted Living Center."

A lump rises in my throat because this man...this sweet, incredible man never stops trying to make my life better, more comfortable, happier.

"There's a waiting list, but they're pretty sure a room will open up before Christmas, which means..."

"I could move Mimi to Haines," I murmur, astounded by this news, by what it could mean for me and Mimi. She'd only be forty-five minutes from Skagway; a quick ferry ride or even quicker puddle jumper flight.

"Something to think about," he says.

"Last week, after her fall, I started thinking that I needed to be closer to her," I tell him. "When she first started going downhill, I prioritized her care over us living close, but I'm missing out on time with her. And we're running out."

"Maybe you don't have to choose," he says. "If she lived in Haines, and you lived with me—"

"Tanner."

"What?"

"Think about what you're saying."

"I don't need to. I know exactly what I'm saying."

"You're asking me to move in with you?" I confirm.

"Kenna," he says, "I love you, and this is what it means: whatever I have is yours. My home. My life. My heart. It's all yours. Whatever part of it you want or need, it's yours." He scans my face before adding, "Of course I want you to move in with me. I can't think of anything worse than you leaving Alaska."

I gulp over that lump in my throat, but tears still spring into my eyes.

"I don't deserve you."

"I'm yours all the same," he says. "And yes, you do. You deserve every good thing life can offer, and if that includes me, I'm all yours, baby."

I squeeze his hand, then lift it to my lips to kiss him.

"Let's go home?" I suggest, my need for him inside of me sudden and blinding.

A fire ignites behind his eyes. "Let's go."

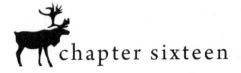

chapter sixteen

Tanner

A blissful week passes in a blur of sex and sleep, of flirting and talking and happiness.

And yes, the end of the season is rapidly approaching now, but it doesn't loom over my life as it used to. Little by little, brick by brick, we're building a path toward a future together.

McKenna joined me in Haines on her day off to visit St. Anne's, and she felt strongly it could work for Mimi. Right now, we think that McKenna will probably go back to Seattle and teach for the fall semester, but she plans to give her notice in November and move up here with Mimi by Christmas. There's still a lot of planning and work ahead of us but knowing that she wants to be with me—that building a life together is a goal for both of us—means everything to me.

August is our second busiest month of the year in Skagway, and the cabins are filled every day with tourists, adventurers, family reunions, retreats, honeymooners, and random travelers passing through Skagway. We've had a boon summer for animal sightings, and yes, there's been a typical amount of Alaskan rain, but all in all, we'll make a tidy profit which will see us all comfortably into next year.

I'm feeling satisfied as I help Gran and Reeve with chores on a Friday afternoon. We put away the groceries, move a huge load of bleached-white towels into the dryer, sweep the cabin floors, set a campfire for tonight's activities and update cabin availability on our website.

As I'm working on the computer terminal in the kitchen, my mouth watering from the smell of bread baking for tonight's dinner, I notice an alert in the corner of the screen; there's a red bubble on the icon named TRAIL/CAMERA.

Huh! I'd all but forgotten about installing the two little cameras on my cabin, and I certainly didn't expect to see activity so soon, but something must have triggered them. Excited to see what I'm dealing with, I click on the icon, which tells me it's loading up the photos.

A second later, the first photo appears.

I blink at the screen in surprise and horror as my blood runs cold.

Clicking on the mouse, the next picture loads.

Click. Another.

Click. Another.

Holy shit. I can't believe what I'm seeing.

Is this a joke? Is this for real?

I look around for someone to tell me I'm not going crazy, but I'm alone in the kitchen. My father, Hunter, Harper, Parker, Sawyer, and PawPaw are all out on tours or errands, but I've got to get a second pair of eyes on this. I pick up the walkie-talkie next to me.

"Reeve. Reeve, come in."

"I'm folding towels. What do you need?"

"Come to the kitchen. Please."

"Why? I'm busy."

"Reeve, PLEASE! Come to the kitchen now."

"Fine!"

Two minutes later, I hear the front door slam, and ten seconds later, Reeve is stalking through the kitchen.

"Gran wants the towels folded by three, Tanner! What do you—"

"Come here," I say, jumping up from the chair. "Sit down and look at this."

She gives me a look. "Is it gross?"

"It's fucking troubling."

She eases into the seat, staring at the screen. I use the mouse to click back to the first picture.

"What do you see?"

She squints, leaning closer to the screen. "What's this? A night vision camera?"

"I put two on my cabin last week."

"Is that..." She looks up at me, her face stricken. "Is that Ramona?"

I clench my teeth together and gulp. "I think so."

In the first picture, Ramona, dressed in dark leggings, a dark top, and her hair in a bun with a dark cap on her head, rounds the corner of my cabin.

Reeve moves her hand to the mouse and clicks.

In the next picture, Ramona is doing something to the

252

hot tub. Hard to know exactly what she's doing since the quality is so grainy, but it's clear she's lifted the corner of the cover. Is she putting something in it?

Reeve clicks again.

The next photo shows Ramona's feet on the stair railing; it looks like she's climbing up onto the roof.

Reeve clicks again.

The next photo shows her crawling on my roof toward the skylight.

My little sister looks up at me. "This is seriously fucked up, Tanner."

"I know," I say, fisting my hands by my sides.

"And beyond creepy."

"Yeah."

Reeve clicks again to see Ramona lying on my roof and cupping her hands around her eyes as she looks through the skylight at my bedroom below.

"Holy shit."

"I know," I say, my breathing shallow and quick.

In the next picture, she appears to be using a small object to scratch at the skylight window.

And the final picture shows the top of her head as she lowers herself back to the railing below.

Reeve looks up at me, wide-eyed. "We have to go check your hot tub!"

We race out of the lodge, my sister on my heels as we run to the back of my cabin. I tear the hot tub cover off to see a pigeon guillemot, probably dead for a little while, floating around on top.

"Ugh!"

"It's young," says Reeve, grabbing the skimmer.

My mind goes to gruesome places. Did Ramona kill it? Or did she go foraging on the beach for something dead and disgusting to put in my hot tub?

"Makes you rethink the hare, huh?" asks Reeve, plopping the guillemot's body on the ground.

The Arctic hare we found weeks ago! That could have been Ramona too. My stomach flips over and my lunch threatens to come up.

"This is so fucked."

"You gotta go talk to Joe, Tanner. This is scary."

"Trespassing," I say. "Destruction of property."

"Stalking," adds Reeve.

"Jesus," I mutter.

"I'll tell Gran it was an emergency," says Reeve, pulling the plug on the hot tub to let the water out. "Save those photos and take them to Joe."

"Thanks, Reeve. That's exactly what I'm gonna do."

***

An hour later, Joe's printed out the photos from the cameras and put the memory stick in an evidence bag. I took pictures of the damaged skylight and of the dead Guillemot, too, which I email to Joe.

He puts on his sheriff's hat. "I'm going over to the Krazy Kone. I need to bring her in for questioning. Stay here."

"Joe!" I say, as he leaves the station house. "What happens after that?"

"Stalking's a felony. The rest are misdemeanors."

"What are we talking? Fines? Jail time?"

"Yeah. I mean, this is serious stuff, Tanner. You've got her on trespassing and stalking, but also criminal mischief for the damage to your skylight, and—if she took pictures of you and McKenna—voyeurism. Plus, there's a possible animal cruelty charge in there if she killed the hare or the guillemot. All together? That's one to five, one more, one to five, another...best guess if she's convicted for everything? Three to twelve years behind bars and up to fifty thousand dollars in fines. She's in deep shit. Deep, deep, deep shit."

I nod solemnly as Joe heads out to find Ramona, disbelief and disgust giving way to relief.

"It's finally over," I whisper.

Except, as soon as the words leave my lips, I realize they're not true.

Ramona won't be remanded to custody following her chat with Joe today. There'll be an investigation and charges filed. She'll get a lawyer. I'll need a lawyer. She'll be arraigned and let out on bail. Then what? How long before she gets a trial? How long after that until she's sentenced?

This could go on for years.

I take out my phone.

Tanner:

I need to talk to you. Any chance you could meet me at

the police
station?

***

<u>McKenna</u>:
Police
station! Are you
okay?   Did
something
happen?

***

<u>Tanner</u>:
I'm   okay,
but   yes,
something
happened.
Remember
the cameras
I installed?
They picked
up Ramona
putting
dead
animals   in
the hot tub
and   using
something
to   scratch
the skylight.
She's been

**watching
us.**

***

<u>McKenna</u>:

...

...

**That is so
fucking warped
and gross.**

***

<u>Tanner</u>:

**I know. I'm
so sorry,
baby. Joe's
bringing her
in for
questioning
. Can you
come here?**

***

<u>McKenna</u>:

**Give me two
minutes.**

I know that Ramona should be held accountable for her actions, but at the same time, I just want to get on with my life.

If I thought she'd leave Alaska and never come back again? That'd be enough for me.

I just don't know if it'd be enough for McKenna. If she

wants Ramona charged, then we'll take this all the way. I just need to know how she feels.

"Tanner?"

I leap up from the guest chair in front of Joe's desk and meet McKenna in the waiting area near Vera's desk. We sit down side by side, and she looks up at me with worried, furious eyes.

"Are you fucking kidding me with this?"

"Unfortunately, no. Reeve and Joe looked at the pictures, too. It's definitely Ramona. She put a dead bird in the hot tub two nights ago; probably left the hare, too. She's been scratching marks in my skylight, too. And…" I wince. "And watching us."

"I am so skeeved out."

"Yeah."

"And angry! What right does she have to invade our privacy like that?"

"None."

The door to the police station swings open, and Joe enters dragging a handcuffed Ramona behind him.

"Ms. De Alicante didn't want to come peacefully," he explains, pulling her toward the back of the police station where I know there are four small holding cells. "Vera! Give me a hand, please."

"FUCK YOU ALL!" Ramona screams, staring daggers at me and McKenna when she notices us. She stumbles as Joe pulls her forward but rights herself before falling. "I'm not a fucking criminal! I will not go in that fucking cell."

"Yes, ma'am, you will," says Joe, his voice firm. "You

need to calm down a spell before we talk."

Vera follows behind them, unlocking the cell door. Joe gently nudges Ramona inside. As soon as the door slams shut and Vera locks it, Ramona collapses to the floor in tears. She wails and sobs, curling up in the fetal position, unresponsive when Joe says her name.

"Keep an eye on her," he tells Vera, then gestures to us. "Let's give her a minute. Come and wait in my office."

We sit down in front of Joe's desk, and he takes a seat facing us. "I'm going to need statements from both of you. Who saw the hare in the hot tub? Was that Hunter? Maybe we can get him in here later—"

"Joe," I say, leaning forward. "Can I ask you a question?"

"Sure. Anything."

"You said stalking's a felony, right?"

"Yes, sir."

"What's the statute of limitations on pressing charges?"

"Ten years."

"Okay. We have ten years. And on the rest of the stuff?"

"Voyeurism, criminal mischief, and trespassing can all be charged up to five years after the fact. And the animal cruelty stuff? We'd have to launch an investigation into whether she killed them or found them, but they could be a problem for her, too. Alaska takes that stuff very seriously."

"Okay. So, even if we decided not to press charges now, we still could press charges, at any time, up to five years for most of it, and up to ten years for the stalking?"

"Correct."

"Tanner," says McKenna, laying her hand on my arm.

"You aren't thinking about letting her go without pressing charges? This is serious. She's dangerous."

"I know. But Alaska, by design, is safe," I tell her. "It's hard to get here. It's expensive. What if she knew that the second she stepped foot in Skagway again, she'd be charged with enough shit to land her in prison for over a decade? I mean, would *you* come back? Or would you just go home and get on with your life?"

"We're not dealing with someone rational," says McKenna.

"I know that. But statements and depositions and lawyers and trials? Oh, my God, she'll be getting exactly what she wanted: attention from me. I mean, if anything, she'll become more obsessed. But if I don't even care enough to press charges?"

McKenna looks uncertain. She shifts her gaze to Joe. "What do you think?"

"I can see both sides," says Joe. "On one hand, Tanner's probably right. A trial gives her an audience. A platform. She'll be photographed. She'll get attention. Weirdos will come out of the woodwork to take her side as the 'jilted girlfriend.' It's possible she'd enjoy it all and even ramp up her bad behavior." He sighs. "But at the same time, it's a gamble letting her go. Yes, you can still press charges after the fact, but your case will be weaker. And there's always the possibility that she'll escalate on her own if she isn't held accountable."

"I honestly believe," I say, choosing my words carefully, "if we give her the chance to leave and never come back, she'll take it. And I think if she knows that we'll press charges to the max if we ever see her in Skagway again, she'll never return."

"What do you base that on?" asks McKenna.

"The fact that she never once reached out, visited, or contacted me from last September until May. She didn't text me, or send a Christmas card, or friend me on Facebook. I didn't hear a peep from her. I think she got back here thinking we might pick up where we left off last summer, and when she realized McKenna was in the picture, she got mad and lashed out." I shift in my chair to look at my love. "If you want me to press charges, baby, I will. In a second. I'll do it. But I feel like—if she understands that coming back will mean a world of shit for her—she'll go home and leave us alone."

"If we go that route, I want her phone and laptop destroyed. And anywhere else she might have saved pictures of us."

"Done," I say. "We'll make sure."

"And I want for her to understand that this is a *one-time offer*. If she ever shows her face in Skagway again—for any reason—she's going down."

"Agreed," I say. "Joe, what do you think?"

"I'm more than happy to let her know what's waiting for her if she returns," he says. "I'll scare the pants off of her."

"For your sake," I say, "I hope she keeps them on."

Joe chuckles, then nods at us. "Okay. So, we're in agreement? No charges pressed if she gives up her electronics, leaves today, and never comes back?"

McKenna takes a deep breath and lets it go slowly. "I hope we're not making a mistake."

"I don't think we are," I tell her, taking her hand in mine.

"I just want to get on with our lives. I don't want to get bogged down in court cases and lawyers and trials for the foreseeable future."

"Okay," says McKenna, squeezing my hand and nodding in agreement. "Let's do it."

***

McKenna

I wasn't there when Tanner and Joe talked to Ramona, but I heard that after an hour in a jail cell, she broke down completely, crying about how hurt she was about Tanner getting engaged and how she just wanted to scare me out of Alaska with the dead animals in the hot tub.

"I thought I could make her hate it here and leave," she'd wailed.

As for the skylight?

When she'd realized how much it bothered Tanner to have his car keyed, she wanted to "key" something else.

"So she admitted to keying my car in front of Joe," said Tanner. "The skylight was an encore performance."

Joe had laid out the charges for her, and Tanner told me that she'd started hyperventilating when he added up the prison time and fines.

"I can't—I can't go to *jail!*" she'd screamed. "And I don't have fifty thousand dollars! Where am I supposed to get that? I'm sorry. I'm so sorry! I promise I'll stop! I'll pay for the skylight. I'll pay for the car door. I'll never go to the campground again. I'm sorry, Tanner! Please don't do this!" Finally, Joe had explained that if she left the state of Alaska and never set foot in Skagway again, Tanner and I were willing to give her a one-time pass. She'd cried grateful tears, sobbing that once she left, she never *wanted* to come back to Alaska again.

"I hate it here!" she'd cried. "I only came back for Tanner, and he didn't want me anyway."

Joe had accompanied her back to her apartment, watched her pack, taken her electronics, and driven her to the airport. He didn't return to the police station until her plane was safely in the air.

"And you really think it's over?" I ask Tanner as we sit in Adirondack chairs with his siblings by the dying campfire.

"I do," he says. "I really think she's gone for good. She doesn't want to go to jail. You should have seen her face. She was terrified. I genuinely believe she was sorry, too. She just wanted to hurt me for hurting her and took it too far."

"You let her off too easy," says Harper. "I would've pressed charges."

"Yeah, I agree. She should have been held accountable for what she did," says Sawyer, checking his phone, then pocketing it quickly with a frown. "But on the other hand, I'm glad she's gone."

"Heard from Ivy yet?" Tanner asks him.

"No. But I sent her a text asking how she's doing. I'm sure it was weird to go home after her shift at work and realize her roommate was gone."

"I bet she writes back soon," I tell him. "I hope so."

"Me too. Night, guys," he says, getting up from his chair and heading to bed.

"You okay?" Hunter asks me. "That was some pretty weird stuff, her watching you guys and putting dead animals in the hot tub. I mean, '*Fatal Attraction*'-style dead bunny stuff. Literally."

"Yeah. I'm still pretty creeped out," I tell him, "but Joe's keeping her laptop and phone as evidence. She never posted pics of us anywhere that we could find. I'm not even sure she took any. She said she was only on the roof to scratch the glass."

"Psycho," mutters Parker. "Glad she's gone."

"Amen, sister," says Reeve, who's sitting on Parker's lap.

"Bedtime for you," says Parker. "Or Gran's wrath."

Parker walks Reeve back over to the lodge and then heads to her own cabin, leaving me, Tanner, Hunter, and Harper alone at the campfire.

"What's next for you two?" asks Harper.

Tanner takes my hand. "We've been talking about McKenna moving up here permanently sometime this fall. There's a care center in Haines that may be able to take her grandmother in November or December."

"Are you serious?" asks Hunter, momentarily distracted from his phone. "That's awesome news!"

"Not a word to Iz," I tell him. "I haven't talked to her about it yet."

"Mum's the word," he promises.

"I'm happy for you guys," says Harper, her voice soft, her eyes staring blankly into the glowing orange embers.

"How're things going for you, Harp?" asks Tanner. "You and Joe had an intense moment at the Parsnip last week.

264

Everything okay?"

She looks up at her brother, tries to smile, fails, then looks back at the fire.

"Leave it," she whispers.

The four of us sit in companionable silence as the fire dies, and finally, when stars fill the sky, and Tanner and I are the only ones left, he takes my hand and leads me home.

***

Buzz.

Buzz, buzz.

Buzz, buzz.

For a second, I can't figure out if the buzzing of my phone is part of a dream I'm having or my actual phone buzzing on the bedside table.

It's not dark, but it's not quite light out yet, which means it's around four or five o'clock in the morning.

I reach for my phone, which vibrates in my hand, connecting me to the reality of the moment. My eyes fly open, and I sit bolt upright in bed.

"Hello?"

"Ms. Cabot?"

"Speaking."

"This is Leroy Huggins, the night nurse at Memory Quest Care Center."

"Yes." My hands start to shake.

"I'm sorry to tell you that your grandmother had another fall tonight."

"How bad? Is she, um, is she…?"

"She's alive but unconscious. She's been taken to Yakima

Memorial by ambulance."

I whip the covers off, ignoring Tanner, who grunts in his sleep and rolls onto his back.

"How bad is it, Mr. Huggins? I need you to be honest with me. I'm in Alaska. I need to know if I should come down."

"I haven't had an update from the hospital yet."

"How bad?" I ask through gritted teeth.

"Bad, Ms. Cabot. It was a very serious fall."

"If you were me—"

"I'd get on the first plane to Yakima."

His words knock the wind from my lungs. *I can't breathe. I c-can't breathe.*

"McKenna? Kenna? Are you okay?"

Why does Tanner sound like he's underwater? I feel him pry my phone from my fingers as I sink to the floor.

"Hello? Yes, this is her boyfriend. Yes. I see. Okay. Yep. Yep. There's a flight at six a.m. I'll make sure she's on it." Cradling the phone against his ear, he sits down on the floor next to me and pulls me onto his lap. "Thank you. Any updates, please call. I see. Okay. We'll contact the hospital. Yep. Thank you, again."

He ends the call, puts the phone on the bed, and rubs my back. I finally draw a deep breath and let it out with a wail.

"*Mimi…*"

Tanner holds me tight.

"Kenna, listen to me. We'll get on the six a.m. flight to Juneau. From there, we can go to Seattle and rent a car or get a flight directly to Yakima. Either way, I'll get you there by this afternoon. I promise, baby."

I backhand my eyes with the sleeve of my sweatshirt and take another deep breath. *Focus, McKenna. Focus. You can cry later.*

"F-first f-flight's at six?" I ask.

"Yep. And we'll be on it."

"We?" I ask.

"I'm not letting you go alone."

"You're going to l-lose your job."

"Side benefit of working with family," he tells me, gently swiping a tear away with the raspy pad of his thumb. "They can't fire me, baby."

"He s-said it was b-bad," I manage to say between sobs and hiccups. "The n-nurse."

"I know."

"What if..." I can barely speak because I'm snotty and sobby and getting to that point where I can't suck in a deep breath. "What if I'm t-t-too late?"

"You won't be," he tells me, cupping my cheeks gently and staring into my eyes with determination. "You get dressed. I'll pack us a bag."

"What would I do without you?" I ask.

"Not a question you'll ever need to answer, baby." He kisses my forehead. "Now, let's get moving."

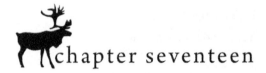

chapter seventeen

Tanner

We get to the hospital in Yakima a little after two-thirty and beeline for the information desk, where we ask about Mimi, whose full name is Madeleine McKenna.

"Mrs. McKenna was admitted a little after five a.m. this morning," the receptionist tells us. "And it looks like she's in CCU, which is our Critical Care Unit." She looks up from her computer. "Are you family?"

"I'm her granddaughter," says McKenna, "and her guardian."

"I see," says the receptionist. "Well, visiting hours go until eight p.m., so you have plenty of time. She's allowed to have two visitors at a time. Did you both want...?"

"Yes, please. Two passes," says McKenna.

"Of course. I'll just need your IDs."

A few minutes later, we're headed upstairs to the CCU, McKenna's cold, clammy hand ensconced in mine. She's been relatively calm during our travels today—from Skagway to Juneau, from Juneau to Seattle, from Seattle to Yakima—but once we hit the ground in Yakima, I felt her nerves and fears start to get the better of her. She ignores the tears that keep sliding down her cheeks, wiping them away as she moves forward, step by step, toward Mimi's bedside.

We were able to talk to Mimi's doctor from the Seattle Airport and know that she went wandering last night and ended up slipping on a recently-mopped back staircase. She wasn't found for at least an hour when the night nurse noted that she wasn't in bed during a standard, hourly bed check.

The care center's theory is that the nurse doing the three a.m. bed check inadvertently woke Mimi up when she closed her bedroom door. Mimi woke up confused and wandered to the stairway door near her room, which hadn't been latched. They believe she slipped and fell down the stairs soon after three o'clock and wasn't discovered missing until the four o'clock bed check. Care center staff found her a little before four-thirty and called the ambulance, which took her directly to the hospital.

What I've realized—though I'm not sure McKenna has—is that no one has given us an actual account of Mimi's injuries or current status. So I'm not surprised when we're intercepted upon entering the Critical Care Unit. But my heart sinks. Because when a doctor wants to speak to you one-on-one before your patient visit, it's not generally a good thing.

"Are you Ms. Cabot?" asks a young doctor in a white lab coat. "Mrs. McKenna's granddaughter?"

"Yes. Are you Dr. Singh?"

"I am." She nods. "I'd like to update you if that's okay. Can you come and sit with me for a moment? Then I'll take you to your grandmother."

I squeeze McKenna's hand as we follow Dr. Singh to a family waiting area furnished with vinyl loveseats and a flatscreen TV playing a cooking show.

Dr. Singh leans forward, her face grave, her hands clasped together. "I left out some details when we spoke over the phone."

McKenna gulps softly. "What details?"

"Your grandmother suffered a very severe TBI—that's a traumatic brain injury—when she fell. She didn't receive treatment for at least ninety minutes after the accident. By the time she arrived here at Yakima Memorial, she was—for all intents and purposes—gone."

"She's...*dead?*" murmurs McKenna, swaying beside me.

"No. She's on life support."

"So, she might be okay?"

Dr. Singh looks sorry. "No. She won't be okay, Ms. Cabot."

"I'm sorry. I can't..." McKenna blinks rapidly. "What—What are you saying?"

"When your grandmother arrived, her heartbeat was thready and slow, and it was a matter of hours, if not minutes, until she passed away. But when I heard from Mr. Huggins that you'd already left Alaska for Yakima, I made the call to place her on life support. I wanted you to have the chance to say goodbye." Dr. Singh clears her throat. "To be clear, her brain shows no activity...and when she's unhooked from the machines, I expect the rest of her organs to fail quickly. But saying goodbye is..." Dr. Singh pauses, and I sense that she has experienced this sort of loss personally. She seems to understand, on a deeper level, the value of saying farewell to a loved one. "It's important. I believe that. And I wanted you to have the chance to see her, to speak to her, to say goodbye."

"I just—so, heart's still beating?"

"For now."

"But her brain is...dead."

"Yes." Dr. Singh grimaces. She has more to say. "Er— Ms. Cabot...in the interest of full disclosure, I need to tell you that your grandmother signed a DNR several years ago. Technically, I shouldn't have made the call to keep her alive, but—"

"Thank you," McKenna whispers urgently, leaning forward to cup her hands over Dr. Singh's. "Thank you for giving this to me. I'm so grateful, Dr. Singh."

The doctor takes a deep breath and sighs. I think I see relief behind her eyes. She made the right call. McKenna releases the doctor's hands and leans back into me.

"How long do I have?" she asks.

"Today," the doctor answers. "We'll unhook the machines tonight."

McKenna nods, reaching up to swipe at tears. "There's nothing else you can do?"

"I'm sorry, no. But Ms. Cabot, your grandmother doesn't feel any pain," says Dr. Singh, her voice gentle.

"W-was..." McKenna sobs, then takes a deep, shuddering breath. "Was she in p-pain? Do you th-think?"

"I don't," says Dr. Singh. "I think she went wandering, walked through a door, slipped, fell, hit her head, and then…nothing."

"Nothing?"

"No more pain. No more loneliness. No more confusion."

I put my arm around McKenna, drawing her close to my side. "You okay, baby?"

"May I be blunt?" asks Dr. Singh.

"Please," whispers McKenna.

"For a patient with late-stage dementia, this sort of quick ending can be a blessing both for the patient and their loved ones. I am so sorry for your loss, Ms. Cabot, but I am not sorry for her. I am relieved for her."

"I understand," says McKenna, wiping her tears and lifting her chin. "Can I see her now?"

"Of course," says Dr. Singh, standing up. "And again, I'm very sorry for your loss."

When we stand up, McKenna sways again, and I realize that she hasn't really eaten anything today. I put my arm around her waist and guide her back down to the couch.

"Dr. Singh," I say, "can you get us some juice? And some crackers, maybe?" I turn to McKenna. "You have to eat something."

Dr. Singh leaves the room, saying she'll be back in a second with provisions.

"I'm not hungry."

"You may not feel hungry, baby, but your body is starving. Eat and drink something. Then we'll go see Mimi."

She inhales sharply, looking up at me with red, watery eyes. "She's dead, Tanner. Mimi's dead."

"Hey, hey, hey," I say, taking her hands in mine. "Her heart's still beating for a little longer. And that's a heart that loved you your whole life. Talk to her heart. Tell her heart how much you loved her, how grateful you were for her, how much you'll miss her. I promise she'll hear you, McKenna. I know it. I promise."

"You c-can't promise that, T-Tanner."

"I can, because I know *my* mother heard *me*," I say, remembering the day Gran and Dad drove us up to Whitehorse General to say goodbye to my mother.

She lay still and quiet on white sheets, a tube in her mouth, her head bandaged, and a monitor over her bed pulsing in regular beeps. "My dad took us up to say goodbye. Me, Hunter, and Harper. And I can't tell you how I know, but I do. She heard me. She knew I loved her. She knew I would miss her. She knew she was a good mother. Saying goodbye matters, Kenna. For her and for you."

McKenna leans her head on my shoulder and cries in deep, heavy sobs, her sadness an alive thing, her grief too overwhelming for words. Her tears well forth from the broken, abandoned little girl inside of her, from the confused teenager she became, and from the profoundly scarred adult she is.

I rub her back and tell her I love her and promise I'll be here for her, now and after, always and forever.

Dr. Singh opens the waiting room door and discreetly places a bottle of orange juice and a plate of graham crackers on the opposite loveseat, then leaves quietly.

McKenna cries for a long, long time.

And then, when she's ready, we go to Mimi's bedside, and she says goodbye.

***

McKenna

Dr. Singh and Tanner were right—I feel certain that Mimi heard me say goodbye, and the gratitude I feel for that space and time with her will never fade away.

I spoke to her heart, thanking her for loving me when no one else did. I thanked her for taking me in and making sure I always felt loved. I said I was sorry for the two years we lost after my college graduation. I said I wished we'd had more time together, but that I would cherish every moment we'd had. And I told her she was the best grandmother and mother I ever could have had and that the love I had for her would last until my final breath. I would remember her lessons and example in my own life and honor who she was with who I am and will become.

I held her hand when they removed the tube from her throat and unplugged the breathing machine. My ears listened for one last heartbeat, and my eyes filled with tears when the drone of the monitor told me that I'd already heard it.

I kissed her bruised and wrinkled cheek, holding her soft palm against my cheek one final time, and then I let Tanner lead me away from her room to a future that held her memory instead of her presence.

We arranged for Mimi's body to be transported to Seattle, then took an Uber to Isabella's condo since my place was still being sublet. Tanner and I fell into the made-up futon in Isabella's home office and slept for hours, still dressed, in each other's arms.

And when I woke up ten hours later? My eyes were sore and tired from crying, but my heart was surprisingly full. For a girl who felt unloved for so much of her life, I felt surrounded by love. From Mimi's spirit. From Isabella's friendship. And from Tanner's strong and steadfast love.

And that's when I knew.

That's when I knew—for sure and forever—that I loved him, too.

"You're awake," he says, putting his phone on Isabella's desk and kissing my forehead. "How're you feeling?"

"Tired. No. Exhausted."

"I know," he says softly. "Hungry?"

"Yeah," I say, surprised to discover my appetite's already back. "I think I am."

"Isabella's working at a summer camp this week," he tells me, "but she said she left a box of your favorite donuts in the kitchen."

"Raised Donuts," I say with an appropriate amount of reverence. "They're amazing."

"You want coffee, too? I can make a fresh pot."

He swings his legs over the side of the futon to go and get us food, but I place my hand on his back to stop him.

"Tanner. Wait."

He looks at me over his shoulder. "You okay?"

I nod, gulping over the sudden lump in my throat. "I need to say something."

Turning to face me, he takes my hand. "What's up?"

Say it. Go ahead and say it. It'll be okay. Mimi's voice in my head is loving and sure, a reminder that she'll always be with me and the encouragement I need to say the words on the tip of my tongue.

"I love you," I whisper. I look him in the eyes, clear my throat, and say it again, louder and stronger this time: "I love you so much, Tanner Stewart."

His smile is small at first, like he can't believe what I just said.

"Say it again."

"I love you," I say, the words easier the third time.

"Again."

"I love you, I love you, I love you," I say, waiting for lightning to strike me dead and delighted when it doesn't. "I'm in love with you, Tanner."

He whoops and chuckles, lying back down and pulling me on top of him. He pillows his arms behind his head and grins up at me. "You love me?"

"I do," I say, leaning down to kiss him. "I love you."

"I love you, too," he says.

"I know," I say, leaning my elbows gently on his chest. "When did you know?"

"This morning, when I opened my eyes, it was the first thing I thought." I kiss him again, marveling that this beautiful, kind, smart man is all mine. "You welcomed me into your family, into your life. You took care of me and protected me. You stuck around, even when I pushed you away. You brought Iz to Skagway and found a care home for Mimi in Haines. And you came with me to Washington. You dropped everything to be here with me."

"That's what you do when you love someone," he says. "All of that."

"You *are* love," I tell him. "You *live* love. Every day."

"Speaking of every day," he says, "what do you need from me *today*?"

"Donuts," I say. "And coffee."

"Done."

"And help with arrangements for Mimi."

"I'm here, Kenna. Whatever you need."

"I need *you*," I tell him, leaning down to press my lips to his, and it turns out I left something off the list of what I needed.

I need his touch and his taste and the solid, sure strength of his body covering mine, moving inside of mine, and bringing mine to that sacred place where two become one, where Tanner and McKenna blur into we, into us, into love, into always, into forever.

***

Four days later, the morning of Mimi's funeral is bright and sunny, the sky a striking cerulean blue and the sun bright and warm behind fluffy white clouds.

I choose to believe this is because Mimi is happy now. She's not in pain. She's no longer confused. She's finally at peace.

It's a small graveside service with a few of Mimi's friends from her old neighborhood, her cousin from Portland, another cousin from Tacoma, her primary caregiver from Memory Quest, Dr. Singh, Isabella and her mother, Tanner and me. It doesn't surprise me that Sheila doesn't show up, and frankly, I'm relieved she doesn't. I don't know how I would have handled seeing my biological mother today, on the day I lay to rest my *real* mother.

We gather at a nearby café after the service, where Tanner and Isabella have arranged to have coffee and pastries served in a small private room that overlooks the harbor. It's a small, warm event, with Mimi's friends and cousins telling stories as I sit flanked by Isabella and Tanner, surrounded by love, held upright by its strength and promise.

Afterward, Isabella and I drive Tanner to SeaTac for his flight back to Skagway. We say goodbye on the curb outside of Alaska Airlines departures.

"I'll see you soon?" he asks.

"I'll let you know when. I need to let my landlord know I'm not renewing my lease. Memory Quest sent two boxes of Mimi's things to Isabella's apartment, and I need to go through them. I want to stop by the college and give them my two weeks' notice in person. And I need to get my things out of storage and pack them up."

"And your car?"

"Sell it, I guess. I don't know yet. I haven't gotten that far." He's trying to look confident, but I see the worry behind his eyes, like he's afraid that the moment he leaves for Alaska I'll fall in love with Seattle and decide to stay here instead. "Tanner. I love you. You're my future."

"I know," he says. "The only life I want is the one that includes you, Kenna."

"Me too," I tell him. "So trust me when I say I'll be back

in Skagway in two weeks or less. And when I get there, I'm staying. For good."

"Little but fierce," he says, his face relaxing as he leans down to kiss me. "That was the first thing I thought when I saw you. Turned out to be true."

"You had no idea what you were in for."

"I wouldn't change a day," he says. "Even that week in the middle that sucked so bad. I still wouldn't trade it if it brought us here."

"Agree," I say, looping my arms around his neck. We kiss for a long time before I finally let him go. "Travel safe. And text me when you get there."

"I will," he says, pulling away from me but turning around just before he goes through the revolving door to mouth, *I love you*, one more time.

***

Two weeks later to the day, I follow his steps through the revolving door at SeaTac Departures, ready to start my life—*for real, this time*—in Skagway.

It's Labor Day Weekend, and people are traveling in droves, one last hurrah as the fall breathes cool air down the neck of summer. With my affairs in Seattle settled, and after a few nights at Isabella's and my favorite Whidbey Island B&B, I'm rested and relaxed, and ready for life's next adventure.

As I take my window seat, bound for Juneau, I think about a conversation I had with my best friend three days ago, sitting by the inn's pool, soaking up the last of the summer sun.

"So, you finally said the words," Isabella had said,

grinning at me. "Harder or easier than you thought?"

"Neither," I'd said. "Just...necessary. It was like I couldn't help myself."

"So...*easier.*"

"Compulsory. I couldn't have stopped myself if I tried."

She was quiet for a few minutes, then said, "I like the Stewarts."

"Yeah," I'd said, nudging her arm playfully. "I know."

"I just mean that they're good people."

"Absolutely. I agree—"

"But Hunter and I are cooling it."

Wait. What? How did I miss that?

"Huh. Did something happen? You seemed pretty into each other."

"I don't *do* long distance," she'd said, adjusting her sun hat so her cheeks wouldn't burn. "I'm a fourth generation Seattleite."

"Yeah, I know. But—"

"No buts."

Whoa. Okay.

"So...that's it?"

"I told him we could be friends. I mean, you're probably going to marry Tanner and have half a dozen little Alaskans running around Skagway a year from now. You better believe Tia Isa's going to be in the picture."

"So...you left the door open? For someday?"

"No! No doors. No openings. I don't *do* long distance, Ken," she repeated, her tone getting testy.

Eeek. Okay.

"Gotcha."

"So don't, like, say hi to him from me or anything."

"Should I let you know if he finds someone else?"

She had taken a deep breath and huffed softly. "Shut up, Ken."

Ah-ha! The door may not be *open*, per se, but it wasn't locked and bolted either. Isabella only got touchy about stuff when it was unresolved and still bothered her.

"I feel your big brain whirring next to me, girl. Stop trying to psychoanalyze me, McKenna Diana Cabot."

Stop being an idiot, Isabella Maria Gonzalez, I'd thought to myself, but I'd left it alone.

I'm not looking forward to seeing Hunter. I don't think I'm going to like mopey Hunter very much.

Once in Juneau, I text Tanner, letting him know that I should be in Skagway on time at 5:40pm.

Tanner:

Can't wait to see you. Travel safe, baby. ILY

***

McKenna:

ILY2

We're sappy as hell, but I don't care. This is the first and last time I'm ever falling in love with someone; I'm leaning into it, not away.

As my seaplane comes to a stop at the Skagway Airport, the butterflies triple in my tummy. I grab my bag and climb down the plane's stairs, my steps faster and faster until I'm running into the terminal and leaping into Tanner's waiting arms.

It's only been two weeks, but it felt like eternity. I wrap my legs around his waist, locking my ankles together as we kiss hello. We're making a scene in public, but I don't care, and neither, it seems, does Alaska. We get a thunderous applause from the good folks at Skagway Seaplanes, and when Tanner puts me down, our eyes dilated and cheeks pink, we take a little bow.

"You're here."

"I'm here," I say, grinning up at him.

"Thank God," he tells me, kissing the tip of my nose.

He grabs my bags, and I follow him out to the car. As he puts my suitcases in the truck, I open the door and start to get in the car, but he stops me.

"Hold on! We're not going yet," he says.

"What? We're not?"

He closes the trunk and holds out his hand. "Come with me."

"Where are we going?"

"You'll see!"

Threading his fingers through mine, he leads me away from the parking lot, toward the footbridge we crossed on the Fourth of July en route to the axe-throwing competition at Smuggler's Cove. At the time, I'd stopped our brisk walk to look for salmon, but we didn't have time to linger on the view of Yakutania Point and the mountains beyond. Today, not in a rush to be anywhere, we stop in the middle of the bridge. I stand at the railing, the wind in my face as chilly today as it was when I first arrived in May, and Tanner stands behind me, a buffer against the breeze, my bulwark from any storm.

"Welcome home," he says close to my ear.

"It's good to be back," I tell him, taking his hands from the railing and putting them around me. "It's good to be home."

"This is one of my favorite views," he says.

It's going to be one of mine too. I already know it.

"Remember when you got here in May?"

I turn around in his arms, smiling up at him. "I was just thinking about that! It's just as cool today as it was then."

He nods, grinning back at me. "The season's almost over. Fall's coming."

"Whoever thought that day would lead us here?"

"Speaking of then and now," he says, a twinkle in his eye. "Do you remember the first question you asked me after we said hello?"

I think for a second. "Um...I don't know. Something about it being weird? Our situation?"

"You mentioned that," he says, "yes. But your first question was: 'Got a ring for me?'"

"Right," I say, holding up my hand, which still bears the opal ring he gave me that day.

His face sobers and he swallows nervously. "Ask me again."

"Ask you..." My voice trails off as he takes something out of his pocket and bends down, kneeling on the bridge in front of me. I cup my hands over my mouth and gasp. "Tanner!"

"Ask me," he says again, smiling up at me, his eyes

shining bright with love.

I take a deep breath, blinking the tears from my eyes and blaming them on the wind and not on my feelings for this sweet man at my feet.

"Got a ring for me?" I whisper.

He opens the little black box in his hand, and inside, I find a ring identical to the one I'm wearing, except that instead of an opal in the middle, there's a brilliant diamond.

"I do," he says.

"Tanner."

"I love you, McKenna. I'm going to love you forever, no matter what. You're my person, my woman, my love. Will you be my wife, too?"

"Y-Yes," I murmur as he slips the ring on, pushing it up against the first one he ever gave me. "Yes, yes, yes, yes, yes!"

He stands up, pulling me into his arms and kissing me until I'm breathless.

"Let's go home," he suggests, a million promises for now and forever in his eyes.

My summer in Skagway is over, I think, holding his hand as we cross the bridge back toward his car. *But my life in Skagway has just begun.*

THE END

epilogue

Harper

I'm happy for my brother.

I am.

I promise.

It's been three weeks since he got engaged to McKenna, and honestly, they're the sweetest couple I've ever seen: burly, blonde Tanner and tiny, dark-haired McKenna. I'm sure their kids will be beautiful.

In fact, I'm positive.

Oh, my heart.

Positive, because I already know what a blonde Stewart and a dark-haired—

"Cheers!"

Hunter finishes his toast and everyone at the engagement party clinks their glasses together and whoops with glee for the happy couple. Reeve, sitting to my right and drinking sparkling cider by order of Gran, clinks her glass with mine and rolls her eyes. She wants champagne something fierce, but Gran won't have it; not until Reeve turns eighteen, which is still ten days from now.

Hunter steps down from the mic that Bruce has set-up for toasts, and Sawyer, sitting to my left, leaps up to give the next speech before I can stop him. Since Ivy Caswell went back to Fairbanks, Sawyer's been partying like it's his life's mission. Night after night, drink after drink, girl after girl. That'll stop soon. By October 10th, the cruise ships will be gone and the rest of the seasonal help with it. All that'll be left in the quiet off-season is the 1,200 souls that live in the borough of Skagway.

The locals.

"Harper!" cries Parker, who slides from her seat into the one Sawyer's just vacated. "He's drunk as a skunk! We should have stopped him."

"Tammer 'n Muh-kenn-ya...you guys are...so great," says Sawyer, clutching the mic like he'll fall over if he lets go. "An' it's so great that, um, ya' know...you live *here*. In Ssssakway. Because if one of you lived in Farawaybanks, it would be a bummer."

Sawyer starts laughing hysterically at his dumb joke, which prompts Hunter to get back up. He steps onto the little platform and puts his arm around Sawyer. The mic picks up his voice when he whispers, "Awesome job, l'il bro. That'll do it."

"I'm big," says Sawyer, frowning at Hunter.

"Yep. You are, but—"

"Don't silence my love, bro!" yells Sawyer into the mic, pointing a finger at Hunter and sloshing his beer onto the floor. "I love Tan, man." He chuckles, raising a fist in the air and pumping it. "Tanman, Tanman, Tanman!"

"Let's hear it for Tanman!" says Hunter into the mic, helping Sawyer off the platform. They stay over to the side, Sawyer leaning against Hunter, close to the bathroom just in case.

As the applause dies down, I know it's time for another Stewart sibling to step forward and say a few words. I feel the pressure of being the oldest girl, the one who looks the most like Tanner, the one who's closest to him in age.

"I think everyone's waiting for you," whispers Parker, nudging me.

"Go on, Harper," says Reeve. "Give a little toast!"

I'm not the showy type. I'm happiest on the trail. Or skiing a double black diamond. Fishing. Hunting. Anything but this. But then...Tanner, my first little brother, who's sitting at the table in front of mine, turns around. His blue eyes lock with mine. He half-smiles, then shrugs. And I don't have a choice anymore. *Okay. Okay. Okay.*

I stand up to the hoots and hollers of my sisters first, and then my brothers, and then everyone else in the room, who clap and yell my name in encouragement.

"Whoot! Harper!"

"Yeah, Harper!"

"Go Harp! Go Harp!"

I step up onto the little podium and take the mic from its holder, scanning the room.

I've been coming to the Purple Parsnip since I was a baby, and yet I can't ever remember a time that Bruce closed it for a private event as early as September. I appreciate it that he made an exception for my brother and his fiancée, former

Parsnip employee, McKenna, who now works for us.

"Hi, everyone," I say.

More whoops. More hollers.

I think I recognize every face in the place tonight...teachers from grade school through high school, coaches, business owners, lower-48 transplants, and seasonal workers.

"The mayor's here tonight," I note, waving hello to Sam.

"Hey, Harper!" he shouts. "About time one of you Stewarts tied the knot!"

The crowd loves this, of course. It's a cacophony in the room for a good thirty seconds of clinking glasses, guffawing, and revelry.

While everyone else goes nuts, I grin at Sam, then track the faces of the people at his table, which is populated by civil servants: Assemblymembers Ginny Roe and Harold Kluge, Borough Clerk Avery Wells and...*(shit)* Sheriff Joseph Raven.

My breath catches.

My cheeks flush.

My heart stutters.

I haven't seen Joe in a handful of days, which has been good for me. But maybe not for him.

His cheeks are cut from marble and his midnight-black hair is held back in a leather strap. His eyes are trained on mine, fierce and focused, but under them are deep, dark circles; because his skin is a lot darker than mine, they're easier to miss unless they're bad...which they are. I lift my gaze to his eyes, which are blacker than brown, stone cold like a brick wall in January. They give away nothing.

"I love you, Harp. I'll never love anyone but you."

The words slide through my brain; old and expired and taunting.

I blink my eyes and gulp softly, darting my glance to Tanner. Tanner, my brother. Tanner, who loves me.

"Hey, now! My little brother got engaged, everyone!" I say, lifting my champagne flute high. "How about some 'Cheers'?"

The crowd goes wild again and without meaning to, I slide my gaze back to Joe, who is surrounded by revelers, but stares at me steadily, like a marksman waiting for the perfect moment to pull the trigger.

Please don't hate me, I think. *I can't stand it.*

But there's no conversation between us—just his cold, steady stare. That, and my reaction to him, which, despite his obvious rage, is soft...is desperate...is full of the kind of longing that will eventually kill you.

I force myself to look away from him.

"Okay," I say. "Okay, now. Let's quiet down."

Tanner lifts his chin, grinning at me like a puppy who just earned a treat. It's so much easier to look at Tanner than Joe.

"Hey, Tan."

"Hey, Harp!" he says.

"I'm happy for you," I say. "I'm so damn happy for you!"

"Thanks, sis!"

I raise my eyes to the crowd, making a point not to look at Joe.

"When McKenna got to town," I say, "we didn't know

what to make of her. We liked her a whole lot better than Tan's last girlfriend..." The crowd laughs, many of them remembering Ramona. "But that's not saying much." They laugh again. "Then we got to know her. And she is—I swear—one of the best people I've ever met. She loves hard." I pause for a second, looking at my future sister-in-law. "She's one of the good ones."

Hunter and Sawyer lead the whooping and clapping this time, repeatedly smashing into each other like rival quarterbacks. Ridiculous. Sawyer's going to get sick any second if they keep it up.

"And my brother," I say loudly. Then, in a normal voice as the crowd calms down. "My brother, Tanner. He's the best."

More clapping. More whooping.

I can't help it—I slide my eyes to Joe.

He stares back at me, waiting for me.

Always waiting for me.

"Love isn't always perfect," I say. "Love can make a lot of mistakes. Love can break your heart. Love can make you wish you'd never ..." Joe leans forward. My voice trails off. I down the remainder of my champagne forcing myself to look back at Tanner and McKenna. "Love can be the best thing that ever happened to you, too." I smile at my future sister-in-law and then at my brother. "That's the kind of love I hope for you! Cheers!"

The crowd goes wild...again.

When I slide my eyes back to Joe, he's gone.

Six siblings.
Six love stories.

The Stewarts of Skagway
A New Series for 2024

A small but mighty outpost on the very edge of the Alaskan wilderness, Skagway has been a favorite stop for prospectors, adventurers, and cruisers for over a hundred years. It's also the home of the midnight sun, grizzly bears and the six Stewart siblings who are about to spend 2024 falling in love! Meet the sexy, sharp-witted, fun-loving Stewarts of Skagway – Tanner, Harper, Hunter, Sawyer, Parker and Reeve – who have no idea how much their lives are about to change as they each find their very own happily-ever-after.

TANNER, #1

When Tanner learns his crazy ex is returning for a summer in Skagway, he places an ad in the *Odds Are Good,* looking for someone to pose as his fiancée for the summer. Enter McKenna Cabot, a commitment-phobic college professor from Seattle caring for her aging grandmother. The promise of seasonal money is too good to pass up, so she heads north only to fall head over heels for tall, blonde, and handsome Tanner.

HARPER, #2

The love story of Harper Stewart and Joe Raven

HUNTER, #3

The love story of Hunter Stewart and Isabella Gonzalez

SAWYER, #4

The love story of Sawyer Stewart and Ivy Caswell

PARKER, #5

The love story of Parker Stewart and Quinn Morgan

REEVE, #6

The Christmas love story of Reeve Stewart and Aaron Adams

Odds Are Good
Stand-Alone Romances

SINGLE IN SITKA

When Seattle journalist Amanda heads north to Sitka to research a story, she answers the *Odds Are Good* personal ad of single dad Luke, hoping for some no-strings-attached fun. But could the sweet, widowed father of three—who just happens to be a smokin'-hot state trooper—turn out to be the man of her dreams?

NOME-O SEEKS JULIET

Upon learning that his entry in the Qimmiq Dog Race will be canceled if he doesn't have a female teammate, Cody places an ad in the *Odds Are Good* magazine, desperately searching for a woman in the Lower Forty-Eight to enter the competition with him. Luckily, he recruits Montana-born Juliet, a veterinary student with an agenda of her own.

A FAIRBANKS AFFAIR

Tired of being treated like a freak when men discover that Faye is a thirty-year-old virgin, she answers an ad in the *Odds Are Good* magazine, hoping to trek up to Fairbanks over New Year's and turn over her v-card to a sexy Alaskan. But when her chemistry with businessman Trevor turns out to be stronger than she ever could have imagined, what started out as a one-and-done mission becomes much more complicated.

MY VALDEZ VALENTINE

When Los Angeles lawyer Addison receives a desperate voice mail from her adventure-seeking brother, Elliot, she hires Alaskan helicopter pilot Gideon (whom she first discovers via an ad in the *Odds Are Good*) to take her to her brother's last known location. As the two uncover more and more details about Elliot's last days, they find themselves falling deeply for each other.

CATFISHED IN CRAIG

Tony moved Craig, Alaska, three years ago in the hopes of disappearing from his uncle's mob associates in New Jersey. But Alaska ain't home. And he misses the Jersey girls he grew up with. Tessa answers Tony's personal ad, intending to teach its cocky, conceited author he ain't all that. But when she finds herself in danger, she flees to Craig to disappear with

Tony.

DR. DAN IN KETCHIKAN

Dr. Dan's waiting room is always full on port days, but he's all business when it comes to his patients until he meets quirky cruise guest, Ruby, who injures herself on a lumberjack excursion. Will these two adorable misfits discover that they're only at the beginning of a journey toward forever?

SUMMER IN SKAGWAY

When Tanner learns his crazy ex is returning for a summer in Skagway, he places an ad in the *Odds Are Good,* looking for someone to pose as his fiancée for the summer. Enter McKenna Cabot, a commitment-phobic college professor from Seattle caring for her aging grandmother. The promise of seasonal money is too good to pass up, so she heads north only to fall head over heels for tall, blonde, and handsome Tanner.

KODIAK LUMBERJACK

Influencer Nola positions herself as the beauty behind a big bucks Instagram page, while lumberjack Soren declares himself the muscular hottie behind Kodiak Island's most coveted carvings. But what if Nola was the victim of a devastating accident, hiding behind the anonymity of the internet? And what if Soren lives in his lumberjack brother's shadow, just an accountant posing as a testosterone beast? Could they somehow make it work when they meet in person?

ALSO AVAILABLE
from Katy Regnery

J.C. and the Bijoux Jolis

THE STORY SISTERS
(Blueberry Lane Books #15–17)

The Bohemian and the Businessman
The Director and Don Juan
Countdown to Midnight

THE SUMMERHAVEN SERIES

Fighting Irish
Smiling Irish
Loving Irish
Catching Irish

THE ARRANGED DUO

Arrange Me
Arrange Us

ODDS ARE GOOD SERIES

Single in Sitka
Nome-o Seeks Juliet
A Fairbanks Affair
My Valdez Valentine
Catfished in Craig
Dr. Dan in Ketchikan
Summer in Skagway
Kodiak Lumberjack

THE STEWARTS OF SKAGWAY

Tanner
Harper
Hunter
Sawyer
Parker
Reeve

STAND-ALONE BOOKS:

An Amazon Affair
(a stand-alone travel novella)

After We Break
(a stand-alone second-chance romance)

Braveheart
(a stand-alone suspenseful romance)

Frosted
(a stand-alone romance novella for mature readers)

Unloved, a love story
(a stand-alone suspenseful romance)

**Under the YA pen name
Callie Henry**

A Date for Hannah

ABOUT THE AUTHOR

 *New York Times* and *USA Today* bestselling author **Katy Regnery** started her writing career by enrolling in a short story class in January 2012. One year later, she signed her first contract, and Katy's first novel was published in September 2013.

Over fifty books and three RITA® nominations later, Katy claims authorship of the multititled Blueberry Lane series, the A Modern Fairytale collection, the Summerhaven series, the Arranged duo, and several other stand-alone romances, including the critically acclaimed mainstream fiction novel *Unloved, a love story.*

Katy's books are available in English, French, German, Hebrew, Italian, Polish, Portuguese, and Turkish.

Check out Katy's Website here:
http://www.katyregnery.com

Made in the USA
Middletown, DE
31 January 2024